THE HAWK

Clearly she did not want to think herself mad, for now another thought occured to her. At first she resisted it, but it grew more insistent as the warmth crept back into her body. She did know where he'd been, of course she did. The sales records that until recently she'd kept for him showed mileage, accommodation and meals, all covered by bills. They were locked in the bureau in the front room, away from the children. She knew he'd been in one place where there had been a murder – Manchester on Christmas Eve – because he'd told her. Why? had he been trying to tell her . . . or was he more clever than she ever took him for, casually mentioning it, because it was exactly the sort of thing an innocent man would say?

About the author

Peter Ransley is one the most highly respected writers in television. His work includes the award-winning KATE THE GOOD NEIGHBOUR and MINOR COMPLICATIONS and the immensely successful series, THE PRICE. Peter Ransley comes from Pudsey, Yorkshire, and now lives in London with his wife and family. This is his first novel.

The Hawk

Peter Ransley

CORONET BOOKS
Hodder and Stoughton

Copyright © 1988 by Peter Ransley

First published in Great Britain in 1988 by Hodder and Stoughton Ltd

Coronet edition 1989

British Library C.I.P.

Ransley, Peter
  The hawk
  I. Title
  813'.914[F]

  ISBN 0 340 50059 X

Printed and bound in Great Britain for Hodder and Stoughton Paperbacks, a division of Hodder and Stoughton Ltd., Mill Road, Dunton Green, Sevenoaks, Kent TN13 2YA.
(Editorial Office: 47 Bedford Square, London WC1B 3DP) by Cox & Wyman Ltd., Reading.

For Margaret

Contents

Debbie Bright

It had been a bad summer, bookmakers even taking bets on whether there would be one dry day in August. But autumn was mild and dry. People relaxed. They went out and spent more, enjoying the sun and the warm evenings before winter set in. In Leeds, the strip clubs and prostitutes in Chapeltown had a little rush of business.

The hour had gone back and it was suddenly dark earlier: also good for trade. On the last night of October – Hallowe'en – Debbie Bright did four quickies from her beat in Spencer Place. She was wearing a white miniskirt – visible from the bottom of the street – a black leather jacket, and carried a red shoulder bag.

Spencer Place is close to the city centre, off Roundhay Road, a main route running north-east out of Leeds.

"She preferred commuter run," said Jill Rawcliffe, another prostitute who knew her well. "The men have a few, feel like it, but they're not that pissed. They have to get back to their nearest and dearest, so you have a faster turn-round."

By just gone half-past-seven, Debbie had done sixty-five pounds' worth of business. She went to Goodfood Supermarket, at the junction of Roundhay Road and Deanmere Lane, where she picked up groceries she'd selected earlier but had been unable to pay for. She slipped Doreen Williams, the checkout supervisor, a couple of quid – a regular arrangement – and on the way out bought the off-licence special offer, a bottle of Lutomer Riesling, which she liked to drink with lemonade.

"She were quite sophisticated, really," said Jill Rawcliffe.

She was home in a crumbling two-up and two-down in Back Molton Terrace just after eight, and put her two children to bed. Milly was five and Jason two. They had been with a neighbour, Mrs Giles, who had four children of her own but often was a minder for three times that number.

Debbie Bright was twenty-two. She had come to Leeds from Edinburgh with Jason's father, Michael Bright, described as a musician, for a job which had not materialised. He had drifted south and she had not heard from him for four months.

She intended to stay in that evening. Jason had an ear infection but two spoonfuls of Actifed had sent him to sleep. Perhaps it was because she had seen the film on television – *Alien* was on again. Or perhaps, as Jill Rawcliffe asserted, it was her "Jimmy". Sooner or later, if you worked that area of Chapeltown, you got involved with one or two West Indian pimps. "First they sweet-talk you," said Jill Rawcliffe, "and want peanuts. Then they want productivity."

Whatever the reason, Debbie gave Mrs Giles a fiver and asked her to pop in on the children. She never saw them again.

She said she was going to the "28", a reggae club at Sheepscar, but shortly after half-past-ten she met Jill Rawcliffe in Spencer Place.

"Working over?"

"This is my last."

Afterwards Jill Rawcliffe said: "It were right awful she should say that."

She wasn't sure about the car that picked Debbie up, but she thought it was red, newish, and the man was white with black hair. She didn't catch a glimpse of his face. One thing she did remember was that there were a number of cardboard boxes piled on the back seat; she remembered thinking: she'll not be able to do it in the back.

Early next morning Jack Samuels, a garage mechanic, was taking his dog for a walk to a drab strip of common near the Gipton Estate, when it vanished into a cul-de-sac of condemned houses and wouldn't come out.

"I thought he'd caught a rat. He's always rooting and there's rats as big as that in Gipton. Whole place is a tip."

The dog eventually ran to him with something white in his jaws – Debbie Bright's mini-skirt. Samuels followed the dog to the girl's body. Her blouse and jacket had been pulled over her head. Between her legs there was what looked like a wooden stake. The girl had head wounds, but the cause of death was suffocation. Nearby, among the rubbish spilling from the empty house, a pillow was found with blood on it which matched the girl's blood group. Also found near the body was an unused rubber sheath. The pathologist stated that the girl had had intercourse with someone either shortly before, or shortly after, death. West Yorkshire Police did not disclose any details of the killing, which made just two paragraphs in the *Yorkshire Evening News*.

The second murder was in November. The body of a woman was found on waste ground, used as a car park, near Manningham Lane, Bradford. Her name was Paula Chapel and she, too, was a prostitute. She was last seen alive drinking at a pub called the Perseverance near Lumb Lane, Bradford's red-light district.

Paula Chapel had been hit on the head, and then repeatedly stabbed. A piece of wood had been forced between her legs. On the wall nearby, standing out amongst the graffiti, was a freshly sprayed scrawl: THE HAWK.

The West Yorkshire Police linked the two murders in a cautiously phrased statement, but the press, in a dry period for news, seized on the story. One paper printed a photograph of the wall and said The Hawk was the killer's "grisly trademark", although the police had strongly expressed doubts, and, in fact, soon established that it had been painted there by a nearby street gang before the crime. But the name stuck.

Another paper discovered that the "28" club, where Debbie Bright had said she was going, and the "Persie", where Paula Chapel had had her last drink, had both been haunts of the Yorkshire Ripper. The fact that Debbie

Bright had only mentioned going there, and had never turned up, was not allowed to spoil the story.

HAWK FOLLOWS RIPPER'S BLOODY TRAIL was the headline.

Some people even believed that the Ripper had escaped, and that there was a gigantic cover-up. Even incontrovertible evidence that he was still safely behind bars was not believed by some, and the popular press continued to feed the terror. Prostitutes began to work "team-handed" again, and many left, as they did before, to work in the Midlands or London.

The body of the third victim was found in Manchester on Christmas Eve.

Part I

DOUBT

doubt n. 1. uncertainty about the truth, fact or existence of something. 2. lack of belief in or conviction about something. 3. an unresolved difficulty. 4. *obsolete:* fear.

1

Afterwards, Annie Marsh could remember exactly the moment when the nightmare began, although she was not aware of it at the time. Annie was thirty-three and lived with her husband Stephen, who was a year older, and their two children at 6 Hillthorpe View, Hillthorpe, a small sprawling town half-way between the red-brick terraces of Leeds and the stone houses of Bradford.

The moment was during that period of crisis on Christmas Day between the unwrapping of presents and the serving of dinner. Matthew, who was four-and-a-half, had spilt paints on the carpet.

"I told you not to let him have them!" said Annie.

Stephen was peeling the outer leaves from sprouts. "It'll come out. Water-based."

"Not with water from our tap it won't."

"It doesn't show."

"It does show, Stephen!"

It was stupid, but she was nearly in tears. There was so much to do! The sprouts, they should be on, baste the turkey, the potatoes, had he put the Asti Spumante in the fridge? In five minutes he had to pick up his mother. She was on her own, and they always did Christmas dinner for her, and somehow or other the old cow always wrecked it.

Well, she wouldn't wreck this one! It would be ready on time, for a start, to suit her royal highness. Family Christmas! At moments like this Annie had a wincing memory of herself in the children's home; well, they'd had a good time, they'd had chicken and crackers and pud, but there'd always be a moment when she'd go to her room and think, when I'm grown up, I'll have a family and then I'll have a real Christmas.

A real Christmas! Well, this was a real Christmas all right!

She pulled out the huge turkey, and teased the foil aside carefully, so it could be used again. Everything had been going smoothly until those paints. Stop thinking about it, she told herself! Hot fat splashed on her hand. She jumped in pain. More fat went on the oven lid, on the floor. There! One thing led to another.

"Where are you going?" she said to Stephen, running water over her stinging hand.

"I'll get mark off."

He had some solvent cleaner and a bowl of water.

"Oh, finish sprouts for God's sake!"

He had no sense of urgency. If it was left to him, they'd be carving the turkey at tea-time, with Mrs Marsh right sympathetic: "It takes a bit of organising, does Christmas dinner."

Well, it would be organised. It would be served on the dot of one, with gravy as the old bitch liked it – not a shimmer of grease on the surface – mounds of Brussels, peas, roast and mashed, parsnips and her special thing, Annie's stuffing, none of your packet rubbish, but made fresh that morning, she'd been up since six, a mixture of chestnuts and chopped walnuts, onions, parsley and orange rind. No turkey was ever big enough to satisfy the demand for her stuffing.

"More stuffing, Mum!"

Even Mrs Marsh had to admit: "There's nowt like your mother's stuffing."

She checked the water steaming the pudding, helped him with the sprouts, God he was slow, he was a perfectionist was Stephen, even in peeling sprouts, but don't get on at him, no talking, half-past-twelve, were there going to be enough potatoes, the kids were quiet, up to something, check them in a second. Ah! The little buggers had switched television on, not one of their programmes, but it was Christmas Day, and if it got her through this crisis . . .

She had a sixth sense when something like that was coming on the telly.

"A woman's mutilated body was found . . ."

She was in the front room like lightning. Even in her rapid motion to switch off the television her eyes went to the stain on the carpet. It wouldn't come out, they'd have to put that chair over it.

"What are you looking at that rubbish for? Wash your hands."

"I've washed them," Matthew said, without conviction.

"You could plant spuds in them. Lay the table, Jackie."

Jackie was seven, clever and old for her age. "I'm reading."

"No you're not. Your gran's coming!"

Twenty-to-one. It was going to be close. The sprouts should be on. He was still peeling, slicing the tails off carefully.

"I was over that way other day," he said.

They weren't going to do it. It took twenty minutes to collect his mother. She shovelled the sprouts into a pan.

"Moss Side way."

"Your mother will be waiting. I said half-past." Turkey. A wave of heat hit her as she checked it, turned down the oven a notch.

"Where that woman was killed."

She stared at him, not comprehending for a moment. She thought nothing about it then, although later she must have thought about those few seconds a thousand times. There was a little stillness and silence, in which the clink of knives and forks could be heard as Jackie laid the table. Water dripped from Stephen's huge hands in which dirt was permanently ingrained; her only regret about the job he had was that she had always wanted a husband who would come home with nice, clean hands. He was still holding the knife.

"I never know where you are."

"You do my figures," he said.

His expenses. They were just figures to her. The ringing of the phone galvanised her back into action. What were they standing there like idiots for?

"That'll be your mother."

She could predict what the old cow would say when she

saw the paint on the carpet: "You'll not get that out." And there would be a sort of satisfied gleam in her eye. For some reason her mother-in-law resented their success, the semi in Hillthorpe, the gleaming kitchen, the garden, with its view over the valley, looking down on Bramley and Armley, where Mrs Marsh lived.

"He'll never get a proper job, you know," Mrs Marsh had said to her about Stephen. "Still, I suppose he can draw dole as well as anybody else."

She'd said that about her own son, on their wedding day! Well, Annie had proved her wrong there all right, although it hadn't been easy. He could read, so long as they were words of one syllable. And he could write, if you called printing writing. Put a pen in his huge hand and he was like a child. Put a spanner in it and he was transformed. He was never happier than when he was taking a car engine or a bike to bits.

"My dad can fix anything," Matthew would say proudly.

He was right, he could, but it had taken Annie to see how his talent could be put to use. She had been secretary to Mr Bradshaw, sales manager at Hallet's, the big plastic machinery distributors in Rothwell. She'd chatted up Bradshaw desperately when she was leaving, pregnant with Jackie, pestering him to work on personnel to give the out-of-work Stephen a job. He was unskilled, he had no qualifications, no nothing. And he wouldn't try!

"Summat'll turn up."

"It won't, Stephen, it won't. You'll have to turn it up!"

If she had pestered people in the firm, she had to go down on her knees to Stephen to fill in the form for Hallet's, which would get him an interview.

"You fill it in."

"I can't fill it in for you! You've got to do it!"

On and on for a week. The form got butter on it, and she had to get a new one.

"Have you filled that form in yet?"

They were living with his mother then. It had been dreadful. All Mrs Marsh could talk about was the stillbirth before she'd had Stephen. Finally, Annie filled in the form herself and took him to Hallet's and stood outside until he'd had his interview.

He got a job sweeping the machine room floor. That's what it amounted to. She swallowed her pride. She didn't know how long the job would last. Mr Bradshaw wanted her to go back after she'd had Jackie. He said she was the best secretary he'd had, but she'd been ill. In hospital. Those were right dark days.

Then a miracle happened.

One day an injection moulding machine broke down on a test run, prior to an urgent delivery to a customer. All the engineers except two were out, and they were dealing with another emergency. While the machine room supervisor was bellowing to someone on the phone, Stephen had a look at the machine. He stopped it in mid-cycle to examine the barrel. When the supervisor returned he heaped swearwords onto Stephen – until the tool-setter found the machine was working again.

Stephen couldn't explain what he had done. For a year he'd worked on the machine room floor and every idle moment – of which there were many – he spent watching the engineers work, humping tools for them, clearing up after them. One thing he did have was patience, endless patience. In helping and watching and waiting he had absorbed every detail of the machines, learning how to trouble-shoot them without going through the technical manuals, which he could scarcely read anyway, and without being able to describe what he was doing.

Eventually he got called over, even when the engineers were there.

"What does tha think, Stephen?"

He didn't seem to think. It was his big, oil-stained fingers which seemed to think, checking, probing, pausing, unscrewing. That was what she learnt from Mr Bradshaw when they made him technical services assistant – the others were called engineers – and sent him on the road.

They were highly dubious about it at first because, as Mr Bradshaw said, he hadn't the presence, the conversation,

19

but soon customers began asking for him – he got on with it, there was less chat, and he got the machine back into production.

Mrs Marsh was late, but the turkey was even later. "So long as I haven't kept bird waiting," she said. "I thought our Stephen were never coming."

She was a small woman – God knows how she ever had Stephen – with small black eyes resting on soft, wrinkled cheeks. She hadn't, to Annie's knowledge, done a stroke since her husband had died. She was barely seventy, but she walked with a stick, which seemed to grow out of her hand, and when she took off her coat, with its imitation fur collar, the pockets rattled with tablets. She took them for the arthritis that knotted her fingers, for indigestion and angina. The first thing she did on a visit was to put them in a row on the mantelpiece – she called them "her soldiers" – together with her sweeteners, cigarettes and lighter.

"What do you need your sleeping pills for?" Annie would ask.

"You never know."

"You never know what?"

"You might ask me to stay."

"You wouldn't stay if I asked you."

"I might."

There was no reason why such exchanges should irritate Annie, but they did. Stephen adored her, and while she was there waited on her hand and foot. She had two other children, Ken and Jean, and they didn't give twopence for her, so she was always landed with her, every Christmas Day. Well it would be different next year, she vowed to herself bitterly, as she drained sprouts and mashed potatoes. Custard, get custard ready. Brandy butter, where was it . . . oh bugger brandy butter! No, she'd better look for it, Mrs Marsh always spotted what was missing and had you running back into the kitchen.

"Don't bother getting up for me, love," she'd say.

They were nearly there. She went into the dining room.

"Not those glasses, Jackie! The coloured ones we got from Schofields!"

She heard the rustle of paper from the front room and Matthew's cry of delight. She couldn't believe it! She'd told Stephen to leave his mother's presents in the car. Now they'd never get Mat to the table.

"Mum, Mum, look what Granny's bought me!"

It was an Autobot which could transform to a radio transmitter, linking two rooms. Annie had bought it for Mrs Marsh to give to him. She rarely went out, and never further than Bramley Town Street. Annie bought all the presents, and Stephen picked out the two best for his mother to give the children.

Oh, what did it matter? The dinner forgotten for a moment, she enjoyed Matthew's ecstasy, there was no other word for it, as, with Stephen's help, he rigged up the transmitter between the front room and the dining room.

"Space station to galaxy . . . space station to galaxy . . . "

"Shame about the carpet," Mrs Marsh said.

She'd meant to put the chair over it! "It's nothing. It'll come out."

Mrs Marsh shook her head. "It's gone into fibre – look."

As she was bending reluctantly over the multi-coloured stain she smelt burning. Of all the stupid things, she'd left the drained sprouts in butter over a light! The pan was burnt, and so were half the sprouts.

Stephen's big frame loomed over her. "Can I do anything?"

"Get them to the table. Get the wine. Jackie!"

Then it happened. He was opening the fridge to get the wine, and she was opening the oven to get the turkey. It was the one thing about her kitchen: when you were moving from the oven to the table, someone at the fridge blocked you. She was backing, half-bent, with the turkey, when Stephen opened the fridge. If she hadn't let go, she would have been splashed with fat.

"You bloody idiot!"

He slipped on the fat, his shoe hitting the turkey, which slid across the greased cork floor.

Matthew came in at that precise moment and laughed with glee. "Good shot, Dad!"

"Get out."

Matthew took one look at his mother's face and left hastily, bumping into his grandmother. "Oh dear," she said. "Oh dear oh dear oh dear."

"It's ruined," said Annie. "You can have the stuffing. I'll do some sausages."

"Nay, it's all right," said Mrs Marsh. "Your floor's clean enough to eat off."

She screamed: "It's not all right! It's bloody ruined!"

Stephen put his arm out tentatively towards her. She moved sharply away, putting her back to them. From that position she could see the apple tree which she had rejuvenated, fed and sprayed, saving it from rot and apple scab. The wind that came across Valley Top bent it over and in winter it was sometimes her fancy that it looked like two hands praying. She never talked about it because, to tell the truth, she thought it too daft even to think about, but the tree was her friend. When things got too much, just looking at it would help.

When she turned round, Mrs Marsh was ushering away the children and Stephen was wiping the turkey with a tea-cloth.

"Not that cloth! I'll do it!"

It wasn't dirty, not that she could see, but she was always worried about the children catching something; she'd seen a programme on the telly about what they could pick up from the floor. So she cut away the skin, and, when that made the bird look forlorn, she carved it there and then.

You wouldn't have thought it was Christmas when she brought the plate in to silence and a ring of apprehensive faces. Normally there was a cheer when the steaming bird arrived, surrounded by roast potatoes and Brussels. She felt wretched and guilty when she saw the children staring at the bird, dismembered to its ribcage.

"Wine!" said Mrs Marsh, as she always did, when Stephen thumbed off the plastic cap of the Asti Spumante.

"It's sweet, it's all right," said Annie, shovelling meat

onto plates. That was always Stephen's job. "Who's for a leg?" he would say. What a cow she was being! She pushed the meat over to Stephen and glanced at her mother-in-law as she mumbled: "I'm sorry."

"Don't be daft," Mrs Marsh said. "Sorry? For what? For cooking this lovely meal? Three cheers for the cook!"

"The cook!" everyone cried.

"It's a Job is cooking a meal like this," Mrs Marsh went on, sliding the gravy in its boat to check there was no grease before pouring it. "I should know. It used to be only a quart of light ale and a chicken from Bevan's in Town Street when prices dropped on Christmas Eve, do you remember, Stephen? It weren't much, but I did it for six people, next door, on his own, he came in and it were always ready, on the dot!"

It was twenty-to-two. Annie stared at her plate. There was a knot in her stomach, and it was as much as she could do to taste the stuffing. Even that didn't taste right – had she left out the orange?

All around her rose murmurs of appreciation: it was lovely, moist, better than last year, it had a real flavour, fresh; this one had walked about a bit. She couldn't look up from her plate, and the knot in her stomach grew tighter the more their compliments flowed.

When Stephen said: "Any more stuffing?" and Mrs Marsh said to the children: "There's nowt like your mother's stuffing," she couldn't stand it any longer.

"It's not so hot," she said.

"It's great," said Stephen, "like it always is."

"No it's not," said Annie, controlling her irritation. "I've left the orange out."

"Oh, is that what it is," Mrs Marsh mumbled through a full mouth, "I thought it wasn't quite up to your usual."

Annie felt a rush of hatred for the old woman for so readily agreeing with her. Oh, this was absurd! What did it matter if she'd left the orange out of the stuffing? But it did, it did. She dropped her fork. The blood sang in her head as she bent to pick it up. At any moment she would have to leave the table. It was Matthew who saved the day.

His bright black eyes stared at her from beneath the thick tangle of hair she always wanted to take a comb to. He began to grin, then, as she stared at him, splutter. A fragment of turkey hit the tablecloth.

"Here," said Mrs Marsh, as another fragment hit her arm.

"Matthew. What's up with you?"

He got out some words which only Jackie caught. She began to giggle.

Annie's fury mounted. "Stop it. What *is* the matter?"

"Playing . . ."

"What?"

"Playing football wi' turkey."

There was a moment's silence. The children's giggles froze. Then, although she struggled against it, she felt her face twitch. The children picked it up instantly, and their laughter redoubled.

"Now stop it! You daft beggars."

But Matthew, who was already into rugby – the wall beside his bed was Blu-Tacked with Leeds' stars – yelled: "It were a real drop kick!"

Now Stephen began to laugh. It took a lot to get him going, but once started he never stopped. It always surprised her how good a mimic he was; she supposed it was all the listening he did, sitting there quietly, in the background of any conversation. Now he mimicked her getting the turkey out of the oven, bending and being hit on the bottom.

"Oops!"

"Stephen, stop it."

He got her expression to a T. For an instant it gave her a funny twinge. It was her, and it wasn't, there was a mocking twist to it that disturbed her but was forgotten in a fraction as she gave way gratefully to the gales of laughter. Mrs Marsh smiled benignly rather than laughed, nothing would crack her face, but from that moment, my goodness it was Christmas! The pudding came in to the applause that the turkey had lacked. The children clamoured to light it and, for once, indulgently, she gave them matches.

"Strike them away from you."

Woosh! There was a great cheer, followed by "aws" as the blue flames flickered out. She'd remembered the brandy butter, and for once there was enough custard. They pulled crackers, groaned at the mottoes, listened to the Queen and agreed she was looking older and her spectacles didn't improve her. Her little tree present from Stephen was a miniature Benedictine. She loved sweet liqueurs, and was persuaded to drink it there and then, so that when he brought out the new Polaroid camera she had given him, she protested only feebly about having her photograph taken.

"Take the children . . . Your mother's looking nice . . . "

She always shied away from cameras; God knows, she was nothing much to look at in the first place, and somehow the camera cruelly seemed to lengthen her already long nose, stiffen her square jaw, and give her a double chin. Her smile went and her eyes stared.

"Prisoner 99," the children always said.

She did a deal with Matthew that he could take a Polaroid of her kissing Stephen under the mistletoe if he would write under it in the album. He was slower than Jackie at getting into reading and writing and Hillthorpe Primary, where he'd just started full-time, was no help. All they seemed to believe in was creative play! There were no desks, no system, no order, just thirty kids milling around, gawping at stick insects or splashing paint.

"Here! What are you writing? Don't help him, Jackie!"

Annie flushed. The two of them had written, in wavering writing: "Mum LoVes DaDTru." Jackie was completing shading the arrow piercing a bleeding heart.

"Don't be so soft!"

"You're not going to rub it out, Mum!"

No, she couldn't. There it would stay to be seen whenever the photograph albums were pulled out, as they were now. It was dark now, but they hadn't switched on the lights, gazing at the photographs by the light of the imitation coal fire. The Benedictine spread a warm, sleepy glow over her.

"Hey up. Prisoner 99 again."

They'd got to the wedding photographs. She'd really looked hunted, no, in that one she looked proud, hanging on to Stephen's arm. He took a good picture, in the tails she had insisted on him hiring. Mrs Marsh thought she was getting above herself as usual, but hadn't she been proved right? It had been a bit of a sensation in Bramley. They had only afforded it by her borrowing a friend's wedding-dress; it hadn't really fitted her very well, but who had been looking at her? He looked like a film star with his thick hair, dark eyes and funny, far-off smile.

Surely it wasn't that time! Mrs Marsh was scooping up her pills from the mantelpiece and putting them in her coat pockets.

"Ah well," she said, as Stephen took her out to his car, "New Year next."

"I expect so," said Stephen, and for some reason they all found this hilariously funny.

2

The children were asleep. The house was silent. Stephen wasn't back – fussing around his mother, no doubt. She would find him any job, any errand to keep him there. She gritted her teeth, and attacked the last of the washing-up. Then – bliss! She made a cup of tea and put her feet up. She was going to look at the new gardening book Stephen had given her, and plan spring. What a lovely idea, planning spring! She had a brief picture of what she would plant under the apple tree; it was a difficult spot, very shady, but then she was diverted.

The photograph albums hadn't been put away, and she couldn't rest with that mess. She found herself looking through the wedding pictures again. She never thought

26

she'd marry anyone as handsome as that. Here she was as a girl, gawky, resentful of being photographed, as usual. That was the home in the background.

It was probably taken about the time she'd finally lost contact with her mother. She had never known her father; her mother, who had drifted from one town in the north to another, had always been vague about who he was. She drank, that was the long and short of it. And, when she paid one of her infrequent visits to Annie, she usually had a man in tow; usually a different one.

Yes, she must have been about fourteen then. Everyone had seemed to be going out with boys except her. Wasn't that the time she'd decided her life was over?

She'd gone up to – God knows it was still painful to remember – David Crowther. Like her, he was not much to look at. In fact he was repulsive. A luminous little pear of snot hung permanently from his nose. He picked at the crusty spots that decorated his forehead. About the only thing he had going for him was that he had parents.

At the canal bridge, which was a sort of meeting ground – you could walk down to the dam, or along the tow-path – she went up to him. He was smoking, and he flicked ash casually from his already browning fingers as she leant on the bridge next to him. She might not have been there, for all the notice he took of her.

"Hello."

He blew a narrow, suspicious stream of smoke in her direction, and turned away to gaze down at boys skimming stones into the canal.

"Are you going down to the club?" she said.

He scratched on the parapet of the bridge with a stone and finally said: "Yeah. Maybe."

"Will you walk me down?"

The stone stopped scratching. He threw it into the canal and turned to stare at her. "Where?"

"To the club! Are you deaf?"

The club was the youth club. For the two of them to walk in together was as good as saying they were going out. He picked at a spot.

"Don't pick at it."

He pulled his hand away in astonishment at her sharp tone of voice. A huge lorry came over the bridge, the wind from it blowing at her skirt. She moved away from the road and was now close to him. The spot he had picked had a little streak of blood coming from it.

"Come on then!"

"Where?"

"To club!"

She began walking and at first, automatically, he followed her. Then he stopped. She glared back at him with mounting irritation. "Come on!"

He held his cigarette, now reduced to a stub, between finger and thumb, sucked the last drag of smoke from it, flicked it into the traffic and said: "I'm not going wi' you."

It had never occurred to her for one moment that David Crowther would reject her. The traffic went by in a continual stream, tugging at her hair, her skirt. All she could think of saying was: "Why not?"

He shrugged, put his hands in his pockets, shuffled his feet, picked at a spot, then suddenly ran towards the stone steps that led down to the tow-path. At the top of the steps he turned and, before vanishing down them, shouted: "Because your face is like the back-end of a fucking bus!"

She ran to her secret place, down by the dam, where she could burrow between the tall purple fireweed. She didn't often cry, but she cried then. It seemed to her then, with a terrible finality, that if David Crowther rejected her, what hope was there? She would never marry, never have a home, never have babies. The tears she mopped from her face seemed to mingle with the water frothing in the dam below. She would be like Betsy, the old tramp the children baited, as she walked over the bridge with her plastic bags, in an enormous baggy overcoat, winter or summer. No. At least she wouldn't be that.

She remembered drying her eyes on her dress and setting back with determined steps for the bridge. Why was it so painful after all these years to see that fourteen-year-old girl, averting her swollen cheeks from people, convinced that she would never marry, deciding to take a commercial course and save every penny so she could buy a house, however small and poky, since she would be on her own?

She put the photographs away. Her tea was cold and she made a fresh pot. Still she didn't open the gardening book. Why she was in this unusual mood she didn't know. She was always one for getting on with it, but again she felt compelled to return to the photograph albums.

Here she was, in that awful cardigan she had worn for years, bought in that Kirkgate shop that took local authority clothing vouchers. You felt a right pauper going in there, with someone from the home handing over the vouchers. The caption underneath primly said: "With friend outside college. 1970."

Wasn't that Michelle? She hadn't looked at these for donkeys! Wasn't she looking at this because she had been with Michelle when she had first met Stephen?

She had put her files in the basket on her bike and had actually jumped on and said: "Tarar then," when Michelle said: "Come to pub?"

"What for?"

"A swim. What d'you think what for? A drink!"

Michelle wasn't too brilliant to look at either, but she was leggy, with lovely blonde hair down to her shoulders. Above all, she had chat.

"I don't drink."

"Time you did."

"I've got no money."

In fact, she had one hundred and twelve pounds five shillings in her Leeds Permanent Building Society book, mostly earned from her Saturday job at Boots in Briggate, but every penny of that was being saved for the house.

"I'll buy you a bag of crisps. Come on. Please."

Annie was flattered by this attention. She had few friends and rarely went out. She found herself drawn into the pub, clutching her shorthand notes and some shopping in her bicycle basket.

"What d'you want to bring that in for?"

"I can't leave it out there, can I?"

She felt everyone was looking at her. Men turned, holding pints. One winked at her. She looked away. A juke box was hammering out "Jumping Jack Flash". A notice in front of her asked: RU 18? She didn't know where to put herself, or her bicycle basket. She was just eighteen, but she felt like a criminal, certain no one would believe her. Meanwhile Michelle was leaning on the bar, laughing with the barman and ordering two snowballs.

"I told you I didn't drink."

"This isn't drink. It's cold custard. Put the bloody basket down, for Christ's sake."

They had barely sat down when it became apparent why Michelle so desperately wanted her company. Two boys came in who went to the tech down the road. One of them stopped when he saw Michelle.

"Fancy seeing you here."

"Fancy seeing you."

Michelle introduced him as Pete and his friend as Mike, who was clearly meant for her.

"I thought Doreen was coming," said Pete.

Annie caught Michelle in the middle of making an alarmed face at him. "Shurrup," she said. "Annie has the best speed in the whole class."

"Fast is she?" said Pete, and everybody laughed. Annie managed to, although her face was burning. It was all horribly clear. Doreen was Michelle's best friend. Something had gone wrong and she, Annie, was a last desperate stop-gap. She had seen the look of disappointment on Mike's face, and when he went to the bar to get drinks, she felt she couldn't stand it any longer and bent to pick up her bicycle basket, but it wasn't there.

"I put it over there. What d'you want it for?" Michelle said.

By the time she found it, Mike was back with the drinks. She just stood there, trying to form words, but nothing came out.

"Shall I take that?"

He put the basket down under the table. Dumbly she

30

moved to sit down, kicked against the basket, and grabbed at the table. Beer slopped.

"Drunk again!" cried Pete.

"You and your bloody basket," said Michelle. "What have you got in it – gold bars?"

The worst, the cruellest thing was that Mike was so nice. He didn't ignore her and talk across her to the others. He was ever so polite and well-spoken, and asked her about the course she was taking and what the college was like. And here she was, in her terrible old cardigan, conscious of the darn in the front which she kept trying to hide with her sleeve. She was sweating inside it, but her blouse was even worse. Why oh why hadn't Michelle told her what was going on? Because she knew Annie wouldn't have come in, that's why. She grew angrier and angrier at Michelle.

Four years ago, by the dam, she had convinced herself she would never meet anyone like Mike. Now, suddenly, here was her chance, her opportunity! Desperately she tried to listen to him, be intelligent, smile, but her swelling anger at Michelle and her shame at how she looked dried up any conversation she might have had. There were more drinks – how much was all this costing? – and she swallowed her snowball in the hope that it might help, but it just made her feel swimmy and a bit sick.

The juke box never stopped and the pub filled up. Some friends of Mike and Peter came in and it became a party. One, Steve, she knew by sight. He'd been in the stream below her at school. He was big, with thick curly hair and the faint beginnings of a moustache which the others joked about. Girls fancied him, but he had no chat, no go, and was never seen out with anyone. After a long, complicated conversation about a motor-bike he was apparently repairing for Pete, to which he contributed mainly monosyllables, he lapsed into silence, sitting on a stool at the edge of the group. Unlike the others, he had a half, not a pint, which he sipped slowly. Like her, he seemed out of it, but unlike her he seemed content just to sit and watch. Several times, as she struggled to talk to Mike, she caught him glancing at her, and once he smiled.

31

It was a strange smile, unnerving somehow, and she felt as if he knew what she was going through, and was actually enjoying it; it was as if he was watching a performance.

"What?" she said.

For minutes Mike had sat there without saying anything, ground to a halt by her unresponsiveness. He was glued there, she was sure, by sheer politeness. Each moment she told herself she must go, release him from this agony, but each moment she thought she might say something, well not brilliant, but normal, interesting, that would bring a nod, or even a smile to those nice cheeks, and, as the silence between them had lengthened she had become so panic-stricken in her desperate search for a subject that she had completely failed to hear him when he did speak.

"What?"

"Do you like Fleetwood Mac?"

"I don't know him."

She knew it was stupid, as soon as she opened her mouth, but the words still came out. There was a great howl of laughter. Someone drummed on the table. On the edge of the group she could see Steve's grinning face. From somewhere she managed to bring out a smile, trying to indicate it was a joke.

"It's a group," Pete said.

"I know it's a group, stupid!" she yelled at him. There was a little silence round their table.

"All right," said Michelle. "No need to bite his head off."

She fumbled for her bicycle basket. Mike helped her. For a moment they were pulling in the wrong direction to get it out from under the table. He laughed and she found herself laughing with him. It was as if, at the last possible moment, she had found a formula, an approach to him. But then he said: "Nice to meet you" and she replied "Nice to meet you" and she was moving to the door while he was moving to the bar. Before she left she turned to see him join another group where a girl began chatting to him.

In the porch of the pub a boy asked her for a ride in her basket. She could still hear the juke box: "I'm a king bee, baby, buzzing round your hive, I'm a king bee baby, let me come inside."

Her back tyre was down. She had a slow which she'd kept meaning to mend. It wouldn't pump up.

"Shall I have a go?"

It was Steve. Even now he was standing quite a way from her, as if he was still on the edge of the group.

"It's all right, thank you."

"Hang on."

He unclipped the light from the front, spun the tyre slowly and stopped it. In the shaft of light, his dirty fingers worked with a surprising delicacy to extract something. A little dagger of glass gleamed in his palm.

"Tha'll not pump that up," he said. "Have you a kit?"

She shook her head. "I'll walk it."

"Hang on."

He went back into the pub and borrowed one from God knows where. He ignored her completely while he upended the bike, only saying: "Hold light." She stared as he took the outer off with his fingers, where anyone else would have struggled with tyre levers. He pumped and spat to check the puncture. A tiny gob of spit hit her hand holding the lamp. He remained silent until he'd forced the outer back on.

"Is he your boyfriend then?"

"Who?"

"Mike."

"No. I don't go out with boys."

Was his face amused? It was just outside the circle of light, and it was difficult to tell.

"Never?"

"No."

"Your spindle's wearing and your chain's slack. Do you want me to fix them for you?"

"It's all right."

"I could come round."

"It's all right."

"See you then."

"See you."

Her mind was in a turmoil. It was only when she was half-way down the street that she realised she had never thanked him. Mike, not Steve, remained in her mind. From the moment she woke up she went over the scene in the pub over and over again. If he'd been like everyone else she could have forgotten, but she couldn't forget his kindness, his gentleness. She could have asked him about his work, the tech, what he planned to do in life – now she rehearsed talking to him about a thousand subjects.

She even pillaged her building society account to buy clothes and, wearing jeans and a Fleetwood Mac T-shirt which she had hunted through the arcades for, she cycled past the tech every day while the students were leaving. She saw him once. He had his arm round a girl. She was convinced it was the one he had talked to in the pub, directly after she had left.

He stopped and smiled. She wobbled to a stop.

"Remember me?" he said.

"Oh, yes, yes, of course. How are you?" Her shorthand pad fell from her basket.

"Still the same old bicycle basket."

"Yes. Yes. Still the same."

She put a chair under the knob of her bedroom door and lay on the bed and cried for an hour, until her cheeks were puffed and swollen. Then she threw cold water over her face and told herself not to be stupid. She sold the Fleetwood Mac sweater top to someone in her class for a pound, and put the money back into the building society.

It must have been a year later when she saw Steve again. At first she didn't recognise him. She'd just given herself her Saturday treat, coffee with cream and a Danish at Oliver's in Albion Place when this crowd of lads bumped into her. They thought they were Leeds United, kicking a Coke tin and scoring goals into litter bins. Her bag dropped and she rounded on them, thinking they were about to take it and prepared to fight for it, when a right scruffy looking fellow held it out to her.

She took it from him with bad grace. "Go and lake in fields, can't you?"

34

He grinned at her and she realised who he was. He had dirty great sideburns down to his chin, a Mexican moustache, and wore a sweatshirt covered in oil and dirt. The others kicked the tin. One whooped and leapfrogged over a litter bin.

"Come on Steve."

"Are you still going around wi' Mike?" he asked.

Since that disastrous evening she'd left college with top speeds and just started as a junior at Hallet's. Proud of her success, she looked better and dressed better and felt much more sure of herself. For a moment, that one word knocked it all away.

He kicked at a cigarette packet with a trainer that was splitting at the seams, and corrected himself. "Oh no. He's engaged, isn't he?"

"Is he?"

"Well I heard he were. Lass at Oakwood. Posh."

His mates had got bored with football and were flicking lighted matches at one another. "Come on Steve! We'll miss match!"

"See you then."

"Thank you," she said.

He stopped, puzzled, picking up something from her tone of voice.

"For mending my bike. I never thanked you properly," she went on, awkward and confused. What on earth was she saying all this for?

"Is it all right?"

"What?"

"Your bike."

"The three-speed's broke."

"D'you want me to fix it?"

That was it. To the surprise and horror of her one friend Mary (he was rough and he had no O levels) she began going round with his crowd. On his motorbike. To pubs and even once (only once) to Leeds United. Did it start because he was the only part of the evening in the pub she had left? What a funny thought! She'd never seen it that way before. But they'd grown closer, inseparable.

"Mum LoVes DaDTru."

She read the children's wavering caption and looked at the big man, in his best suit for Christmas Day, kissing her under the mistletoe. He was a sight different from that shambles in T-shirt and trainers who had bumped into her in Albion Place!

She left the kitchen light on for him and potted Matthew, who was still not dry at night. Their bedroom was in the back. She switched out the light and, before getting into bed, gazed out over the Aire valley, cut by the thick yellow line of the M62. That was Bramley. One of those pin pricks of light was his mother's. He was late. He was often late these days. She'd probably had one of her turns.

Annie got into bed. First she went onto her right side, head crooked on her elbow, and then turned onto her left. Was that him? No, it was next door's garage that always creaked, she should have given them an oil-can for Christmas. Why wasn't she sleeping? It was that rest she'd had. What a good day after that disaster! She would like to have made love to him. They hadn't made love for ages, had they? Not that it mattered. She'd never thought much to it, really. It was a lot of fuss about nothing. But for some reason she found herself thinking about it and, when she felt him beside her, she must have fallen asleep, God knows what time it was, she touched him diffidently, but he was well away, breathing deeply, and so she did her left side, crook of the elbow, right side and was soon drifting back to sleep again.

3

Some of the shrubs were a bit wind-lashed, and Annie sorted out sticks to support them. It was the day after New

Year and all the festivities were over, thank God – she could get a bit of tidying up done in the garden.

She looked for the hammer because a couple of the sticks had nasty-looking nails in them. She opened Stephen's tool-box, which she'd bought him two Christmases ago. The hammer wasn't there. He was fussy about putting his tools back, but she thought no more about it, and used a spanner to bang the nails down. It was clumsy to use, and she caught herself a clout on her finger nail, which was still smarting when she arrived at Norma's to get the kids, whom Norma had collected from school.

It was funny how she got on with Norma. She wasn't her friend, she'd no time for friends, but she felt really relaxed with her, although they had right different views. Norma was a teacher, only a primary teacher, but she read books, proper books, not paperbacks. They spilt from the shelves onto the floor, and when you went to sit down, there was usually a book there. At first Annie had tidied them up.

"Don't do that! I know where everything is."

The kids were upstairs playing when she got there, and Norma was on the phone. There was a full pot of tea, cold.

"I don't know," Annie grumbled. The waste that went on in other people's houses!

She made fresh. Norma was still on the phone: God knows what her bill was, she said the same thing eighteen times.

"I don't fancy it," she was saying. "It's right near where that girl was killed and my car's in dock."

Norma was separated from her husband and it was a struggle keeping her old banger going. Stephen had changed the clutch for her that summer. Annie sugared a cup of tea, put it in Norma's hand and shouted to the kids.

"Fifteen minutes!"

She looked out of the window. The weeds seemed to grow in winter here. One of these days she would take a fork to them. Norma had put the cup down. That would get cold.

"What happens if we miss the last bus?" she was saying. "I'm not walking home with the Hawk flying about."

Annie yawned. She'd done some digging which had really flaked her. At last Norma put the phone down, adamant that she wasn't going to go to the evening meeting.

"I don't know what you're worriting about. He only attacks prostitutes," Annie said.

"He might run out of them. Did you sugar it?"

Annie sighed. She didn't want to talk about this, but Norma went on about it, until Annie said she'd had enough of monsters beating children, starving children and killing women, they should shoot a few and that would stop it. She knew that would annoy Norma, and had the satisfaction of seeing her lips tighten.

Sometimes they had a real ding-dong, her and Norma, and she sensed it was going to be one of those.

"He's not a monster!"

"Oh, you feel sorry for him, do you?"

"Well, in a way . . . "

"In a way!"

She did talk some rubbish, even if she was a teacher, not that they did much teaching these days.

"He's a normal human being."

Now she laughed. She had to put her tea down. "Oh come on, Norma! It's normal is it, to kill a woman, to – to – "

"To shove a knife up her vagina?"

She didn't know where to put herself. That was Norma all over. She loved shocking people, making herself out to be liberal and progressive. Upstairs Matthew was shouting that it was his counter, he'd won. She drained her tea and teased a leaf from her lip.

"Is that what he does?"

"That's what they say."

"What does he do that for?"

"Gratification."

She didn't know what the woman was talking about. As so often, she asked herself why she came here. They had nothing in common. Norma's house was like a pigsty and she wouldn't be surprised if that was why Doug had left her.

"Sexual pleasure."

That was it. She got up, shaking her head in disbelief. Norma followed her as she cleared the tea things and took them into the kitchen.

"It's true!"

"Get away." You wouldn't believe it, but there were still breakfast things unwashed. Annie scraped a bowl of soggy cornflakes into the bin. Her kids didn't get the next course until they'd finished the first. Norma was still going on, pacing up and down as if she was in the classroom.

"He must be leading a normal life, or he'd have been caught by now. Look at Peter Sutcliffe. He lived with his wife, saw his parents – "

"He were a nutter."

"Oh God you infuriate me! You don't follow an argument! Nobody suspected him, that's the point!"

"Are you keeping this fat?"

"Don't do the washing-up!"

"It'll give me something to do while you're gassing."

She had met Norma when Jackie first started in the playgroup. Susan, Norma's child, had really created when her mother tried to leave her, until Annie had pointed out she had the same red shoes as Jackie. From that moment the two kids played together, and brought their parents, somewhat unwillingly, together. Annie had thought Norma stuck-up then. She wore beads, brightly coloured skirts – usually with red in them that matched her lipstick – and a suede coat from Sting in Harrogate Road which must have cost a bomb. Her husband was something unbelievable like an architect.

In those days Annie had no car and had to trudge up Moor Lane which was a real hike, but she enjoyed the wind in her face and kept refusing lifts from Norma. One day it was raining heavily.

"We're all right, thank you," said Annie, when Norma pressed her to come in her smart Escort, with red and blue stripes on the side.

"It's pouring down!" Norma protested.

"We're not sugar, we won't melt."

"I will," wailed Jackie.

Well that was it! They all fell about, and from that moment it was understood that they all went back together, whether Annie wanted a lift or not.

That was only four years ago. Now Norma's husband had gone and her car wouldn't start. She looked a wreck. The suede coat was stained beyond cleaning, and her blouses sometimes had a dribble of egg down them, which Annie would scrape off with a finger-nail.

Annie gathered her flock together ready to go out to her pride and joy. It was only a K registration Morris 1100, but Stephen kept it in tip-top running order, and once a week the children had to polish it and remove every sweet-wrapper and drinking straw before they got their pocket money.

"I don't suppose I could borrow your car?" Norma said.

Well that really took her breath away! Of all the damn cheek!

"You suppose right," she said. "It's only insured for me and Stephen."

"I could phone my broker."

"I don't like to, I'm sorry, Norma."

While she got the kids into their coats and found their clothes Norma phoned the baby sitter to cancel her. She was engaged. When Annie came back to say goodbye, there were tears in Norma's eyes.

"What's up?"

"Nothing."

"Oh," said Annie. "That's all right then. I don't know what you do when it's summat."

Norma flew at her. "Oh, I do hate you! You're always so pious, so right, so bloody organised, so mean!"

The last word stung Annie. She was right, more often than not, she was organised, but no one had ever called her mean. No one had ever talked to her like Norma, not since she was a girl, and not often then. She was about to round on her when she saw Jackie at the door.

"What are you staring at? In the car."

"What's happening?"

Susan had appeared.

"Get the washing-up done," Annie told Susan.

"It's not my turn."

"You dirtied them! Get them done!"

Susan went off rebelliously. She obeyed Annie more than she did her own mother. Once Annie had twisted her ear. You only needed to do it the once; and then they felt it if you as much as looked at them. Norma read books like *The Development of the Primary-School Child*, but she knew nothing about bringing them up.

When Annie first met her she said: "I like a home that's child-centred."

She had never heard anything so daft! "I'm the centre of my home," she said. "That's what the child wants, and that's what my Stephen wants."

Norma controlled herself, opened her mouth to speak, and began crying again. Annie despised tears. If you had to cry, you did it in private, except at funerals and weddings, you didn't bother other people. She went to the clock to rewind it before she remembered it was broken.

"What is this meeting?"

Norma searched in her sleeve for her handkerchief, then looked among piled-up newspapers and books for her handbag. Annie handed her tissues. If there was an emergency with children people turned immediately to her. She could produce tissues, plasters and baby aspirins like magic.

Norma blew her nose and mumbled something.

"What?"

Norma said: "Methodism in the West Riding."

Annie looked at the clock. Maybe Stephen could fix it. She turned to the window. The children were fighting in the car but let it go for the moment: it would tire them out for bedtime. She turned to Norma.

"Well I wouldn't weep buckets over that."

"Oh Annie, oh Annie."

Norma was gripping her arm tightly, her eyes shining. She was half laughing, half crying. It was embarrassing. First she was biting her head off and then she was all over her. She moved away.

41

"There's a fella," Norma said.

"You're married."

"We're separated."

"You want to get yourself sorted out first."

"I am bloody sorted!" There she was, flaring up again. "Honestly, Annie. You live in the last century!"

"I wish I did when I look at television."

"Well. I knew you wouldn't lend it to me."

"Then why did you ask?" They were at the door. Susan was clattering pots in the kitchen with a sullen loudness. "Why don't you get him to give you a lift back? This fella."

"Because it'd look right obvious. He'd think I was after him."

"Aren't you?"

"Yes! I think so. I don't know. Any road, I want to keep it flexible."

This was too complicated for Annie, and she started to go, but not before Norma had gripped her by the arm again and said: "Thank you, Annie, anyway." There was such a warmth, such an amount of feeling in that grip that it stayed with Annie as she got into the car and separated the quarrelling children. She resented it bitterly. She felt really rotten. She had been looking forward to the evening all day. Stephen was away again and she had no meal to cook, so she was planning to get out her new gardening book and the seed catalogues. Now all she would think about was Norma! Mean. She was mean, was she?

"Stop it you two!"

Now she was shouting at the kids. They were arguing about the ownership of a pencil. She found another one.

Borrow the car! Who did she think she was! There she was, waving from the window with Susan. She started the car and put it into gear. It was no good. Mean. Her evening would be absolutely ruined. She switched off, got out of the car, and walked back to Norma.

Then of course, as soon as she'd got the children off, mashed a pot of tea and got the catalogues out, she worried anyway. Was it really all right about the insurance? Norma wasn't all that brilliant a driver at the best of times, look at her car, twisted bumpers, a dented wing, and with her mind on that Methodist . . . Was he a Methodist? She got into some weird and wonderful situations did Norma.

Annie tried to decide whether to have another go at cauliflowers. They had been a disaster last year, but should she have one more go, planting "Snowball" under cloches now or . . . No. She couldn't concentrate. Why on earth had she let Norma have the car? What a daft thing to do! She kept seeing Norma go into the back of someone, or parking it without the brake on.

She put the catalogues away – at this rate it would be ummer before she bought any seeds – and switched on television. On one channel was a series she hadn't been watching. On another was a discussion. She was about to switch over when she caught the words: " – killer will strike again."

It was everywhere. You couldn't get away from it. She was too restless to listen properly and picked up the paper. She registered the sentence a moment or two after it was said.

"He hit her with a hammer, or similar instrument, and dragged her into the bushes."

The paper hung from her fingers as she leant forward and stared at the screen. The man speaking had white hair and spectacles and looked some kind of a scientist. He smiled once or twice as he spoke of murderers of this kind being particularly difficult to find. The Yorkshire Ripper had pursued his grisly path for six years before he had been caught by a pair of false number-plates. A young man with a red and yellow tie asked the scientist about computers, and the scientist said yes, all the reports and interviews were being filed on computers, but the computer could only collect pieces of information together. If it wasn't put in there in the first place, there was nothing a computer could do.

This was the cue for the policeman heading the enquiry to speak, the assistant chief constable, Brian Bevan.

"We believe someone knows or suspects who this man is,

and may be sheltering him. If you have any suspicion at all, please phone us on this number. Everything you say will be treated in absolute confidence."

The number appeared, the three men talked together as the signature tune rang out, and then the news came on. Annie made fresh tea and, as usual, cut a chunk of Wensleydale to go with a couple of biscuits. Slowly, a number of incidents came together in her mind. It was like one of those children's puzzles where you have to join numbers together to form a picture.

She stared at her finger nail, now blackening where she had hit it, with a spanner because she couldn't find the hammer.

He was often away, he had been away on Christmas Eve, he had been in Manchester, near where that woman had been killed, he'd told her.

Cutting sprouts. She saw him in the kitchen, holding a knife, cutting sprouts.

"I were there. Over that way."

Is that what he'd said?

She did not, for one moment, take this seriously. It was strange, curious, but it was absurd. A fantasy. Nevertheless, she let her mind wander into this fantasy. It was frightening but compelling, like a late-night horror film which she thought complete nonsense, but could not switch off.

The noises the house made seemed louder. A hot water pipe knocked. There were cracks and creaks which she would not normally hear. Coals settled on the dying fire. She didn't move, in fact she couldn't move; it was as if she was in some kind of a trance. The initial fear had gone. She was quite separated from it; she might have been someone else watching this woman sitting by the fire, enjoying, yes enjoying the unusual intensity of the noises in the house, and the wind in the apple tree.

And then the back door opened.

She jumped up. Her knee had gone dead and she half twisted over, banging against the chair. There was a scream in her throat, but it was stuck there, unable to get out.

44

"What's the matter?" Norma said.

She shook her head, unable to reply.

"Sorry. Did I give you a fright?"

"You might have rung."

"I didn't want to wake the kids. Oh, thank you Annie, thank you!"

"Is it all right?"

"What?"

"The car!"

"I went into the back of a lorry."

She burst out laughing at the look of consternation on Annie's face. She hugged her and told her not to be a fool, of course it was all right. Her cheeks were glowing and she took off the old suede coat.

"Are you stopping?" said Annie, but the sarcasm was lost on Norma, who was turning up the gas fire without asking. "You look as if you've had one or two," she added.

"Wine and cheese."

"In a Methodist church?"

"No! It's a meeting *about* Methodism. And the work ethic. The chapel was a good thing for the mill-owners because it equated poverty with righteousness, and kept wage rates down."

Annie ignored this rubbish. "What's his name?"

Norma ducked her head. "John. He's lovely."

"I thought he might be."

"Oh Annie, you are nice. I wish you'd been my mum."

"What a daft thing to say. You said I was mean this afternoon."

"Did I? I think you're the most generous person in the whole wide world."

"Make your mind up."

"And the funniest."

"Nobody's ever called me that before – will you gerrof me! Stop pawing me!"

But she was pleased. Normally there was nothing she liked more than her own company, but that had been an odd fancy that had fair frozen her to her chair, and Norma in this mood could be a right tonic, when she wasn't a right pain. You didn't need television when she was around. They sat by the fire and drank cocoa. She was astonished to learn that John was ten years older than Norma – forty-five – and even more astonished to find he had been giving the lecture. He was a lecturer at Bradford Tech, and, because of this, and because Norma described him as kind and gentle, she made Annie think again of Mike, the tech student she'd fallen for on that disastrous night in the pub. For a moment she felt a twinge of envy when Norma told her how John had escorted her out to her car, held the door for her ("He's not from around here," said Annie) and asked: "Would it be possible to see you again?" Norma, suppressing a giggle, imitated his London accent, sounding like a slowed-down BBC news-reader.

"What did you say?"

Norma broadened her natural Yorkshire.

"I said, well I don't know, like."

"You didn't!"

"Of course I did! I've got a lot on!"

"Like what?"

"Kids, PTA. PTA, kids." She imitated his voice again. "I said I'd have to consult my diary. At home."

Annie was hanging on to every word. "And what did he say?"

Norma smiled, and gazed into the fire. "May I ring you then?"

There was a silence. The gas fire puttered, illuminating Norma's face. Annie finished her cocoa. "What happens if he doesn't ring?"

"Of course he'll ring!"

Annie's envy disappeared. What was she thinking about! She was the happy one, with the husband, family, this house, everything. Whereas poor Norma would be distraught again this time next week, hunting for tissues. She was about to say this when she looked at Norma, hands clasped tightly round her legs. She had her shoes off and her big toe poked through her tights and Annie, rather to her own surprise, found herself saying: "I'm right glad for you."

"Thank you."

As she saw Norma out she said: "Will you be all right?"

"What?"

"Walking home?"

Norma had forgotten about the Hawk. Or perhaps she had been playing up her anxiety in order to get the car.

"I'll stick a placard on my back," Norma laughed. "Respectable Woman, in brackets Nearly."

Annie flapped her hand to hush her. It was after twelve! She hadn't had such a late night in ages, and it was school tomorrow and Stephen would be back. There was the whole house to do. And the shopping. And she still hadn't got down to those flaming catalogues! But, as she looked, as usual, over the lighted valley before drawing the curtains she gave herself a little hug, in imitation of Norma. She was glad, so glad she had lent her the car! She had no friends apart from Norma, and she always said she didn't need them, but hadn't this evening been, well, really enjoyable? If she hadn't let Norma have the car they would have stopped seeing each other. Norma wouldn't have stopped. She would. She couldn't have gone round there, after that.

She squeezed the toothpaste onto the children's toothbrushes as she did every night, ready for the morning. She was generous. She was funny. Well, nobody had ever said *that* to her before, maybe she was changing in her old age!

4

It was not that again, it couldn't be that. Her body was frozen, as frozen as when she was sitting in front of the television, newspaper hanging from the tips of her fingers.

Part of her could remember that, so she was awake. But she was not in her bedroom, so it was a dream.

The window was very clear, with drops of water running down it like bars. It was grey, but growing lighter. The door was grey, but growing darker. It was like dawn and evening at the same time.

She had to move, she must move! But not a muscle would respond. She struggled. The silence was terrible. The door was now black, no it was a curtain, a long, fluted black curtain. It moved. There was something behind it.

She struggled. If she could only turn over, but she was completely paralysed!

The blacker the curtain grew, the lighter the window became. There was a moor-top outside. It was Top Withens at Haworth, there was the ruined house, there was the tree waving to her, if only she could move the barest fraction in that direction she would be all right, but she was tied down and something had come out of the curtain, if only she could at least cover her breasts she would be safe, but she was choking, choking and drowning in the curtain.

"Mum . . . Mum."

Jackie's frightened face was staring down at her as she fought off the tangled sheets. At the door, Matthew was standing, wearing only his pyjama top so that she grasped, even in her state, that he had wet the bed again.

So it wasn't that, it was only a stupid nightmare!

"What's the time? Ten-past-eight! Why didn't you wake me? Why aren't you dressed?"

"I can't wear those tights."

"The darn doesn't show, Madam."

"It does."

"Then it will have to show. Go to the toilet when you wake up, Matthew. Don't just pee in the bed."

How could it be that? She wasn't even pregnant. She was having no more children. There could be no fear of that.

She had to nag them into their clothes while she put the porridge on – she wouldn't send them out with sugared cereals in their stomachs on winter mornings. Neither would she have them late for school. The latest they could leave was quarter-to-nine. She packed them in the car clutching slices of Marmite toast and when they stopped at lights, passed them their toothbrushes and a Thermos of water.

"Aw Mum!"

"Do you want toothache?"

"Where do we spit?"

"In cup! Drink from flask. Use your heads."

They were still giggling and spitting when she arrived, forced, like other latecomers, to park on a yellow. Jackie made it, but Matthew's line had gone in. She felt deflated, defeated.

"Tell her it was me. You overslept."

"I'm allus early."

"I don't care! Tell her you're sorry!"

When she got back to the car, Susan was being dropped off by a neighbour of Norma's, with two other children. She didn't know how some people got away with it. Susan had made the line once this term, and that was because Norma's watch was fast.

What was she doing? She was turning to go down Lawson's Lane to go into town, instead of the quicker route down Chapel Street. Was that because the Chapel Street way led her past the hospital?

She was not afraid of that any more. To demonstrate that to herself, she reversed and parked outside the hospital. Norma had left two lipsticked stubs in the ashtray. She put them in the litter bin.

Hillthorpe District Hospital. They had painted the board outside, but a pound to a penny it was just as grotty inside. She felt nothing. This morning she had just had an ordinary, horrible nightmare, that was all. She got back into the car, but did not drive off immediately.

A woman, very pregnant, was going up the drive. Annie watched her waddle up the steps and fit herself into the revolving doors. Probably the other doors were stuck: nothing seemed to work very well in that hospital.

Hadn't she had to use the revolving doors that day?

She'd thought it would crush her and the baby. Her things were stuffed in a plastic bag. It was caught in the door, and her pyjamas, talc and a little doll she'd been given for good luck were flung out into the drive.

How she'd shouted at Stephen, although it was probably her fault as much as his! The last two weeks of the pregnancy had gone on for ever. She dreaded making all that fuss, only for it to be a false alarm. She'd had her case packed and standing in the hall. The night before, just as they were going to bed, she was sure it was coming. The pains were sharp, and every ten minutes. Stephen pulled a sweater and trousers on over his pyjamas and got the old Escort van out – he'd just been taken on by Hallet's and it was all they could afford.

He put the case in the back and helped her in.

"Wait a minute."

"Are you having it?"

"I don't know."

"Let's get t'hospital."

"Hang on, can't you!"

The next contraction was twelve minutes. Then there weren't any. She insisted on going back to bed, and they forgot about her case. As soon as his van disappeared down the road next morning she remembered, and shortly afterwards the pains began in earnest.

They had no phone. They had just moved to their first house, a two-up and two-down in St Jude's Terrace. There was nobody she knew with a car nearby. The phone at the bottom of the street was vandalised: the handset was ripped away. She kept, now she looked back at it, amazingly calm. She went to the bus stop. She calculated she could make it, if she was reasonably lucky, with a bus.

How stupid she was! But she thought she knew it all and she'd had a good pregnancy. She'd felt so fit, more alive than she'd ever been in the middle months. She had grown to feel that there was nothing to it, perhaps to defend herself against Mrs Marsh's gloomy tales of hard labour.

"Steve's was hard. He didn't want to come out, did you?"

"I don't remember."

50

"Well I remember. I shall never forget."

She tried to put these stories out of her head as she stood at the bus stop. With her plastic bag she looked as if she was going out shopping. There was one other person waiting, an oldish man sucking a dead pipe. He said something about just having missed one and she smiled. Then a contraction came. She tried to ignore it. She gasped, dropping the bag.

"Are you all reet?" asked the old man.

"Yes."

"Are you sure?"

She couldn't speak. He picked up her bag. "You're not having it are you?"

"Yes."

"Bloody hell-fire." The old man started out towards the phone.

"Doesn't – " she managed to get out. He stopped. The contraction was easing. It had been so sudden it had squeezed tears from her eyes. "I'll get bus."

"Bus! Bus!" He was frantic, walking round her, wringing his hands. "If you wait for this bus, babby'll be in primary school."

Suddenly he jumped in the road, waving his hands in the air, and stabbing a finger towards Annie. A car narrowly missed him, the driver's cursing face flashing past. The pain had eased, and she had never felt such a spectacle. She wanted to run. People were coming over. A woman said something she didn't hear over the screech of a van stopping. The old man was shouting.

The driver was a short man with a beer belly almost as big as hers. He leant on his horn and drove through red lights. At first he was cheerful. "Makes a change, does this. Normally I deliver car spares." Then as the pain came again, even worse this time as she couldn't change her position in the cramped cabin, he began to panic like the old man. "Don't have it in here love, please. I'm not insured."

After the revolving doors of the hospital had spun her through, but rejected her plastic bag, her disintegration was complete. She, who was never late, never unprepared, was late and in pieces for the most important event of her life.

Even when they were leading her into the labour ward she said: "I've left the kettle on."

"We'll check."

But how could they check? The house, her house, all they had could be burning down. Then the pain came again and obliterated everything. They were heaving her up and pulling her legs open, oh it was dreadful, she was falling apart! They were dabbing grease onto her, clipping on metal suckers: she didn't belong to herself any more. The smiles round her were false, blurring into nothing with the pain.

Then a familiar face appeared: the midwife she'd seen at the ante-natal clinic. She liked her hands. They were always warm and gentle. She didn't wear a false smile. "Your kettle wasn't on," she said. "Your husband's here."

She hadn't wanted him at the birth, but it was comforting to think of him out there, waiting. She gripped the midwife's hand.

"You're well dilated . . . you're doing well . . . lie on your side . . . now relax."

The sponge wiped over her face.

"Now push . . . "

She was sure it was going to come! Surely it would come now!

"I'm going off now."

The midwife squeezed her hand. Going off? What did she mean? Only when she saw that the windows had grown dark did she realise it was evening. She'd never met the midwife who took over. She was rough and brisk, with a mask of jollity.

"Now come on love! D'you want baby or not? If you want baby you'll have to push better than that. I can feel the crown, I want the head, come on, come on!"

She was sweating and straining and pushing and the pain was frightful; she thought she would burst, split apart; if she pushed the baby would come out, but she would be split like an avocado, she would never be put together again; the midwife was a grinning Humpty Dumpty, who wanted to pull the seed from her and chew and spit out the fruit. There was something wrong. She mustn't let whatever it was come out. She began resisting. The pain was now so great she thought she must faint. Somewhere there were screams. To her surprise she realised they were from her. There was something sweet in her mouth and nostrils. Had they given her something? They were overpowering her. They were putting something in her. There was a man now. He was saying something that she couldn't follow because the pain had deafened her and he was pulling, pulling.

The baby came out like a cork from a bottle. She had a hazy picture between the V of her legs of a bawling crinkled face, smeared with a black fuzz of hair, and a red struggling body, still attached to her by a thick cord.

"It's a girl!"

All the triumph, the love she had imagined, was not there. They put the baby on her stomach. She didn't want it. Something dreadful had happened. She knew that. She didn't want to rest. She wanted to escape. The most reassuring thing was a beautiful cup of hot sweet tea. Then Stephen was there.

"Are you all right, then?"

He wasn't jumping about, smiling. He talked about the kettle, the case left in his van. He was undemonstrative, which was the greatest relief of all.

It happened on the third day.

Her milk was slow in coming and her nipples sore. As she picked up the baby to feed it, she saw it had teeth. She put it down and walked away. She went back. The baby cried at the sight of her, opening its mouth to display white, glistening teeth. She walked round the ward, past flowers and cards and babies, all of whose crying or sucking mouths had boneless gums.

When she got back to her bed, a student-nurse was holding the baby.

"Feeding time," she smiled.

"I can't," Annie said. "I can't feed her."

"Oh come on. Try! Poor baby."

"She has teeth."

"Teeth?"

The unsuspecting girl put her finger between the teeth. They were like little knives, razor-sharp.

Annie screamed, wrenched the baby away from her, and dropped it back into the cot.

They put her into a side-ward. That was all part of the plot, to separate her from the other women. She tried to get out but they kept her there until a doctor arrived. He injected her with something. When she woke up she heard the voices. They were arguing about her. There was a man's voice and a woman's. They were shouting so she had to cover her ears. She was not to have the child. It belonged to the devil. That was the reason for the teeth. They saw that she was awake and they laughed. Did she ever think she would have a child? With her face? She had been chosen by the devil. Unless she got rid of the child she would walk the canal bridge like mad Betsy in an overcoat like a tent, winter and summer, weighed down with plastic bags.

When they brought the baby to her she shrank from it. It seemed to have a kind of fur, like a rat she'd seen in the rubbish at the bottom of St Jude's Terrace, where they lived then. She got out of the side-ward but they had taken her clothes. She went out through the revolving doors in her dressing-gown and reached the shops near the hospital before they brought her back.

Now they took her to a different ward, where one of the patients told her that metal plates would be clipped round her head, rubber forced between her teeth and electricity sent through her. She understood that this was to burn out the devil. But they were making a mistake: the devil was in the child, not her. Again she tried to escape. Again they injected her.

Stephen came every day. He talked about his work, he was then sweeping the machine room floor, about wall-paper he was buying. She looked through the pattern book he brought and kept it by her bed. It was a great comfort. Each time Stephen came he fed the baby. She watched him doing so, although she was uneasy, and sometimes frightened.

She saw a different doctor. This was the one she'd been told would give her the electricity, but he didn't. He was unlike the others. He didn't smile. He was casual. His eyes wandered.

"Are you hearing voices?"

"No."

"Have you heard them today?"

"No."

He looked at her notes and then out of the window, as if he was very interested in a passing bus.

"I'm thinking of discharging you at the end of the week. How do you feel about that?"

"What about my baby?"

"Do you want it?"

She was silent.

"It's not the devil's child. It's your child. You know that, don't you?"

"I'm mad, aren't I? Tell me!"

"I've no idea. It's up to you."

She stared at him. Now he looked at a lorry passing, which made the desk tremble.

"Once you say you are, you're probably not."

"Then what's happening to me?"

He got up and put his hands in his pockets. Now he seemed interested in a hospital notice pinned on a green baize board. His shoes were big and clumpy, and could do with a polish. He had catarrh, cleared his throat, and spat secretively into his handkerchief.

"You've had a baby. I'm sorry, that doesn't sound very deep but . . . " He jingled the money in his pocket. "Most of life is small change, cups of tea, rides on buses. It doesn't prepare us for birth and death. Many women have depression after giving birth – you've had this."

"But the voices . . . the baby . . . they were *real*!"

"It doesn't mean you're mad."

55

"It doesn't?" She felt more her old self as the big clumsy man shambled round the room. Now he was shifting the position of the waste-paper basket with his foot.

"A widow hears her dead husband walking up the path. Knocking his pipe out. She's not mad. She's grieving. She gradually gets over it. As you have. It's what we call, in our boring language, a self-limiting episode."

"What am I getting over?"

"Ah. Well. Perhaps you're grieving too. When you take a husband, don't you give up part of yourself? With a child, you give up even more. You're passing yourself on. You find that hard. Like me."

"Like you?"

"I'm not very good at giving myself up."

She looked at him suspiciously. What he was saying was madness in itself. Or was he trying to trap her? Nobody had ever talked to her like this before, at home, school or business college. She pressed thick fingers into her shrivelled belly.

"I can't feed her."

"Of course you can."

"I can't breast-feed her."

Her head hung in humiliation from her taut, rigid body.

"Why should you?" His voice was mild. Now he was looking carefully, full at her. His brown eyes had little gold coloured specks in them. "You have your own way of mothering her, of loving her."

She turned sharply away as she felt the tears sting. "Can I see my baby?"

They went into the ward. She picked up Jackie and held her. At first the baby cried in her unpractised arms but, after a while, caught the glint of the small gold chain she wore and tried to grasp it. She laced it round the baby's fingers. The baby grasped it, tried to bring it to her mouth, and then stared at Annie with a look of such grave intensity that her heart jumped.

She turned to the doctor. His smile was as slight, as cautious as hers. "Can I come back and see you?" she asked.

"If you like." He was casual again, picking up a card he had knocked from someone's locker. "I'm always here on Thursdays."

Dr Seymour, that was his name. She hadn't gone back, but she had seen him when she'd had Matthew. He'd told her the same thing would happen, only worse. He was right. It was worse than the labour, worse because she was anticipating it. But again he saw her through it. Through another — what did he call it? — self-limiting episode. Self-limiting. Episode. That meant there would be no more, unless she had another child, and she didn't intend to do that.

No more.

She must have sat in the parked car outside the hospital for all of twenty minutes, brooding. What a waste of time! As if she hadn't enough to do! She tore through the shopping and determined to make a blackberry and apple pie, everybody's favourite, using the last of the blackberries in the freezer. It had been a silly nightmare, started by that programme the night before, and the missing hammer. That hammer! It was probably staring her in the face! She wiped her floured hands, and went down to the garden shed.

5

She was looking out of the front room window. Her hands were stuck with flour from her second attempt at the pie, which still wasn't in the oven. Stephen had arrived, but he had not come in. He had the bonnet of his car up and she could see his curly hair bobbing. By the time she went to the front door, he was walking up the drive.

"Bloody plugs," he said. "Hello love."

He looked past her at the usually neat hall. She had had

all the boxes out from under the stairs. Spread out on newspapers were tools, toys, plugs, aerosols and a beer kit.

"Been having a clear-out?"

"No, I've been knitting. What's it look like? Is that the time? I didn't know you'd be back now."

He followed her into the kitchen with his slow walk and and his slow smile.

"It were a valve. All it were were a faulty valve. I could murder a mug of tea."

"I'll get it. I were looking for the hammer."

"Hammer."

He sat down at the yellow kitchen table. Spread out on it was a paper she had bought on her way home. It wasn't their usual one. It was open at an article on the killer, and contained a review of the previous night's television programme. There was a picture of Karen Jones, the Manchester victim, a blonde with spiky hair and a rigid smile. Under the picture of the scientist was a summary of his findings, including his opinion that she had been hit with a hammer.

"What d'you get this for?"

"Oh. I picked it up on a bench."

The lie upset her. She never lied. She'd forgotten she'd left the paper out. She put the mug of tea on the newspaper in front of him.

"Hammer's in the shed."

"No it's not."

His eyes were dark, nearly black, and bloodshot at the corners. They were the very first thing she'd noticed about him, his eyes watching her from the edge of that crowd in the pub.

"No it's not," he said. "You're right. Our Ken has it."

His layabout brother.

"You won't get that back."

He was silent. She sliced edges of pastry from the pie. The newspaper rustled. He read very slowly, and she was never sure how much he took in. When she had married him he couldn't read. She had nagged him about it until he had enrolled for a reading scheme, going to see Eddie, a volunteer, twice a week in the evening for two years. She glanced at him as she put the pie in the oven. It was the *Guardian*. He wouldn't manage much of that. Nevertheless, she began to feel hot and uncomfortable as his oil-stained finger moved over the lines.

"Is that why you were looking for hammer? Did you think I were him, then?"

She was astonished. Astonished he had read it so quickly, astonished he had drawn the conclusion, even more astonished he had said it. Astonished and relieved and ashamed in the same breath as she looked at his grinning face and saw the full absurdity of what she had been thinking.

"You daft beggar. Of course I didn't."

"Anyone who travels gets it. Jim had it from his wife, you know, they were having a right joke about it in Albion."

She kissed him, roughly, quickly.

"What have I done to deserve that?"

She was buttoning up her coat. She had twenty minutes to get the kids from school. "You never kiss me when you come in."

"You never want me to."

"I do. Oh look!" There was a smear of grease on her new coat. "How many times do I have to tell you to take your overalls off when you come in! I must go."

"I'll get the kids."

"No. I want to see the teacher about his writing. Watch the pie. Put it near top to brown at four-twenty and have it out no later than four-thirty."

As if to confirm the absurdity of her wild suspicion, Ken returned the hammer that very evening.

"Have you been working?"

"Nay Annie," he said. "You don't think I'd do owt daft like that, d'you?"

"Wonders never cease," she said. "Would you like some pie?"

She cut a slice and deftly squirted it with a spiral of UHT cream.

"Class," he grinned, "real class."

"You don't deserve it," she said.

He didn't. He was quite different from his brother. He'd never done a day's work in his life, although he was clever, or thought he was. He'd been to approved school, and had done six months in Armley Jail for car stealing. He'd borrow anything that wasn't nailed down. She was surprised he'd returned the hammer, until she realised he wanted Stephen to look at his motor-bike.

Sometimes he was in the money, coming round with cans of beer, and lemonade so she could have a shandy.

"I put a squib up a dog's arse and it came in first," he'd say. Or he'd tell them he'd found a telly that worked on Priesthorpe Tip; he was always rooting around the old quarries which the council now used as a dump.

He wore patched jeans and a filthy Rambo sweatshirt – the sort of outfit Stephen wore as a kid. Now Stephen was as fussy as she was about clean shirts and jeans. She knew Ken borrowed money from Stephen and it led to endless rows, with Stephen saying he wouldn't do it any more – until the next time.

"Delicious." Ken scraped his plate. "Can I have another piece?"

"No," she said. "That's your lot."

Stephen came in, holding a twisted piece of metal. "I need one of these pins."

"Oh dear. We'll have to go round corner for it," said Ken, winking at his brother.

Round the corner meant they'd be supping. Well, her Stephen earned it, if Ken didn't. It was his bit of enjoyment, like she had the garden. He rarely drank much, halves while Ken downed pints. What he liked was just sitting, while his brother chatted people up.

Sometimes it drove her up the wall when the two of them were like this, like kids, laughing and winking behind her back. But tonight she felt great, full of energy! She looked at her Stephen, proud of his good looks and his achievement, of the house, the children. It was true, he hadn't half the brains of his brother, but look what they'd done together.

She got his jacket. It was getting chill. She wanted to kiss him, but wouldn't dream of it in front of his brother. Instead she whispered in his ear: "Don't lend him any money. Don't be late."

The killer! What a laugh! The killer was more likely to be someone like his brother, with his gappy, uneven teeth and his shifty look. No one knew what he was up to half the time.

Ken sucked his breath between his teeth, stained yellow with heavy tobacco he rolled. He held up the metal pin from his bike. "I reckon this'll tek some finding."

"Tek you till closing time, will it?" she said.

Everyone roared with laughter.

"Go on. Gerrout," she said.

Once she'd closed the door she could get down to it. Where had she been the last couple of days? What had she been doing? She galloped through the washing-up and at last got down to the seed catalogues. Her order came to twelve pounds! She dithered over cancelling some, but in the end put the order in the envelope and sealed it. She felt guilty all the way through getting their satchels ready and laying out clean overalls for Stephen, but didn't she deserve it, just as he deserved his pub?

He was late, but she didn't notice. In her mind, as she drifted off to sleep, she saw the whole garden full of flowers: the yellow broom that would appear in March, with daffodils, tulips and snowdrops; then as they died, the orange wallflowers and marigolds, the pinks and the pansies, and those curious FI begonias, and the hosta with its stripy purply flowers which would come out under the apple tree, just as the blossom was falling.

6

In the next few weeks, Norma's love life beat the telly hands down. Annie found herself agog every time she met her. It was childish, of course, Norma was thirty-three and her precious John was clocking fifty; childish, but she listened fascinated.

First, he didn't phone, which didn't surprise Annie in the least. Norma said she couldn't go on living, this was her last chance. Annie provided a shoulder until one morning she got so fed up with her she left, telling Norma she didn't want to see her again until she'd got over it.

She'd just got back home and was cleaning the windows when she heard the clank of Norma's car.

"Can I see you?" Norma said.

"You're looking at me, I can't stop you." Annie squeezed out the wash leather.

"I'm sorry. I know I've been a pain."

"Can you hold the ladder?" Annie said.

"You're not going up that, are you?"

"Well who else do you think's going up?"

Up she went, while Norma put her foot on the bottom of the ladder. It was grand rubbing the panes until they sparkled. The sun was coming out, melting the frost on the front lawn. A big blackbird flew past her, surprised. It was as if she was flying too. Below her was the green of one of the few farms left in the valley, running into what she knew as Quarry Woods, although they called it Cockersdale now, and printed a fancy little brochure about it. Beyond that, spread out as far as she could see, were the red terraces and factories of Leeds.

She poured the dirty water on the roses and they went inside.

"I promise not to mention him again," Norma said. "After this."

"I don't want to hear!"

"I'm not like you."

"What's that mean?"

"Nothing upsets you."

She looked out towards the apple tree. Perhaps she should give it another spray. Nothing seemed to get rid of that scab.

"Will you phone him?"

"You what?"

"Will you phone him?"

"You're barmy, Norma." She put the kettle on and got out the biscuit tin.

"–I don't want a digestive biscuit, thank you."

"It's all there is."

"Please – "

"I don't know him, how can I phone him?"

"You're interested in a course. Your friend, Norma Bridesdale, took one on Methodism in the West Riding and it sounded so interesting . . ."

Annie stopped listening. The only thing to do with that sort of talk was let it wash over you. She made the tea and went over the rest of her day. She'd definitely give the tree a spray, then she'd see if the library had that book, *Writing With Your Child*. She'd asked Norma, but Norma couldn't even remember her own name at the moment. As she turned with the tea, Norma was smiling at her pleadingly. Suddenly she'd had enough. You had to be cruel to be kind.

"Look Norma, he doesn't want to know."

"He said – "

"Of course he said, but if he were interested he'd have phoned, wouldn't he? He doesn't – want – to – see you!"

"I can't believe that."

"You don't want to. You're thirty-three. Married with a kid. Men don't want to take that on."

"Some do."

63

"Men aren't like that. They're bad enough when they have their own."

"He's not like that!"

"They're all like that! I know what men are."

"You know nothing, Annie, nothing about men, nothing at all."

The vehemence behind Norma's words took Annie by surprise. Far from there being tears, there was anger in her eyes.

"I've held a man a sight longer than you," Annie said.

As soon as the words had left her lips she felt ashamed. Norma turned away. She picked up her bag and put on her gloves.

"Here's your tea."

Norma said nothing.

It was the guilt Annie felt at her remark, followed by anger at Norma for making her feel guilty, which made her do it. No good would come of it, she knew that, but she would prove her point.

"I'll phone him," she said.

In silence Norma produced from her bag a leaflet with the college phone number on it. "His extension is 392."

"How do you know that?"

Norma flushed. "I just do!"

"Why don't you phone him?"

"How can I?"

Annie went into the hall, where the phone stood on a polished table, with a plastic pop-up labelled USEFUL NUMBERS, and a china money-box pig with a broken tail.

"I'll pay for the call," said Norma.

"Don't be silly."

For some unaccountable reason she was terribly nervous. Her fingers were all thumbs and the first time she dialled she got the wrong number. When the college came on the line she panicked.

"What do I say?"

"You're interested in a course!"

"Hello? Can I help you?" The operator's voice came over a confused background conversation.

She wished Norma would go away and let her get on with it. Why was her heart thumping so much? Perhaps he wouldn't be in. He would be teaching. But she got straight through.

"John Holmes."

She was paralysed. She couldn't say a thing. Oh, this was ridiculous! What on earth was she doing this for? Norma's agonised face was at her elbow mouthing something she couldn't understand.

"Hello?"

"Mr Holmes?"

"Yes?"

Norma stabbed a finger violently at the leaflet. "Methodism," Annie managed to get out.

"Methodism." A trace of impatience crept into the deep voice which made Annie instantly see him as a beautifully suited BBC news-reader. "What about it?"

Norma had her head close to the receiver, straining to hear the conversation. She mouthed and then dug a finger first towards the leaflet and then into her own chest. In making these violent movements, she dislodged the china pig, which broke into several pieces on the floor.

"Oh God," said Annie. Matthew had had the pig since his first birthday, and he would be inconsolable.

"Who's that?" said John Holmes. "What do you want?"

"I'm sorry," said Annie, "I've just broken something. My child's china pig."

"Oh dear," said the voice.

Was there ever a more stupid conversation! Annie went bright red, and felt a trickle of sweat run down her back. Norma was gibbering silently, apparently unmoved by the broken pig. Annie felt a surge of anger.

"Look Mr Holmes," she said. "I'm a friend of Norma Bridesdale. I'm phoning for her – "

Norma writhed in agony. "Course," she hissed. "I told you about the Methodism course."

The deep voice in Annie's ear brightened. "Norma? I've been trying to phone her!"

"She's been waiting for you to call her."

"Oh no!" Norma retreated to sit at the corner of the stairs, and shrunk to a ball, shaking her head continually.

John Holmes laughed. "Has she?" Suddenly Annie felt perfectly at ease as he went on to say that he had dialled the number she had given him, but got someone else and Norma wasn't in the directory.

"That's because she gave you her maiden name," said Annie drily. "Her name's Potter."

Norma's amazed face appeared from the shrunken ball, as Annie smiled and chatted.

"What number did she give you, Mr Holmes? . . . No, it's two five six four. Her twos look like sevens."

"Ah. I must remember that." His voice became halting, uncertain. "Will you, er Mrs . . . Miss . . . "

"Mrs Marsh."

"Mrs Marsh . . . will you be seeing her today?"

"Aye," said Annie, "I expect I shall bump into her."

Norma got up slowly, her mouth open, her cheeks taut.

"Will you tell her I'll phone this evening?"

Annie felt curiously elated as she put down the phone, but she concealed the feeling from Norma (and largely from herself) by lamming into Norma for breaking the china pig.

From that moment she became part of their romance. Was that the right word? Norma never said anything about divorce, and God alone knew what John's position was. Still, she had to admit it was doing Norma good. There was a sparkle in her eyes. She had bought a new coat, wobbled on high heels instead of her comfortable down-at-heel flats and had spent hours poring over magazines before having her hair razor-cut short. It gleamed in the light as she turned anxiously before Annie.

"What's that you've got on your hair?"

"Mousse."

"Mousse? It looks like lard."

"Oh shurrup!"

Norma's manner changed as she turned towards Annie. They were in Norma's house. Annie had collected the kids from school while Norma was at the hairdresser's. Norma's voice became wheedling. "Annie."

"No," Annie said.

"No what?"

"Whatever it is you want."

"I don't want anything!"

There was a scream and running about upstairs. Norma went to the door. Annie thought she was going to shout up to them, but instead she shut the door. She had a casual, it-doesn't-really-matter look on her face which Annie had learnt to beware of over the last few weeks.

"I want to do something for you," Norma said.

"Why?"

"Honestly, you're so suspicious! Why! Because you're always doing things for me! Why don't I babysit for you?"

"Why?"

"Why why why why! So you and Stephen can go out together."

"Where?"

"Oh for God's sake Annie!"

The door suddenly opened and Susan came in. Norma gave a guilty start and then spoke sharply to her daughter for bursting in. Susan, who had grown as sullen over the last few weeks as her mother had grown bright, said she only wanted a tape, found it and went out. Norma examined her nails, polished to match her lips.

"Who's going to babysit for you?" Annie said.

Norma flushed. "Oh, er next door."

"That doesn't make sense, Norma."

Norma walked round the room, hands clasped. She caught sight of her reflection in the mirror and touched her shining hair. It all came out in a rush. Annie, as usual, found it both fascinating and absurd. They hadn't done it yet. Very nearly but . . . not quite. She wanted it to be right. That's why she . . . they wanted to babysit. Annie didn't follow.

"Because of Susan! She's jealous! She can't stand the sight of him."

"She'll be asleep."

67

"I keep thinking she's coming downstairs. You saw how she came in the room just now. Just the thought of it puts me off my stroke."

"You what?"

"Stroke." Norma grinned and thumped her fist into her palm. "When he kisses me I melt."

"How romantic." Annie stared out of the window, where the dead leaves from the sycamore tree had still not been cleared from the front garden.

"Romantic knackers! I melt down here."

She put her hand between her legs. Annie went rigid. Nobody had ever talked to her about that so directly, so crudely, since she was a girl at school.

"It doesn't get any different, Annie love," Norma was saying. "I'm thirty-three but I might as well be eighteen. Sixteen. Oh, bloody hell, I do want him! I can feel it coming on!"

And again she put her hand between her legs.

"What about his house?"

"With his wife there?"

"You didn't tell me he was married!"

"I did."

"You did not."

"Well I knew you'd disapprove."

Annie finished her tea and went into the kitchen to rinse out her cup. Norma followed her. "Well?"

"You're not doing it in my house."

"Oh come on!" Norma was smiling. "Why not?"

Abruptly her temper snapped. "Because I'm fed up with you and I'm fed up with him, that's why not." She got her coat and shouted for the children. "All I seem to do is run around after you, lend you my car, phone him and all I've got out of it is a broken pig."

It was over a week later when Norma turned up again. Annie had enjoyed getting back into her old routines, without the constant interruptions of Norma's love life. She was sorting out Matthew's clothes. There were jeans and sweaters that he had grown out of which would do for the school jumble. She was just bringing them downstairs when the doorbell chimed.

"I'm very busy, Norma."

"Oh, I'm not stopping. I just came to give you this."

She held out something in a paper bag. Annie, who had her arms full of clothes, didn't take it. "What is it?"

"Open it!"

Annie put down the clothes and took out of the bag an enormous china pig, grinning from ear to floppy ear, complete with a question mark of a tail.

"Put it on the table where the old one was."

Norma was so delighted with her present that Annie didn't have the heart to tell her that Matthew would hate it. It was the old pig, without a tail, which he loved, and this pink monster would only remind him of his loss.

"I'm sorry I haven't been around," Norma said.

Annie didn't know what to say. She put the clothes in the jumble bag under the stairs and eventually found words. "How long are you not stopping?"

"As long as a cup of tea?"

As they went into the kitchen Norma told her the pig was John's idea.

"Was it?"

"He bought it."

"Did he?"

"In Halifax when he was lecturing."

It was no bigger than the tiniest of the seeds, the ageratum, that she had bought, but it was there: a sense of unease, a vague uncertainty which she could not put into words.

"That was nice of him."

"He is nice."

Annie put the biscuit tin on the yellow table. While she was doing so, Norma came up behind her and hugged her, whispering in her ear.

"We've done it!"

"Done what?"

"Oh Annie! *It!*"

"Oh. I'd better put the kettle on, then. Did you put something in Susan's cocoa?"

"No."

Norma hugged herself. Each time she came, Annie thought there would be nothing left to surprise her. Each time Norma came out with something that flabbergasted her. They had gone down to Quarry Woods. Norma could scarcely get the words out; she kept shaking her head at herself, at the memory. Annie knew the exact spot she described: early in the year there was a great bank of wild blue hyacinths where the woods broke to let the sun in; later the hedges blazed with willow herb and purple loosestrife; later still, you could pick the juiciest blackberries. She took Matthew and Jackie there with the *Observer Book of Wild Flowers*.

At the top of the quarry was a hole, boarded over. Matthew had discovered you could drop stones through the chinks and it took seconds before they hit the bottom; they called it Matthew's Well. In summer it was one of their favourite places for a picnic, but in winter it was bleak and muddy, and the rocky track down the quarry became a little stream.

"You want your heads testing," Annie said. "You must have got soaked down there. Is that where you got that cold from?"

"Yes. I want this cold to go on forever."

"You daft beggar. Well don't come near me. I don't want it."

"Oh Annie." Norma whispered. "It was wonderful. I'd forgotten what it was like."

Annie set out the cups. "Doug only left you last year."

"Oh, he left me a long time before that, you know what I mean? You know, it got mechanical like. I'd forgotten, I'd forgotten completely what it could be like, you know what I mean?"

Her eyes were shining, and Annie found herself moved in a strange way, her irritation vanishing. There was a silence in which Annie could hear blackbirds quarrelling in the garden, and a car in the street.

Annie was still holding the cups. She put them gently down in the saucers, as if she was in a church or the library, and brought out the cake she had been saving for Sunday tea, for which she always baked something special. This one was Matthew's favourite: a chocolate layer cake.

Norma stared at it. "Oh, don't cut that for me."

"I'm cutting it for me. You can have a digestive if you like."

Norma pronounced it delicious, but Annie, who had had slight pangs of regret at her gesture as she slipped the knife into the cake, felt herself rewarded by finding, as she half-suspected, that the sponge was not her lightest; she could always bake another for Sunday. She thought the surprises were over for today, but as she cut second slices and poured second cups, Norma, through a mumble of crumbs, came out with another.

"Will you come to dinner?"

"Dinner?"

"It's a meal you have in the evening. You and Stephen. I want you to meet him."

Annie stared at her. She licked the chocolate cream from her fingers. "What for?"

"What for? Because you've been part of it! Because I like you! Because you're my friend!"

Annie's eyes suddenly started pricking. She had to get up and side the plates, otherwise she'd have been bawling too. Why did Norma have this effect on her? Why didn't she leave her alone? She'd been having such a happy day, she'd got everything organised, now she'd have to bake another cake, the sponge wasn't too bad, why did she have to come along disturbing her? She didn't want to meet him. La-di-da teacher. No he was a lecturer. Lecturer. Dinner.

"I wouldn't know what to say to him."

"Don't be ridiculous. You did all right on the phone."

"That was awful."

"He thought you were wonderful."

"Get out!"

"He did! You're going all pink like the pig!"

71

She did feel hot and flustered. It had never occurred to her that they would talk about her. She felt even more uneasy. They weren't their sort of people, but it was impossible to get Norma to understand that. In the end, to get her out of the house, she said she would talk to Stephen about coming. She didn't intend to do so. What was the point? They wouldn't go, it wasn't Stephen's cup of tea at all, any more than it was hers. Probably Norma was just being polite anyway, she decided, not expecting her to come for a minute. Yes, that was it. As she began to mix another chocolate cake, the invitation was already receding into a casual idea which would not be mentioned again.

<h1 style="text-align:center">7</h1>

The pink pig was a sensation. To Annie's surprise Matthew was perverse enough to love it. Not only that, he told her the other one was right rotten.

"You loved it! Poor pig!"

"I did never! It were all chipped and it had no tail. I shall save up in this."

"I'll bet."

"I will. You owe me fifty pee."

"I don't!"

"You do!"

He went into a long rambling explanation, involving some money dropped on the floor, taken by Jackie, and a week's pocket money which he swore he'd never been given, until she struck a deal with him that she would give him the coin if he would keep a record of the money, pinned to a board in his room. She tried to tell herself she wasn't giving in and being too soft: it would help his arithmetic, and eventually lead to thrift; but really, what use was a china pig if you couldn't rattle it?

"Thank you Mum!"

He flung his arms round her neck. There were no half measures with Matthew. He was either up or down, unlike Jackie, who had some of her own reserve. He always released something in her when he kissed her like this, and she felt, as she held his wriggling warmth, that she was closer to him than to anyone else in the world.

"Thank you for my pig."

"Don't thank me. I didn't buy you it."

"Who did?"

She ruffled his hair. Who did? What would she call him? She tried to explain, but this produced another stream of questions, once he got on a subject he never stopped, until she said the pig was from his Uncle John.

Next morning was a Saturday. She did the weekend shop with Jackie while Matthew enthusiastically held the spanners for Stephen, who was working on Ken's bike, which had packed up again.

"Here," said Matthew.

Annie was walking past them with a carton of groceries. "Don't here me. Help me carry this "

"Dad says I haven't got an Uncle John."

"It's Norma's boyfriend."

Stephen was in his green overalls: some days he never seemed out of them. Spread out before him on sheets of newspaper was the carburettor.

"Oh. Why did he give him pig?"

She was suddenly irritated. The supermarket had been crowded and she was sure the woman had rung up 64p instead of 46p for that tin of tuna. "God knows, I don't know. Here. Take this."

He spent all his time on his flaming brother's bike but he never thought to give her a hand.

She got the second load and began to run through the prices. She was annoyed with herself for not having queried it, but the queue had been right down to the biscuits. Stephen came in with the last bag.

"Funny."

"What?"

"Giving lad the pig."

"Oh for God's sake. He broke it."

"He's been here? I didn't know you'd met him."

There it was on the receipt! 64p! She knew it! It wasn't the money, it was being diddled: it was always on their side, and always that checkout. She put the tin on the windowsill with the slip underneath it.

"Don't touch that tin. I'm taking it back."

As she turned, she took in his last remark. He was wiping his hands on the rag he always kept in his overalls, his face questioning. She looked at the slow movement of his fingers. There was a simple explanation. Why was she making such a meal of it? Why was she feeling uneasy again?

She knelt down to put the groceries away in the cupboards, and told him the story of the pig, but it wouldn't come out in a straightforward way. She felt as daft as a brush when she told him how she made the phone call, and because it had been a pleasant memory, which was now turning into something else, something silly as she put it into words, she grew increasingly exasperated. When she rose to her feet, the blood pounding in her temples from long bending, and saw him grinning at her, she snapped at him.

"They've invited us to dinner."

"Dinner?" He put the rag back in his overalls.

"It's a meal you have in the evening."

He gave her his long, slow smile: she could never rattle him. "At home, dinner time were twelve o'clock."

"You're at home now."

"We don't eat dinner."

Sometimes he could drive her up the wall! It didn't make it any better that he was right. He had his main meal in the middle of the day, while she had a knife and fork tea with the kids. Sometimes he joined them, more often he didn't.

"What's that got to do with it? Some people dine in the evening."

74

The word seemed right funny when it came out of her mouth. Like the way he spoke. Mr La-di-da.

"With candles?" Stephen said.

Was he laughing at her? "Well we're going," she said. "And that's that."

The next week was dominated by nothing else. Norma was delighted, and said John was right looking forward to meeting her. The main problem was fixing a date. Annie had no idea that arranging a dinner for four people could be so difficult. Mind you, one of the four was married to somebody else so that did complicate matters: he couldn't do weekends. Then Stephen never knew where he was going to be, apart from Christmas and bank holidays.

"I'm on call," he would say.

"You can't always be on call! What about Thursday?"

"I'm in Derby."

"Friday."

"I'm on call."

"Get somebody else to do it!"

"How can I?"

"Tell them you're going to dinner."

He grinned.

"Tell them it's your mother's birthday."

Eventually the great day was settled for Friday week and Annie thought Norma would give the phone a rest, but scarcely a day passed without a call.

"Is there anything you don't eat?" she asked.

"Is there anything you don't eat?" she repeated to Stephen.

"What is this? A quiz? I eat owt you put in front of me."

"I hate tomatoes," chimed in Jackie.

"They give her the pip," shouted Matthew, rolling about at his own joke.

It was typical that Stephen wouldn't give her a straight answer. "There must be summat you don't eat!"

"Why?"

"Everybody has their likes and dislikes."

Eventually she told Norma she wasn't too keen on pork

and he wouldn't eat tomatoes, neither of which was true, but something seemed to be required for what was turning out to be as important as a wedding or Christmas. It was the first time Norma had invited any of her friends to meet John. When she discovered this, Annie wanted to back out, urging Norma to invite someone else. She said Stephen might be on call. She felt awful; she hated lies and had drummed it into the kids not to tell them. She expected Norma to take it casually: she had plenty of friends she could ask. Instead, she was very upset.

"He wants to meet you."

"Why me?"

"Because you're part of it."

That made it worse. But there was no getting out of it now. She went through her side of the wardrobe with increasing anxiety. Mostly she wore jeans and sweaters, with the occasional skirt. The only suitable dress was the one she had worn for her sister June's wedding four years ago, but there was the purple stain where Matthew had spilt Ribena down it. Kids! How could you dress up when you had kids?

She couldn't ask Norma's advice. That would be making too much of a thing about it. After all, it was only an evening at Norma's place for God's sake, what was she getting so het up about?

When she collected her gardening paper from the newsagent she bought *Woman* and *Woman's Own*, hiding them in her bedroom drawer because they would only produce that daft grin from Stephen. She felt that only he knew, not from anything he said, but just from that look, exactly what was going through her mind.

With her morning cup of tea, instead of reading about compost and winter tar oil washes, she read: "If the strains of the party season have stretched you to the limit, slip into something more comfortable for your next evening out."

She stared at the elegant clothes, draped on young, beautiful models, and used the magazines to wrap some dahlia tubers she was taking to her sister.

Half-heartedly, she went round the shops. She, who was

76

so sure of herself and so critical when buying the children's clothes, flicked uncertainly at shimmering ranks of dresses and blouses. She tried on one dress, which looked fairly plain and sensible, and which she thought she would get some wear out of. But her sharp collarbones sticking out of the V-neck, and the severe blue collar made her look like – she could hear Matthew's voice – "Prisoner 99".

She put her jeans back on, noticing now, among all these new clothes, how shabby they were, and slunk out of the cubicle. She gave up. She would get the stain out of that dress. She went into Marks for some socks for Matthew – his feet grew by the day – and there she saw it. It was a paisley printed wrap top with a matching fuschia silky skirt. She looked at the labels. Fifty pounds! Ridiculous! She bought some trifle for tea and passed the clothes on her way out.

"He wants to meet you."

As if that mattered! She fingered the pleated skirt. That would suit her, but she wasn't too sure about the top. Her neck would stick out again and wasn't it a bit too gaudy?

"Are you buying that?"

She stared at the woman, another customer, who had been hovering around her. "It's the only one left in that size," the woman explained.

Suddenly Annie couldn't bear to part with it. "Yes," she said, "yes I am."

Fifty pounds! On something she might wear a couple of times! She hid her guilty parcel in the boot of the car and collected the kids from school. She could always take it back tomorrow. Usually when they got in she listened to Matthew's reading, and did sums with Jackie, who was weak on arithmetic. They were surprised and delighted when she told them they could watch television.

Her hands were shaking as she took the silky clothes out of the green bag. What a lot of fuss about nothing! The skirt wasn't bad, in fact it fitted her well, but the top was a disappointment, showing too much of her scrawny neck. Fool! Who did she think she was? She whirled round as there was a sound at the door. Jackie was standing there, staring at her.

She was about to shout at her for creeping about, when Jackie said: "Hey Mum, that's real."

"Don't finger it! I haven't bought it. I'm taking it back."

"Why?"

"It doesn't fit. Look at the neck. I look like a chicken."

"Take belt out of loops. Tie it across like this."

She was right. She was unnerved into silence when she saw her reflection. She was not one of those glamorous women in the magazines, but she was not herself. She could take the loops up. Of course. She would think about that instantly for her children, why didn't she think about it for herself?

Jackie fussed around her, laughing with glee. She loved new clothes. Annie rarely had this kind of fun with her: it always seemed to happen with Matthew; so much so that she had to make a conscious effort to leave him and play with her.

She couldn't stop looking at herself. Well, she thought, I don't look dreadful. Jackie dashed off to her bedroom as if she had a train to catch and rooted around until she found her favourite necklace. It was only a cheap, white, plastic thing, but somehow it looked more expensive against the purply, paisley top. And it covered her bony bits.

Jackie hugged her. "Ooo, I've never seen you look so nice. It's fantastic."

"Don't pull at it."

"You are going to buy it, aren't you?"

"I might."

"You might – you are, you are!"

Matthew came in and she laughed as he gawped at her, and then retreated before his dirty hands.

"You are you are you are," they chanted, advancing on her.

"Stop it, stop it you two!"

She took it off, frightened now that every touch would leave a mark, locked it in the wardrobe, and put on her old sweater and jeans. She glanced at herself in the mirror, as if some of the change might still be there.

"Is it for Norma's?" asked Jackie.

"Well I thought I might wear it for that, yeah," she said casually.

The day before the dinner Stephen was in Derby. He said he'd be back early evening but he phoned up to say he'd be late. She spent the evening worrying, convinced that something would keep him in Derby tomorrow. She pressed his suit and even ironed the new tie she'd bought him in Schofield's. That were three pounds. For a tie! But it was a nice red and green stripe, and looked vaguely as if he had had some kind of an education.

At two o'clock in the morning she woke up. There was a man in her room. She could see his silhouette in the moonlight filtering through the curtains. She dare not move. Her eyelids were still half-closed, and she felt as she had in her bad dream, but this was real. As her eyes focussed, she saw it was Stephen, of course it was him, but she stayed in her half-sleep, puzzled why she should have thought him someone else, staring through half-shut eyes at his black shape. She could now see the white smudges of his face and hands. He was looking straight down at her. As in the dream, she felt she must move, or something dreadful would happen, but she could not so much as flicker an eyelash. If he moved, then she could move, but the two of them seemed bound together in some frozen silence.

How long they would have stayed like that she did not know, but then Matthew cried out in his sleep. They moved together.

"Stephen?"

"Aye."

"Is that you?"

"Aye."

"What are you doing?"

"Getting undressed."

Matthew cried out again.

"I'll go," he said. "You go back to sleep."

She heard him murmuring to the child. The murmuring comforted her. It couldn't be that again, that only happened when she had children. It was a trick of sleep that stretched out a second into minutes, and anyway, why shouldn't he look at her? She dozed and turned and looked at her watch and could not sleep properly again. She was up before six, cleaning the house.

"Are they coming here, then?" Stephen said.

"No but your mother is."

Stephen collected Mrs Marsh on his way back from work. It was one of the coldest nights of the winter, and the small dumpy woman was muffled up to her curling grey eyebrows.

"You just have a good time," she said, "don't worry about me."

She hooked her stick on the chair, put her pills on the mantelpiece, and peeled off her coat and one of two cardigans while Jackie and Matthew chattered round her.

"It's a special occasion," said Jackie.

Mrs Marsh turned, eyebrows lifting. Stephen was positioning the chair where she liked it, near the fire, in front of the telly, and within stretching distance of her tablets. Annie put Norma's telephone number, in bold figures, next to them.

"It's nothing to crack on about," she said. "We're only going out to dinner."

"If there's anything you want me to do, speak now or forever hold your peace," said Mrs Marsh, settling comfortably in the armchair, and picking up the monogrammed folder containing the *TV* and *Radio Times*.

Ten-past-six and Annie still hadn't changed. Come for drinks at seven, Norma had said, and we'll eat at seven thirty. At this critical point she was suddenly in awe of Norma, whom she scolded and looked down on for being in such a mess. Dinner. This was Norma's territory, not hers. It couldn't be twenty-past-six! She was still flying around, putting tea and biscuits out for Mrs Marsh, getting the children's teeth done.

Mrs Marsh's spectacles had a stalk missing, and her nose was in a permanent wrinkle from holding them on while she marked the TV programmes she was going to see. As she did so, she murmured: "Dinner. My word."

Annie just stopped Matthew from spilling his drink. "I don't see what's so special about the word."

"I allus have my dinner – " the old woman started.

"At twelve o'clock," Annie finished. "But times have changed."

"Not always for the better," said Mrs Marsh.

There was no answer to that. Twenty-five past. She was just on her way upstairs when Jackie said proudly: "Mum's got a new dress."

Mrs Marsh's spectacles slipped. "Have you?"

"No I haven't."

Why on earth did she say that? She saw Jackie's face. She suddenly knew it was impossible. She couldn't wear it. It wasn't her. She couldn't come down in front of this old cow, or Stephen come to that, wearing that! She would wear what Matthew called her Ribena dress. Nearly half-past. She was going up the stairs when Stephen was coming down. He was wearing his Shetland Isle sweater and grey slacks.

"For God's sake," she shouted.

"What?"

"I left your suit out!"

"It's not a wedding."

"Stephen gerrit on, please!"

His mother craned up, staring, as he retreated into the bedroom. Perhaps there was something she could do about the Ribena. If she wet it, it might make it worse. She could keep her legs crossed – oh what was she on about! She was half-way through putting it on when Jackie came in. Her face fell.

"Oh Mum," she wailed, "you can't wear that old thing!" And, plunging towards the wardrobe, she pulled out the purple silk skirt and top.

Stephen, who was knotting his tie, turned.

"It doesn't fit," muttered Annie.

81

Jackie took charge. She could be a right little bossyboots sometimes, but she'd never been like this with Annie before. She dressed Annie in the same scolding way as Annie used to dress her.

"It's not in the loop . . . no, tie it here . . . not like that . . . in a bow so it goes over your hip . . . come here, let me do it . . . That's real! Fantastic! Stand up. Pity you haven't any lipstick."

She had. She'd bought the palest purple shade she could find. She disliked the greasy feel of it on her lips but she had to admit . . .

"It matches!" Jackie cried. "That's terrific. Pat your lips on this tissue."

"Have you been wearing lipstick?"

"No."

"You're fibbing."

"Well you're a fibber. You told Grandma you hadn't a new dress. Look, Dad. In't she terrific?"

She got up, suddenly shy and awkward. He rubbed his head, as if puzzled. "Aye," he said.

"Well kiss her then."

They all laughed as Jackie pulled them together, and then the child kissed them both.

Mrs Marsh's spectacles came tumbling off when she saw her, and she asked the question Annie was dreading: "How much did that cost?"

"Twenty pounds."

Another lie! Why? It was her own money. But tonight belonged to her, or rather to the woman in the purple outfit. She wasn't going to have it ruined by that old cow or anyone else. The woman in the baggy sweater and jeans would tell her how much it cost. Later.

It was wonderful to be out of the house! How long was it since they'd been out together? She couldn't remember. He'd been away for her birthday, when he usually took her to the Cavalier Steak Bar.

She loved the bright moon and the bitter, sharp cold, which had already laid a layer of frost on the car windows. She helped him scrape it off.

"It's nearly seven."

"It's not far."

She laughed. He stared at her.

"Come on," she said.

The children banged on the windows as Stephen started the car. She had laughed because she was happy. Because she had told a lie. Because she had not only spent fifty pounds on an outfit but she was actually wearing it.

Frost sparkled in the headlights. They were on the road where she used to cycle to do her business studies. Abruptly – her stomach lurched as if she was in a lift stopping – the years slipped away. It was both wonderful and terrible. Wonderful because feelings which had been buried under marriage and children and house-buying came rushing back, feelings of hope and tenderness and love. Terrible because everything she had built round herself, the house, Stephen and the children, the £2000 painfully accumulated in the Leeds Permanent Building Society, the garden even, were gone, suddenly blown away in the sharp air, and she was still that girl, that vulnerable, gawky girl, detaching her basket from her bike – oh that basket! – and going into that pub where she had met Stephen.

No, she had met the other boy, Mike.

Stephen had simply watched her, as he had watched her last night, or was that a trick of sleep?

Recently, she'd been unable to get that evening in the pub out of her mind. Hadn't Stephen been amused as he watched her, in that awful darned cardigan, with her feet stumbling over her wretched bicycle basket, as she struggled to say something to Mike? Hadn't he known the torture going on in her head, as only an observer, an outsider can? Hadn't he followed her because of that? So what? What was she getting at? Why did she have that uneasy feeling again? He'd been amused, but he'd followed her because he'd felt sorry for her, and because he had been lonely like her. What was wrong with that?

She lifted up her bottom and smoothed the pleats of her purple skirt so they would not crease. Well, she grinned to herself, no darned cardigan, she was dressed for Mike all right.

His name was John! Mike indeed! What on earth was she dreaming about?

"Here we are." Stephen put on the handbrake and switched off the lights.

But not his stolid silence, not her common sense telling her that her babble of thoughts were all nonsense, nor the night chill as they walked past the larch tree up Norma's front path, could stop her heart beating faster, as fast as that of the gawky young girl with her bicycle basket entering that pub, as if, for once, life had permitted a re-run, had given her a second chance.

8

"Sorry we're late," Annie said.

"I was praying you'd be later," Norma said. "Nothing's ready. Hello Stephen. My God you look posh. I am honoured."

Norma wasn't very dressy. In fact she was very casual: white blouse and her old black slacks. The house looked the same old tip; waiting for the door to be answered, Annie had expected some kind of a transformation, dim lights, music perhaps, after all it was a dinner; but the hall table was stacked with circulars and unopened bills, and coats were thrown haphazardly over the banisters. Annie felt a flutter of panic as Norma removed her coat.

"My God," she said, dipping her head into her clutching hands. "Look at you. My God."

Annie wanted to flee out of the front door. A sound drew her eyes upwards. Kneeling down, with her face pressed against the bars like an animal in a cage, was Susan. She gave Annie an unblinking stare back. She was naked.

"I was going to get all glam and organised," Norma said, "and then I thought – it's you."

She saw Annie's expression, clapped a hand over her mouth and shrieked with laughter at her own clumsiness. Annie felt sick. Norma put her arm round her.

"You look lovely. Doesn't she look lovely? Where is John? I've never seen you look lovelier. Where did you get it? Marks? I don't believe it. Our guests have arrived, darling."

Darling!

Annie caught a flash of hatred in Susan's eyes. A toilet flushed in the bathroom behind her. Stephen pushed two stubby fingers at his tight shirt collar to try and ease it. Annie snatched them away. There was always dirt on them.

As the latch rattled on the bathroom door – it always stuck – Norma shouted: "Come and see what she's bought for you, darling!"

"Shut up, Norma," Annie said. "Please shut up!"

Norma was immediately contrite, clutching at Annie's arm. "I'm sorry, how awful, I'm only going on like this because I'm nervous, Susan has been playing up something terrible, pretending she's ill –"

"I am ill," shouted Susan, jumping up to the top of the stairs, and brandishing her clenched fists. "I'm ill ill ill!"

"Of course you're ill if you stand about with nothing on," Norma shouted back. "Get your pyjamas on!"

"I can't find them!"

"They're on the radiator."

"They're not."

Into the middle of all this stepped a shambling, balding, bespectacled man whom Annie stared at with incredulity. She thought he must be the plumber, or some elderly relative, until he produced the educated tones she had heard on the phone.

"Can I help?"

Susan treated him as if he didn't exist. She stood so he could not come down the stairs and yelled, "I have a temperature."

"I'll give you a temperature – "

"I have I – "

"Susan you are seven years old! Get to your room."

Susan became incoherent, tears spurting, and Norma, darting upstairs, looked ready to explode when Annie stopped her. "Count up to five." That brief moment enabled Norma to control her temper and take Susan in her arms. "Come on then, come on then, come on."

"There spoke the voice of experience," said the man coming down the stairs.

"Oh," Norma half-twisted round and spoke above the sobbing child. "John, Annie, Stephen."

John came forward with a warm firm hand. "It's so nice to meet you at last."

She nodded, smiled, but could think of nothing to say. Stephen also shook his hand in silence. John led them into the front room. It was as untidy as ever. He cleared books from a chair. Stephen stood awkwardly in front of the fire, his hands moving towards his collar again, until Annie gave him a sharp glance.

If Norma was casually dressed, John looked as if he was wearing gardening clothes. An elbow poked through his blue sweater, and his brown cords were wearing thin at the knees. His greying hair bushed out round his bald patch, and the steel spectacles hooked tightly round his ears gave him a perpetually surprised look. Annie still could not quite believe it. There must be some mistake. She couldn't imagine this man in Quarry Woods with Norma, rolling in the wet grass.

When he turned from switching another bar of the fire on and smiled at her, she flushed.

"What would you like to drink?"

"Oh, I'm all right, thank you."

What a stupid thing to say. She should have said: what do you have? She'd rehearsed that.

Stephen asked for a beer.

"Ah." John scratched his bushy hair wildly. "Now that might present a little local difficulty." As he stepped out of the room, Norma passed along the landing. "Have we any beer?"

"Try the fridge."

"Very logical," he said.

When he'd gone, Stephen screwed up his face into an imitation of John's surprised look. "Very logical."

Part of her wanted to laugh, part of her felt a deep, obscure sense of disloyalty.

"Don't start that."

"What?"

"You know."

Once he started his imitating, he could go on forever.

"Where's this dinner, then?" he asked.

"How the hell do I know?"

"I'm starving."

"Shurrup," she snapped, as she caught the clink of bottles.

John came in with a tray bearing several bottles and glasses, which swayed dangerously. He bent apologetically towards them, the light catching his spectacles. "I'm awfully sorry. There's no beer."

"That's all right," she said.

"But we are afloat with wine . . . red or white?"

Stephen stared at the bottles.

"Red," she said.

"Oh good. You've changed your mind."

"No. For him. He prefers red."

John looked a little startled and then said to her: "Are you sure you won't have one? There's an end of sherry . . . "

"All right."

They talked about the weather and agreed it was cold and getting colder, in fact it was cold enough to snow. Stephen was swallowing his wine like beer. John refilled his glass.

"Where do you work, Stephen?"

"Hallet's."

John waited for him to enlarge on this but she knew he

wouldn't. Desperately she tried: "Moulding machines. Rothwell. Stephen's an engineer. He can fix anything that moves, can't you?"

"Usually," he said.

"He'll do owt for anybody, except me," she said.

Stephen grinned, and there was some uneasy laughter before they all lapsed into silence again. One by one, they all glanced towards the door, but there was no sign of Norma, let alone food. John picked up the bottle of sherry.

"No thank you," she said, "I can't drink on an empty stomach," and then blushed furiously at her gaffe.

"I'm sorry," he smiled. "Today has been a real chapter of accidents."

He was really quite posh inside his scrubby pullover, which she now recognised was also Marks, about four years old. How could his wife let him go out like that? Then she remembered she didn't know where he was; it was all very confusing.

He persuaded her to have a second sherry, and poured Stephen a third glass of wine. He asked about their children and she said they had one of each and he said it was nice to have the set and she said, yes, you didn't have to bother any more and he smiled and scratched his head and the conversation died.

She felt more and more self-conscious as they sat there, dressed up to the eyeballs, with him in that old pullover and a pair of Clark's boots in which he looked as if he'd tramped the moors. The silence became more and more penetrating every second and more and more difficult to break. They shifted and looked into their glasses and scratched themselves and then Stephen's stomach began. It started as a tiny stirring which they all ignored, and then climaxed in a full-blown rumble. John started to grin, but she must have looked so agonised that his grin froze.

The rumble faded, and they shifted and drank and waited for the next one. But then came the most welcome sound in the world: Norma coming downstairs.

She burst in. "All right for you, enjoying yourselves.

She's nearly off. She has got a cold. Give me a drink for Christ's sake." She ruffled John's bushy hair. "Oh you useless sod. You haven't given them nuts."

He looked so happy that Annie, for an instant, felt a little stab of envy.

"Nuts?" John said.

"They grow on trees," Stephen said unexpectedly.

There was so much laughter at this that when nuts and crisps and some funny Indian things which tasted of hot curry arrived he was emboldened to cap it by saying, as he took a handful: "Is this dinner then?"

John doubled up, at which Stephen began throwing nuts up in the air, catching them in his mouth and crying: "Is this t'dinner then?"

This was far preferable to that awful, glacial silence, but Annie knew he would go on forever, now he had found something people would laugh at.

"What is for dinner?" she asked Norma.

"Nuts," Stephen said, throwing her one.

She saw from the look on Norma's face and the glance she gave John that something was wrong.

"Can I help?" she asked as Norma left the room.

"No. You're a guest! Sit down!"

But Annie followed her. As she walked through the hall, she could hear Susan coughing. In the kitchen dirty dishes, pots and pans, stood in crazy piles. The extent of the disaster soon became apparent.

Norma took the lid from a large casserole on the stove. Inside was a mush of strips of chicken, spaghetti and sliced mushrooms, flecked with gobbets of coagulated cream. Annie withdrew her nose. It was off.

"What in the world is that?"

"Chicken Tetrazzini."

"What's that when it's at home?"

Norma indicated a recipe pinned on the board, which showed a delicious-looking dish, piping hot, with grilled cheese on top.

"The cream's separated," she wailed. "I did it this morning. I left it on the oven to cool and Susan moved it

89

over the pilot light. That's what the row was about. She did it deliberately because she hates him."

"No she didn't. Don't be ridiculous. You're upset. What are you doing?"

Norma had taken a sieve down from the wall and was attempting to manoeuvre the contents of the casserole through it. "The chicken's all right."

"I'm not eating that."

"You'll go hungry then."

Bits of the mush were slipping into the sink, and onto the floor. Norma was close to tears. Susan, through her coughs, was now calling out.

John came in, followed by Stephen who said: "Come on, Norma. You're missing second course. Crisps."

John squeezed Norma's arm. "Shall I go to her?" Norma looked as if she was going to throw the chicken mush at the wall. Annie took it from her.

"Go see to Susan," she said. "She'll not settle until you do."

"What about the food!"

"I'll knock up something."

"No Annie, this was your treat!"

"Go on, before she gets hysterics. I've done nothing all day and you're jiggered. If you've any Benylin give her three spoonfuls. Stephen, clear those dishes, will you."

"Taking charge, are you?" John said.

She thought from his tone of voice that he resented her butting in, but she didn't care.

"Someone's got to," she said, tying on an apron and making a rapid survey of the fridge.

"What are you going to do?"

"I don't know till I do it, do I?"

It was such a relief, instead of sitting down nattering, or rather not nattering, to put an apron on and get on with it! She was an expert, from those early days in St Jude's Terrace when every penny counted, in stretching food and inventing dishes. The men washed pans and cleared spaces while she fried bacon and sliced onions and mushrooms and cooked spaghetti with practised speed. She even found time to water a neglected plant.

"That's dead," John said.

"It'll live."

"Norma tells me you have green fingers."

"There's no such thing as green fingers." She cubed some little sausages she'd found. "It's all hard work."

He seemed to find this very funny. She looked at him suspiciously. "You mean green fingers have been invented by the lazy?" he said. "You may be right. On the other hand, might you not have a certain flair which rewards your hard work, and encourages you to work still harder?"

She had no idea what he was going on about. Since he had mentioned flair, she supposed it was in connection with Norma, and as she had been invited out to a dinner which she was now preparing, she said: "Flair never filled anyone's stomach."

He laughed even more. Convinced he was laughing at her, she whirled round on him to tell him she was glad he found her funny, but the warm expression on his face stopped her. "Thank you, Annie," he said. "Thank you for saving us tonight. And thank you for making that phone call."

She was moved, not only by what he said, but by his awkwardness; and she suddenly realised that, in his own way, he was just as much out of his depth as she was. But she was so unused to this warmth and awkwardness from men, that her tongue stuck in her mouth and all she could do was push the pan he had given her back to him.

"There's still some muck on that."

"Sorry."

As he went back to the sink, his shoulders hunching as he scrubbed with a Brillo pad, she felt both churlish and strangely excited, she could not say why. She wasn't attracted to him: that was a laughable thought! But he kept glancing at her and she at him as she made the sauce and checked the spaghetti, and once their eyes met, and she looked away sharply, as if there *was* something going on!

"Thank you for the pig," she said.

"Oh. Did he like it?"

"Yes. So do I. He's saved two pounds in it. He never saved anything in the old one."

He was delighted. He poured more wine and insisted on her finishing the sherry while he told her, rubbing his hands at the memory, how he saw the pig in a shop window and knew instantly it was Matthew's.

"But you've never met him."

"I felt I knew him."

"He calls you Uncle John."

"Does he? Does he really?"

He ruffled his wild hair. She could now see what Norma saw in him: they were two of a kind, completely disorganised, with a childish enthusiasm for life which was wonderful if you didn't have to live with it. Now he had put wine in her glass which she was drinking, and really it wasn't at all bad, and he was talking about Methodism in the West Riding, and she was listening fascinated as he brought to life the chapels, those grimy black boxes which still dotted Bradford and Leeds, and painted them not as homes of religion, but houses of repression. It wasn't this idea that held her spellbound, so much as the fact that she was listening to ideas. It was later, only very much later, that she worked out what was happening to her. It was as if some part of her mind had remained frozen since adolescence and was now being melted, as if, in a weird way, she *was* being given a re-run of that awful night in the pub, when she'd first met Stephen.

And that other boy, Mike.

Hadn't she, in some magical way, expected him to appear? And wasn't he here, in the shape of John's kindness and gentleness? The difference was that she was listening, talking, even arguing – about the factory system of the early nineteenth century, for heaven's sake! He made her realise that there was a time when there were no factories, when the view from her window over the Aire valley was green; well, she had known that, of course; but he made her see the view. And now the factories were dying. He made her wonder, think, she who had never seen beyond her garden. She got so excited, and was enjoying herself so much that she let the spaghetti go soggy and the sauce burn.

Instead of being a tragedy, it was funny.

"There's always the Chicken Tetrazzini," he said gravely.

She collapsed with laughter – she was getting as bad as Norma. She tasted the sauce. It was eatable. "Well my family like it a bit burnt," she said.

"I'd like to meet them."

"You must come over."

Just like that! She who never had anybody over if she could possibly help it.

"I'd love to."

"With Norma."

"Well good Lord, you don't think I'd bring my wife, do you!"

She was laughing again, wiping her eyes on the corner of her apron, before she remembered it was plastic, which produced still more laughter until he stopped and she turned to see Stephen standing there.

Watching.

For a brief instant it was as if she was back in that pub years ago, with his eyes on her as she sat with that boy. She flushed and felt guilty, as if they had been flirting. Then she saw that Stephen was quite drunk. He was gripping the doorpost and his face was as white as his knuckles. She ought to have given him, there and then, what his brother Ken called his first public warning, but she didn't. She ought to have put some food down him and got him home, but she wanted the evening to go on, she wanted this wonderful feeling of release to continue, and so she simply said: "It's ready."

As she said every day of the year: "It's on the table."

After all, wasn't she, well not drunk, but a little merry?

Even when she realised that he'd drunk most of the bottle that John had put on the table to drink with the meal, she said nothing. She told herself he was no different from the others. John went up the stairs on his hands and knees, scrambling like a small boy, when he went to get Norma, and found she had dozed off on Susan's bed. What a crew! What an evening!

It really was the worst meal she had ever made, and the most praised. Plates were emptied and refilled. She couldn't drink any more, but the others kept toasting her.

"We must have a name for this dish," John said, raising his glass. "Spaghetti Annizzini."

Stephen found this incredibly funny and produced variations of it: "Annietti Spaghinni." He went on and on laughing at this, and she did give him her public warning look but it made no difference, and she made up her mind to go as soon as they'd finished the sweet. But just as she started making a move the giggling and the laughter died and the conversation became too interesting to leave.

They started talking about marriages: should you go on with a bad marriage for the sake of the children? Annie said you should, John and Norma you shouldn't. John, as part of his argument, quoted a local case where a man, tormented for years by his nagging wife, had stayed for the sake of the children. One night, years of frustration came to the boil over an argument about a scratched saucepan, and he killed her. He was acquitted.

Annie couldn't understand this: it was murder, he should have got life imprisonment! Then Norma remembered the case, only last year, of the man who killed his wife after a dream, when he was in a state a psychiatrist called "night terror". He too had been acquitted, and again Annie found this incomprehensible. So did Stephen. Annie saw to her relief that he seemed to have got a second wind.

John began talking about his own marriage, in a jokey way at first, but gradually became serious. He didn't pretend to know what had happened. It was all very normal and boring. For Annie it wasn't. Nobody talked about their lives, let alone their sex lives like this, in public, in her experience.

"We haven't slept together this year," John said. "I'd feel unfaithful."

"Unfaithful?" said Annie.

"Absurd, isn't it?"

Well it was. He managed to speak lightly about something that was private. He must have been drunk, Annie thought, but he looked quite sober. If she'd been Norma she'd have stopped him, but on the contrary Norma was actually squeezing his leg under the table. And the way she looked at him, it was downright embarrassing, but the words that came out of his mouth as he twisted the stem of his empty wine glass . . . well, she were spellbound.

In fact, he hadn't practised what he preached They'd been married for nineteen years. They had a son at university. Now he'd practically left home there was no excuse for them to remain together. But there was so much between them. They were such good friends. Mary was such a fine person. But the fire had gone out of his marriage. And he thought it had gone out of him until . . .

"Art going to murder thy wife?" said Stephen, broadening his Yorkshire as he did when he was fooling around.

"Stephen!" Annie pushed back her chair.

"No," John laughed. "I'm too fond of her."

Annie had never heard so much nonsense in all her life. "Fond of her? How can you be fond of her?"

"I am."

"If you were you wouldn't be here."

Norma and John both started talking together, disagreeing with her. Out of the corner of her eye Annie saw Stephen reaching for the wine bottle again, but she was too intent on holding her ground to stop him. Normally she disliked arguments, but this was different, somehow invigorating. The three of them were talking at once. She was dimly aware of Stephen laughing in the background, at what, she didn't know.

She shouted above the lot of them: "Have you . . . have you . . . told her this?"

"No."

He was going on but she interrupted him. "Anything? Nothing at all? Then," she shouted as he tried to speak, "how can you be fond of her?"

There was an abrupt silence and he looked so wounded

that she felt a pang of regret at her victory. Norma's hand had left his knee. She looked at the tablecloth, and Annie thought she saw an unspoken argument between them. Then Stephen began laughing. She glared at him, but he wouldn't stop.

John put down the wine glass he was twisting between his fingers, looked at her, and then at Stephen. "Do you talk to each other?" he said.

If the silence was intense before, it was twice as intense now. Stephen stopped laughing. There were small beads of sweat on his forehead, and his chin and lips were shadowy. He came forward as if he was going to join in the conversation. They waited expectantly, but had to watch a drop of sweat roll from his forehead and into his collar, which he had finally prised open, the top button hanging by a thread.

"Do you talk to each other?"

The question still hung in the air. It was Annie who answered it.

"We're happily married," she said.

There was a little pause, and then everyone erupted into laughter. The tension evaporated. She could see it was funny – was it? – but not that funny, but she was happy to laugh with them in sheer relief that the tension had gone and the evening had been saved. John thumped the table and Norma said she was wonderful and then John leant across the table and kissed her, it was such a shock, right boldly in front of Stephen, not on the cheek, but on the mouth, and she stood there confused and he was smiling at her and she smiled back at him and then Stephen was laughing hysterically.

"We're happily married," he slurred. He leant across the table to Norma and John and pulled them together. He was so strong he held them against one another. "You . . . going to be happily married?"

"Well . . . there are one of two obstacles . . . "

"Pakki . . . "

"What?"

"This Pakki," said Stephen.

96

"Come on, Stephen," said Annie, taking hold of his arm.

"Annie Spaghanni, best girl for your marriage."

"And for yours," said John.

"Best man. Best jokes. This Pakki, I saved this Pakki, I was at the baths —"

She tried to pull him away, but he wrenched himself free. She staggered.

Stephen had a beautiful grin on his face. "I saved this Pakki from drowning."

"How did you do that, Stephen?" Norma said.

"I took my foot off his head."

Annie saw the smile freeze on John's face. He saw Annie's mortification and tried to interrupt Stephen, but it was no use. Every joke was about the Pakkis, some inane, some crude.

"What's top of the Pakistani hit parade? Who's Sari now . . . How many Indians can you get in a Mini? Six. Five in the seats, and Mrs Gandhi in the ashtray."

Stephen choked with laughter at the jokes, which came out in a never-ending stream. Where did he get them all from? Ken. He was his brother Ken now, not Stephen. The only time he'd been like this before was at the wedding. Ken had laced his beer with vodka on his stag night. He'd been able to stand up the next morning only after he'd been violently sick. For God's sake, she prayed, he wasn't going to be sick now, was he? His eyes were glazed and his laughter going. Sheer panic at the thought enabled her to get him to the door and half-way up the stairs and she thought he was going to make it when he lurched violently and was sick on the landing.

"Get in."

She shoved him in the bathroom, followed him, got cloths and insisted on cleaning up the mess.

"Please let me do it, Norma, go away. I'm sorry, I'm sorry."

"The meal was so late."

"Please let me do it."

Then she cleaned him up. He was quiet now, his face white, his hands shaking. She said not a word to him. She was calm, but inside she was sick. She couldn't help thinking of Cinderella, a story Matthew was on at the moment, and insisted on her reading to him every night. Or was it that she enjoyed reading it to him? Midnight had struck. There were bits of vomit on the purple skirt. The evening had gone. The coach was a pumpkin, the horses mice.

They would not have believed it, Norma and John, but as they helped Stephen into the car all this grim-faced, self-controlled woman could see was a disintegrating coach, and Cinderella fleeing into the night.

She didn't look at John and scarcely waved as she drove away. That was that. She didn't blame Stephen. She had tried to get above herself. Pride had had a fall. It was her fault he had drunk wine when he had wanted beer and she had known he was drinking too much. That was what men did if you let them. She wouldn't blame him any more than she blamed Matthew if he was sick after a party; what did you expect if some mums loaded the table with so many cakes, crisps, jellies and Smarties? Ch ldren never got sick after her parties. They had just enough to have a good time, and no more. She hadn't been watching, she'd gone off into some fantasy world, and that was her problem, not his.

His head lolled and his chin bumped on his chest as she took the car past the school and along Hillthorpe Road. There was almost no traffic. The moon was still out, bright and clear.

Norma and John were not their sort of people, that was the long and short of it.

She parked in the drive. Home. She felt as if she'd returned from a long journey. Somehow or other she had to get him in and Mrs Marsh home. The crisp air cleared her head. She shook him, gently at first, then more vigorously.

"Stephen. We're home."

His head lifted and his eyes opened. To her surprise they were not bleary and he did not seem particularly sleepy. The irises of his eyes were completely black in the dim light, and gleamed up at her. Was there a smile in them, twitching at the corners of his mouth? There was no mistaking the word that came from it.

"Dinner."

It was impossible to describe how he said that one word; the nearest she could get to it was triumphantly; but that couldn't be right. How could he feel triumphant over such behaviour? But whatever it was in the look and the word, her control went like a dam breaking and the more he grinned the harder she hit him with her large bony hand, slapping him until his face and neck and ears were scarlet.

Maureen Nelson

The story the police pieced together from various witnesses was as follows. Maureen Nelson, a nineteen-year-old checkout assistant at Kwik-Save went with a friend, Pat Stainton, to Thirties, a disco near the centre of Leeds.

It was a Saturday night and the disco was crowded. They met a couple of boys and Maureen, a vivacious red-head, danced with one of them, Trevor Boyle, most of the evening. Afterwards the four went for a hamburger and Trevor Boyle had an argument with the staff about a cheeseburger which he claimed had no cheese in it.

By this time it was quarter-to-twelve and Pat said she was leaving to catch the last bus from Briggate. Maureen said she'd see her on the bus. The argument went on, Trevor Boyle apparently wishing to assert himself before the new girl he had met, until a fresh cheeseburger was produced.

They ran like lunatics towards Briggate, only to see the last bus moving off, with Pat Stainton shouting from the crowded platform. The bus did not stop. Trevor and Maureen joined the straggle of other people who had "just missed it" and who faced the long walk home. Maureen lived in Cross Gates, on the east of the city, and Trevor in Kirkstall. She phoned her older brother, who was married and had a motor-bike, and had picked her up more than once in similar circumstances, but he was out.

They walked towards the Headrow, eating the large chips and cheeseburger which was the cause of their predicament, and he suggested she came home with him. She refused, saying her mother would kill her. And she didn't dare ring up her father and ask him to get the car out: he would already have been asleep an hour.

She said she would get a taxi as far as it would take her. She had two pounds. Trevor chipped in with another two.

He wanted to go with her, but she said she would be all right. He kissed her, and they agreed to go to the pictures on Monday.

At around twenty-five-past-twelve she ran towards a taxi driven by Hanif Patel, but was just beaten to it by another couple. There were no other taxis in sight. Patel said he would radio for another cab but, tired and cold, she must have set off walking, for a girl matching her description – she was wearing blue court shoes, a black skirt and a blue PVC jacket – was seen getting a lift in Regent Street from a man in a red or brown-coloured car, possibly an Escort.

The car went off in the direction of the A58, which goes through Chapeltown and Roundhay, from which Crossgates can be reached by the ring road. Quite suddenly the huddled red terraces of Harehills and Roundhay Road give way, after the Oakwood Clock, to substantial Victorian stone houses, and the huge green lung of Roundhay Park.

The car left the A58 at Askett Hill, and went along Elmete Lane, which passes between fields attached to schools, and a golf course. Maureen must have known this was wrong, although they were still heading in the direction of the ring road. Perhaps she was reassured, perhaps threatened. At all events, the car pulled into a side turning by a clump of trees.

It is not clear if he attempted to have intercourse with her at that stage. She was struck a blow in the face which had such force a tooth broke off. She was then stabbed with such manic ferocity her left breast was half severed. It was then that the murderer was interrupted.

A courting couple drove into the side turning. The car came in very slowly, the beam from the headlights lighting up the trees, and only glinting on the bumper and one headlight of the other car as it stopped. The girl gripped her boyfriend's arm. At the edge of the headlights there was a movement. He began to grin and she to giggle. They could see the red glint of a woman's long hair, and the vague shape of a man on top of her.

After a whispered conversation – he wanted to stay, she wouldn't – the couple drove off. The man did have intercourse with Maureen Nelson. It was not possible to establish whether he was doing so when the couple drove in, or whether he lay on top of her when he heard the car in order to conceal the dead body.

Maureen Nelson was not, in fact, dead.

The murderer must have been in an absolute panic when the couple left. He did not bother to move or conceal the body. Maureen's knickers and tights were found in nearby bushes, twisted in a ball where he had thrown them, smeared with blood. It looked as if he had used them to wipe the blood from himself.

Another couple who had left a late-night party discovered Maureen Nelson at just after half-past-two. By great good fortune the driver, Denis Clegg, was a CB radio fanatic and an ambulance was on the scene in twelve minutes. The victim had lost a massive amount of blood but her heart was beating faintly, and she began to respond to a transfusion. There were three main stab wounds, in the breast, left lung and, most seriously, one which pierced the pericardium and entered the left ventricle.

Emergency heart surgery was carried out, and the surgeons were still working as people got up for breakfast. The case became a cause célèbre because of the police efforts to talk to the victim late on Sunday evening. Part of the trouble arose because of a disputed prognosis. The police (according to the police) were told that Maureen Nelson's chance of survival was not high. On the other hand, the distraught parents had the impression (or the hope) that Maureen had a fifty-fifty chance of pulling through.

Detective Chief Superintendent Peter Daybury, head of Leeds CID, stayed in the hospital with a team of officers all Sunday. When Maureen began to regain consciousness at about four o'clock, he put enormous pressure on Roger Stead, the consultant in charge, to allow him to speak to her. Stead refused.

Daybury, whose placid, rather jolly face belied his ambition and determination to get his own way, switched the pressure to the parents. Maureen had seen the attacker. She would be able to describe him. They must get him before he attacked again. Or there would be other victims like Maureen, other parents like them. Would they ask her questions about the attack, in his presence?

Eventually they agreed, and the consultant allowed a limited amount of questioning.

Maureen was still in shock, and her eyes remained terrified during the interview, as if, said her parents, she was still seeing the killer. If it was agony for the girl's parents, it was agony of a different kind for Daybury. There had now been three, possibly four murders by this man, with an escalating degree of violence. Over five thousand interviews had been carried out, without results. The press were talking about the "Yorkshire Disease" and, once more, about the incompetence of the West Yorkshire Police.

This girl had seen the killer, talked to him.

It was impossible to be sure whether she understood their questions or not. For minutes she said nothing at all, staring up at her parents, who were watched by Daybury, who in turn was watched by Stead, the surgeon.

What made it worse was that her mouth and face were so swollen that when the few words came, they were mumbled and distorted.

"Over . . . all over," she said.

Her mother said that it was not all over and Daybury, unable to keep back, smiled at her as gently as he could, and asked what the man looked like. The terror in the girl's eyes increased, and she said one word.

"Black."

Daybury could scarcely restrain his excitement.

"You mean he's coloured . . . Asian? West Indian?"

The girl's voice caught in her throat and the surgeon pulled savagely at the policeman's arm.

The girl lapsed into a coma. She died in the early hours of Monday morning, without saying another word.

Black. The word gave Daybury many tortured moments. Had she been saying he was coloured (as he had been absolutely certain of at first)? Or did she mean the killer had black hair, black eyes, a black beard or wore something black?

In the end, his superiors decided that it would be too dangerous and misleading to release what Maureen had said, but it got out. Perhaps it was a nurse or doctor at the hospital who was responsible; more likely it was the embittered parents, but the rumour soon spread round Leeds that the new Yorkshire Ripper was Asian, and the police were concealing the fact for fear of racial trouble. The story reached the national press. Some Asians were victimised and one, who was going out with a white girl, was badly beaten up, knifed, and nearly died.

In Bradford there was a riot, and Asian shops were looted.

One television commentator pointed out that a mass killer at one time could put a whole city in a panic. Now, with the network of motorways, city was linked so swiftly to city that he could terrorise half the country. So far he had killed in Manchester, Leeds (twice) and Bradford. Where would he strike next?

More prostitutes – the younger ones, those without ties – drifted south. Others worked in pairs: when one was picked up by a kerbie the other, in full view of the car driver, wrote down his number.

The police repeatedly said that someone must know the killer. He had been disturbed, he had left in a panic, and he must have been covered in blood. He would have had to wash, destroy his clothes. The car seats might be bloodstained. If he lived in a family, they must know, or at least suspect. If he lived alone, what had the neighbours seen? If only the public would cooperate, the police were "cautiously optimistic" they would find the killer.

The public cooperated, deluging the police with phone calls and letters, but did not believe the police were getting anywhere at all. They were wrong. The police had arrived at the murder site at the same time as the ambulance and a bright sergeant had quickly worked out where the killer's car had been parked. The earth round the bushes was soft, and a good tyre print was obtained. It was made by a Pirelli tyre of standard saloon car size, fairly new (it had probably done not more than 10,000 miles), wearing on the inside, and with an area of damage no bigger than a thumbprint, probably caused by a large tack, or by broken glass which had worked into the tread.

On top of this were the descriptions of the killer's car given by the couple who had disturbed him. Unfortunately, when questioned singly, the pair disagreed, the man saying the car was dark red, the woman black. She didn't know what make it was. The man said it was a Cavalier. This did not tally with witnesses who said Maureen Nelson had been picked up by an Escort. But the man was prepared to swear it was a B registration car, and was vehement enough for Chief Superintendent Daybury to believe him.

He was chary of making assumptions. He had bitter memories of what had happened in the first Yorkshire Ripper case when anonymous tape recordings had led everyone, through massive publicity, to believe that the Ripper was a Geordie. That must not happen again. Claims to be the killer were filed, but disregarded. Anonymous letters (of which there were shoals) were treated with extreme suspicion.

But that tyre was solid evidence. The print was unique. Find the tyre and you found the car. Find the car and you found the killer. The logic of that was inescapable, thought Daybury. The killer might get rid of the car, but the tell-tale tyre would trace it back to him.

The print became the most closely guarded secret in the West Yorkshire Police. The police computer extracted from Swansea all owners of B registration Cavaliers and Escorts within 100 miles of Leeds. It was a huge task, but the majority of owners could be eliminated immediately, since they could not possibly have been at the murder spot at that time.

And, since the last murder, police had been scrupulously logging all cars seen kerb crawling in the red light districts of Yorkshire and Lancashire. All registrations were immediately checked to guard against false number plates. Some cars were logged many times. If they were Cavaliers or Escorts they were given red — top level — interviews by officers close to Daybury. In the first three weeks, more than 500 people were interviewed, the police never revealing the basis on which they were chosen: it was always routine, house-to-house checks.

Secretly, Daybury was more than cautiously optimistic. The killer couldn't possibly know that his off-side front tyre would give him away. Sooner or later, Daybury believed, they would have him.

Part II

APPREHENSION

apprehension n. 1. fear or anxiety over what may happen. 2. the act of capturing or arresting. 3. the faculty of comprehending; understanding. 4. a notion or conception.

9

It happened one evening about a month after that disastrous dinner. Annie had her evening all planned. It was half-past-seven. The kids were in bed, and would soon be asleep. At a quarter-to-eight, Stephen would go out, and a delicious silence would descend on the house. She would do the ironing and recollar Matthew's shirt while she watched the gardening programme.

Everything went according to plan, except her.

At a quarter-to-eight Stephen folded the *Evening Post* and put it on the table next to her chair, as usual. As usual, he had a little yawn and a scratch and looked at his watch.

"Well. I'll just go round the corner."

"I'll come with you."

Why on earth did she say that? Was it because she had been brooding over a photograph of him which showed his now famous black eye? Yes, she had given him a black eye that night she had hit him! Or had she?

The next day, Ken had come over. "Clock you one, did she?"

"Aye," Stephen said, in his flat deadpan voice, and they all laughed – his mother was there as well. Annie tried to smile, but it froze on her face. Annie felt Mrs Marsh's eyes boring into her.

"I were getting out of car, well I'd had one or two, and I were half-sitting like, you know, and I slipped and grabbed for door and it caught me such a bloody whack, didn't it Annie?"

He demonstrated, using the back of the chair as a door, and throwing his hands up to his face. Matthew was enchanted.

"How did you do it Dad?"

Well, as usual, once he got a laugh he was set to do it

forever, elaborating the pantomime, pulling the chair towards him, falling, clasping his face in agony. Annie found herself laughing too, both relieved and disturbed. After all these years, she had no idea he could lie like that. Once he got her to help him up, and there was no wink, no conspiratorial look. It was so completely convincing, Annie almost began to believe it herself.

She'd been thinking about the lie when he'd yawned and stretched himself, preparatory to going out.

Was that why she said: "I'll come with you"?

Nevertheless, she was as surprised as he was. He stood staring at her.

"Where?"

"Wherever you're going."

"I'm not going nowhere."

"All right. We'll go there," she said.

She told him she would get Mrs Crowther to babysit. Her children had just left home and she always looked lost. She had offered several times, but Annie had never taken her up on it. Stephen hummed and hawed, saying he was worried about Mrs Crowther; she'd gone a bit scatty since her kids had left; she smoked; she might fall asleep and set the place on fire. These were exactly the reasons Annie had given for never getting her to babysit; but now she scorned them.

"She's brought up two kids and they're still breathing."

Perhaps if he hadn't put so many difficulties in the way she wouldn't have persisted, but the more he went on, the more she was determined to go; she even put on the purple outfit, deciding she might as well get some wear out of it.

Annie was more worried about Mrs Crowther than she now dared admit; the woman had lit up before they'd even left the house! Apart from leaving ashtrays everywhere what could you do? She couldn't ask her not to fall asleep with a fag in her mouth. And she, Annie, normally the worrier, had insisted on going out!

Then they began to argue about his company car. A

week or so ago he'd brought home an A registration light blue Cavalier, instead of his B registration red one. It was the first time she'd ridden in it.

"There's a tear in the seat," she said.

"Aye, it's a bit of a mess."

"When d'you get your own car back?"

"I don't."

"What d'you mean, you don't?"

He explained that the generator on Macdonald's car had packed up. Macdonald was one of Hallet's London reps and had to get back in a hurry. So Stephen – of course it had to be Stephen, she thought – had swopped his carefully looked after car for this wreck. She was incensed. It was a kind of demotion, dropping a letter of the alphabet. He said it was his suggestion but she knew Hallet's; it was dog eat dog there, they put upon Stephen, he just wouldn't stand up for himself.

They were driving along the Leeds Road and she thought he was taking her to a pub when he said: "Where do you want to go?"

"Where do you want to?"

"I'm not bothered."

She was still worrying about Mrs Crowther, and mad about him being sat on by the reps. They all thought they were God's gift, but he was worth ten times as much as them. She was about to tell him to go to the Farmer's, a steak bar with wine-red carpets and horse-brasses, and waitress service with the drinks, really nice, when she thought, no, let him decide, let him assert himself for once. Swopping his car, indeed!

"Go where you were going," she said.

"I wasn't going anywhere."

"You must have been going somewhere."

"What about the Farmer's?"

"I don't *want* to go to the Farmer's!"

Why did she say that, when she did? When she was looking forward to the warmth, to the luxury of walking over a thick carpet and being served a snowball by a smiling waitress. And why did the next words come out of her mouth, as unexpected as her saying she wanted to go out with him?

"Let's go to the Mucky Duck."

A pub she'd heard him and Ken mention. The last person she wanted to see was Ken, but if it was the sort of place Stephen liked, they'd go there. If that dinner at Norma's had been a disaster, one good thing had come out of it. She had realised how much Norma and John went out together, and how much they shared things. That was why she had reluctantly given up the idea of the Farmer's: it would then be her evening, not his. Didn't she sit on him just as much as the reps? Well, she'd had to. But he had a secure position now. What he needed was to assert himself. To help him do that she would have to shut her trap a bit. Do things he wanted.

The car was slowing, stopping. She stared at him. Headlights swept past them, illuminating in snatches his still faintly discoloured eye.

"You won't like it."

"It's where you go."

He made a face. "Sometimes."

In spite of her good intentions she exploded at him. "Well let's go somewhere before it's time to go home! Go to the Farmer's if you like."

He put the car into gear but still didn't move off. She noticed in the silence that his hands were tight on the steering wheel, making his knuckles dead white, except for faint scorings of dirt which he could never get out, however much Swarfega he used. Suddenly he grinned.

"All right."

Without another word he drove off in the direction of Leeds. Soon they were leaving the brick and stone semis and travelling past old mills and streets of terraced houses, some still cobbled. She didn't know the pub, but she knew the route he was taking only too well. It was the road home – funny how she still used the word about such a place.

The orange street lamps seemed to be dimmer and less frequent as they went from Bramley into Birchgate. She huddled in her seat. Why on earth did he want to come

114

back here for a drink? There was a little rain in the air, and from time to time he switched on the wipers until they squeaked, a noise that always put her teeth on edge.

The Pavilion Cinema, long closed, had now failed even as a bingo hall and was boarded up and covered with thick layers of tattered posters. The streets next to it had been demolished as part of a housing programme which had never materialised, and the waste ground was used as a car park.

He left the main road to cut through a warren of back-to-backs. The children's home was near here, and in the dim light the district seemed grimmer and more poverty-stricken than she remembered it. At some corners little pools of light came from shops still open. There was the fish shop where she used to clutch sixpence for a bag of chips. She thought she caught a whiff of the rank, cheap fat they used (one of the social workers called it axle grease) and in an instant she remembered the smell of those days: a smell which greeted her in the hall of the home when she came back from school: a mixture of disinfectant and watery cabbage, seeping up from the kitchen below.

She looked at Stephen. He stared straight ahead, whistling tunelessly. Where was this pub? She knew the area so well, but she couldn't place such a pub.

They weren't going down to the canal? He grinned at her again, as if he read her thoughts. They drove over the iron bridge, where David Crowther had rejected her, and she thought she'd never marry, never have children. She touched his arm.

"Where are we going?"

"The Mucky Duck."

The penny dropped. Past Pretoria Mill was The Swan, an old canal-side pub which the social workers used to warn the children about. It was a bikers' pub, and there were sometimes fights there.

Tonight there were no bikes, but as they bumped down the cobbles into the shadow of the pub anger rose in her that he could think of bringing her to a place like this. She was about to open her mouth when she caught the look on his face: it was only for an instant, as he got out of the car, but wasn't it an echo of the mocking look he'd given her when he'd said "dinner" and she'd hit him? She couldn't be sure. In fact almost certainly she was imagining things, for now he was smiling at her and taking her arm as he helped her from the car.

She was being silly. She'd asked to come here, after all! Yet, as he fussed around making sure all the doors were locked, the thought crept into her head that he was hesitating, waiting for her to say: "I'm not going in here!" She was tempted to. The place gave her the creeps.

The rain was still a thin drizzle which did not mark the black, smooth surface of the canal. Scarcely a sound came from the pub, and nobody could be seen through the dimly lit glazed and curtained windows.

"Shall we go somewhere else?" he said.

She was about to say yes, when a taxi drew up and a woman got out. She looked about thirty, and wore a red leather jacket and a white skirt split at the sides so it gave glimpses of her thighs. She gave Stephen a smile and a wave before she hurried into the pub.

"Who's that?" said Annie.

"She drinks in there."

"I can see that."

"We'll go somewhere else."

"We'll not."

"I don't think it's your sort of place, Annie."

"Then why did you bring me?"

"You asked."

She must have been mistaken about that mocking look, for now he just looked gormless, helpless, lost. He opened the car door.

"What are you doing?"

"I'll take you to Farmer's."

"For God's sake come on! I'm getting soaked."

He caught up with her, and entered the pub before her. It was fairly empty with groups of people round a circular bar, an imitation log fire and, in what had originally been

116

the public bar before it had been knocked into one, a pool table.

Ken was at the bar, pint in hand, talking to the woman with the split skirt who was perched on a stool. With them was a Pakistani in a beautifully cut grey suit and a striped tie. Ken saw his brother first.

"Steve, you bugger! You're late!" he cried. When he saw Annie, a split second later, his face was a picture. For a moment he couldn't speak, then he quickly recovered. "Well well well, surprise, surprise surprise! I didn't know you were coming, love, what are you having?"

The pub was not what she expected, for all its sinister exterior. It was warm and comfortable and if the glass that the scrubby barmaid hooked down looked none too clean, the snowball was the best she had ever tasted. They sat round the fire. Ken was pleasanter than she'd ever known him, putting his arm round her and saying she was the best sister-in-law he had.

"Tha's only got one," she said, and they roared with laughter, laughing even more when she added: "How much do you want?"

She had a second snowball, which tasted even more delicious than the first, and talked to the woman whose skirt, well, really, when she crossed her legs you could see the line of her knickers, she was as common as muck really, but she was complimentary about the purple outfit and had two kids a bit younger than Matthew and Jackie, so they had a good old natter.

"Is your husband looking after them?" she asked.

The woman, whom everybody called Jan, crossed her legs and picked up her gin and tonic. "He's away."

"On holiday," said Ken.

There were nods and winks which Annie didn't understand. Jan spun a beer mat across the table, catching Ken on the nose, a shot that drew applause. Stephen wandered off to look at the pool table. He was on his half-bitters and had scarcely said a word. Annie felt as if she had gone back to before they were married; in fact, wasn't that one of the lads Stephen used to go about with, with a T-shirt stretched over his vast beer-gut? They were chatting to several women who sat alone at a table; two of them Annie had noticed leaving as she had come in, but they had now returned.

"Do you live in Hillthorpe?"

It was Jan. Annie realised that, under the thick layer of blusher, powder and lipstick she was much younger than she'd first thought.

"It must be great."

She was wistful and envious and Annie warmed to her as she described their house and garden, and their early struggles to get out of Birchgate. She advised her about the best building society to go to for a first mortgage.

"Of course you have to pull together," she said. "I couldn't ask for a better husband."

Jan gave her a curious look, which didn't register at the time, because she was coping with her third, or was it her fourth snowball. The pub had filled up, the juke box was playing Crystal Gale and she could feel the sweet, yellow froth leaving a soft fur round her mouth every time she drank. Birchgate was a dreadful hole but she'd forgotten how warm and, well, *real* the people were, compared with Hillthorpe, with Norma and her la-di-da John.

Two of the women at the nearby table were leaving. As she passed, one, with razor-cut hair and earrings that brushed her shoulders, said: "Are you working, Jan?"

"Not fucking likely."

For a moment Jan's lips were curled back from her teeth, and you could see how thin they were beneath the enlarging smears of lipstick. Then she looked at Annie and said: "Sorry."

This deference made Annie feel even better. "What job do you do?" she asked.

As she reached for her glass, the table seemed to come up to meet her, and she almost spilt her drink. She couldn't be drunk – you couldn't get drunk on snowballs! She realised there was a silence at their table. The Pakistani, whose name was Bahnu, was looking at her with

118

a smile on his lips. He hitched up his beautifully creased trousers and said: "She works for me."

"And what do you do?"

He studied his carefully trimmed nails. "Dry cleaning is my game," he said.

"Tha's a good advertisement for it," she said.

Well, the table fair exploded. You could never tell what people would laugh at. As at Norma's dinner, it didn't seem all that funny to her, but she supposed it was the way she said it. Or maybe she was getting sociable in her old age. They were calling last orders, it surely couldn't be that time, where was Stephen?

People were thronging round the counter and, impossibly, among the squashed-together glasses and overflowing ashtrays, another snowball was placed in front of her.

"From Bernie," Ken said.

"To dry cleaning," said Bahnu, raising his glass. His smile seemed to blow up his face like a balloon, which floated in front of her through the haze of cigarette smoke. Jan seemed upset about something, and was gathering up her things to go. Annie wanted to talk to her but she was dying for a pee and found it beyond the pool table, down a long draughty corridor.

There were four women waiting, and she leant against the cold tiles. They were talking about the Hawk. One said they'd worked it out, it was always on full moon, and it was full moon tonight.

"I wouldn't go out tonight," said one, which Annie, half-listening, vaguely thought was an odd thing to say, since she was out.

Another took out of her handbag a black-handled kitchen knife. The women crowded round giggling, and one was scornful saying she'd never use it when suddenly the woman brought the knife up to the scornful woman's face.

"Wouldn't I? I'd kill him, I'd cut him, as he cuts women!"

All the women were silenced. Water dripped from the pipes above Annie, a spot grazing her cheek so that she jumped. The knife-blade caught the light as the woman put it back into her bag. From that moment the laughter went

119

and women went quickly in and out of the cubicles. Annie was the last to leave. She must have taken a wrong turning because the noises from the bar grew fainter and when she pushed at a door she found it was locked. Another led to an unfamiliar corridor, shrunk by a line of crates which she had to squeeze past. The memory of the knife and the conversation sent a little shiver of fear through her: it was uncannily like her nightmare where there was something behind a curtain, but she could not move to escape from it.

The shouting and laughter from the bar were increasing. Here she was! She opened a door and stood confused, behind the bar, staring at the turning, startled face of the barmaid, who was in the act of dropping a tea-towel over the pumps. Beyond her, in that moment, she saw a little tableau of Stephen, Ken, Jan and Bernie or Bahnu. Ken was giving money to Bahnu. Or was it the other way about? There was a lot of it – or was that her imagination afterwards? For as they saw her the money vanished and Ken was shouting was she going to work for pub? and she was laughing with him, her little fear gone, melted in the warmth of people leaving the pub, swearing undying friendship to each other.

Oh it was lovely to be part of that warmth, to be holding on to Stephen's arm, to be part of other people for a change, so what if she was a little bit – woops, she bumped into someone and they both laughed at one another as if it was the greatest joke in the world. Someone touched her elbow. It was Jan. Beyond her was Bahnu, holding open the door.

"It was nice to meet you," Annie said.

"It was nice to talk to you," the girl said, and there was something so sad and wistful in her face that Annie impulsively said: "Come and see us."

Jan stared at her and then turned sharply away, but not before Annie saw tears blur her eyes. She went swiftly out, her thin legs flicking out her split skirt, and by the time Annie got outside she and Bahnu had gone.

The rain had increased, and the surface of the canal was now pock-marked with it. Cars were leaving.

"What did I say?"

Stephen shrugged. "Her husband's away."

"Oh. Is that it?"

She held on to Stephen as he helped her into the car. As he started the car, she kissed him.

"What's that for?"

"Nowt. Does there have to be summat?"

Poor Jan. Lucky her. Tonight they would make love. Perhaps she could steer his hand up to stroke her nipples. What a crude thought! She slipped down further in the seat as he drove past the now dark corner shops. People were walking home. Once or twice they passed a woman walking alone. She thought of the knife in the handbag, shuddered, and leant her head against his shoulder until the motion of the car jogged her into a doze.

10

Winter didn't normally leave the hill until mid-April, but mild cloudy weather brought out bursts of white magnolia blossom in her front garden, and the big yellow forsythia next door was in full flower. She was frantically busy dashing out in dry spells, sowing, weeding, cutting back the hydrangea and wondering, as she did every year, whether she should uproot it, and deciding, as she did every year, that it was part of the garden whether she liked it or not, and should stay. She felt full of energy and that was, she was sure, because she was going out more, and getting more involved with other people — including Stephen.

She felt closer to him than she had for a long time. They had been out several times, using Mrs Crowther to babysit. She had proved very reliable and, in fact, smoked very little — that cigarette the first night had been a sign of nerves. They had not been back to the Mucky Duck, because, he said, he wanted to show her other pubs. They went to one on the moors near Howarth, and one in Shadwell. They even went to the pictures to see *Back to the Future* and came back to tell Mrs Crowther, by, they did enjoy it, they never thought they made pictures like that any more, and when Mrs Crowther told her that Matthew had woken up and she'd cuddled him back to sleep, well that made the evening seem even more enjoyable. She felt freer, more relaxed than she'd been for years.

To crown it all Stephen got a C registration car! Well, it showed you what they thought of him. And maybe, give him his due, she'd been wrong and he'd been right. Giving up his car so unselfishly got him as far, in his quiet way, as the pushiness of the Jack-the-lads. He was even writing better, at long long last. It was still laborious but, shortly before the Mucky Duck evening, he had said he could do his own reports now. She'd been sceptical and apprehensive about what the company would think, particularly when he wouldn't show them to her, knowing – quite rightly – that she'd interfere. She forced herself not to. Perhaps she had been holding him back by doing everything for him.

She saw the newspaper in Armley which smashed this mood and brought the nightmare back. She had picked up the kids from school and gone there to get a repeat prescription for Mrs Marsh, who couldn't get out because of her arthritis. She seemed lively enough with the kids, but explained that her activity was due to taking extra tablets, from which she would suffer when they'd gone.

On the way back Annie stopped at a greengrocer who always chucked on an extra potato when the correct weight had been reached. As he was lifting up the pan with her three pounds of reds, she was about to tell him just to tip them in her plastic bag when she saw the top sheet of the torn-up newspapers he used for wrapping. On it was a rather fuzzy picture of a woman she thought she knew. Before she could look closer, potatoes and a little shower of dirt covered it.

"You can have a Smartie when you see the next red pillar box," she said.

Mrs Marsh had given them a tube each, although she was always asking her not to give them sweets. She saw in the driving mirror that Matthew had taken the top of his tube off, but she said nothing. She was staring at the crumpled newspaper, which she was brushing the dirt from and smoothing out on her knee. It was torn from a local paper which circulated round Birchgate. For a moment she didn't know how she knew the woman, and then it clicked. It was Jan at the Mucky Duck.

WOMAN FIGHTS FOR CHILDREN was the headline, and the story ran: A woman who assaulted police when her children were being taken into care was given a two-year suspended sentence in Leeds last week. Twenty-four-year-old Janice Stephenson of Birchgate, described by Mr James Taylor (prosecuting) as a common prostitute, bit the finger of WPC Welch and tore a button from the jacket of PC Brooks.

"We can't see a pillar box unless we move," Jackie said.

"Have one now and one when we get to a pillar box."

"I'm having a yellow one. They're the best."

"No they're not. Red are the best."

"She took two."

"I did not!"

"You little liar! I didn't put it in my mouth – ner!"

She rounded on them. "Will you both shut up arguing or neither of you will get any! Put them away!" Silenced by her glaring face, they pushed the tops back on the tubes.

As she drove back to Hillthorpe, the two words drummed in her head. Common prostitute. Described by James Taylor (prosecuting) as a common prostitute.

At home she switched on the television for them and didn't remove the Smarties, although normally they were never allowed sweets before tea. She spread out the newspaper on the kitchen table and, not even putting on the kettle, read the item through.

George Buchan (for Stephenson) said that the defendant was in a highly distressed state at losing her children.

Her husband was in jail for manslaughter, there were rent arrears for which he was responsible, and she had been forced into her present way of life to pay them off. The judge said that but for the children "to whom she did seem attached, the care order not ruling out the return of them to her" he would have sent her to jail too for this serious assault. He would not hesitate to do so if she broke the terms of her probation.

Annie read it again and again until she felt dizzy and had to keep blinking her eyes in order to decipher the print. Slowly the pieces of that nice evening at the canalside pub began to reassemble into a different shape. As they did, she moved from astonishment, to bewilderment, to a feeling of humiliation and, finally, anger.

She felt no pity for the wretched woman, only a burning anger that she had been hoodwinked by her. By her? By Stephen. By the lot of them. They had all been laughing at her, all of them. She could feel her face going crimson. They must have thought she was bloody naive!

And it was not only Jan who was a prostitute. She walked about the kitchen bumping into things, filling the kettle but not plugging it in, each memory giving her a fresh shock. The woman in the lavatory with the knife in her handbag, was she one? The woman with the earrings brushing her shoulders . . . oh, she was going too far . . . but what had the woman said?

"Are you working tonight, Jan?"

"Not fucking likely." Then she'd turned to her and said: "Sorry."

The hypocrite! The little bitch! The deference she'd pretended to show her when she was laughing at her behind her back! And Bahnu, or Bernie, and the money changing hands, what was going on there? Was Stephen involved? She felt sick. He'd lied to her. He'd said he wasn't going anywhere. But hadn't Ken said he was late? They were clearly expecting him.

Hadn't she gone out that evening because of a lie – the lie he had told about his black eye? That had led her to another one. What else was there? Oh, she was getting herself too worked up! They'd been out often since then, to normal pubs, having normal drinks – she had a vivid imagination, that was her trouble. Unless that was to put her off the scent. Oh come on, she berated herself, what scent?

"What are you doing?" Jackie said.

She jumped. The children were staring at her. She'd totally forgotten about them. She stood, unable to speak for a moment, realising that water had been slopping out of the full kettle on to the floor. The children wore innocent expressions and chocolate round their mouths. She said nothing. Mechanically she fried fish fingers and frozen chips, which she normally only used in an emergency. The kids described her as the last woman in the world who made chips from potatoes, but tonight she couldn't do it, didn't want to touch the potatoes which still lay on the table. Matthew lost the head of his Optimus Prime Transformer Robot, and refused to go to bed without it. She was desperate to be alone, to think, and began shouting at him, forcing him into his pyjamas. She heard him sobbing in his bedroom and, unable to stand it, searched systematically until she found the head under one of the radiators. He was ecstatic with happiness and threw his arms round her. Jackie was asleep, but Matthew was so hyped-up she had to read him another story before he would settle down.

It was nine o'clock. She didn't feel like eating, nor could she sit down at first. Every muscle in her body was a solid knot. As she went over and over the scene in the pub she became so livid she hit her clenched fists against her sides. If she had known where he was she would have phoned him, but she didn't, she never knew where he was! When he first started going away he used to phone up just before the children went to bed. When had that stopped? She could phone Hallet's and get his number. No. She wanted to see him face to face. As soon as he came back she'd have it out with him. Going to that sort of pub! Mixing with that sort of woman. And taking her! That was a stupid thing to do! But he was stupid. She'd asked to be taken there, insisted. But then hadn't she said she'd go to the Farmer's? Oh she couldn't remember. Perhaps he'd *had* to go there, for some reason . . .

She made a pot of tea and sat swallowing cup after cup, listening to the wind in the apple tree. It blew spatters of rain against the windows. He was stupid? She was stupid not to have realised what was going on! No. She slowly lowered the cup to the saucer, and the saucer to the floor. She had been drunk, but not on three or four snowballs. No wonder they'd been so delicious! No wonder she'd had such a hangover the next morning! What had Ken put in them? Vodka – as he'd done with Stephen's beer on his stag night, so that he could scarcely walk next morning? What an idiot she was. Of course it was Ken getting Stephen involved in something, and Stephen, as usual, had been led by the nose. Well, that was easily dealt with. He wouldn't be seeing Ken any more, she'd see to that.

It was after eleven. The wind was increasing as she put out the rubbish and locked up. If she didn't have something, hunger would wake her. She poached an egg and dipped fingers of toast in it; the food brought on her appetite so she poached another and went to bed feeling a little better, falling asleep surprisingly quickly. She did not make the obvious connection; she had so thoroughly discounted it before, and was so eager to see Ken as the villain of the piece that it never occurred to her. Later she was to think that if she had phoned him that night, things might have been very different, very different indeed.

The wind woke her, hurling the rain like so many little hammers against the windows. Hammers. The hammer. No no, she'd been through that ridiculous notion. Ken had returned the hammer. Now she was worrying about something else, about that pub, but she'd settled what to do about that, about Ken. Think about being warm and comfortable while the wind howled. She pulled the sheets over her head, and curled up on her left side.

Through her tent she could still hear great gusts tearing up the hillside, whistling in the branches and rattling the door of the garden shed which was not properly shut. Somewhere a dustbin lid clanged and rolled.

Slowly the thought wormed its way into her mind. It didn't have to be the same hammer. There were plenty of hammers. It was a strange coincidence that Ken had turned up with it shortly after she had voiced her fears to him. Was Ken involved? No no no. That was impossible. What was not impossible was that Stephen had phoned him . . . She couldn't remember going out, but she might have gone across the road.

"Shall I do your bike this evening? . . . Oh, can you bring us a hammer . . . I've lost mine . . . "

For didn't a murderer always get rid of the weapon, the incriminating evidence? A sudden crash made her jump out of bed. If she hadn't bit on the sheets she was holding she would have screamed. Convinced someone was outside she thought wildly that he knew her thoughts and had returned to kill her. She crept silently into Matthew's room and peered out of the window. Stephen's car wasn't there. In a lull, the wind moaned softly, and then she heard a sliding noise above her, followed by a crash on the path below. A tile, she'd told him the tiles were loose, how many times did she have to tell him?

Matthew's mouth was open and his face, like Stephen's, wore a frown in sleep. He was lying on Optimus Prime. She removed it and tucked him in. The children would sleep if the house fell down. Seeing to them slowed the thumping of her heart. It was the violent night outside that was giving her these thoughts. Stephen! The idea was absurd. He was the last person. He wouldn't hurt a fly! What had he done when she'd hit him? Nothing.

She had a pee, drank water from the tap, letting it run over her face and chin and then remade her bed. As she turned out the light she glanced, as usual, over the valley, bisected by the motorway, a snake marked by orange lights. He knew prostitutes. He was away regularly. She never knew where he was. The hammer.

She put on her raincoat and unbolted the back door, staggering back into the kitchen as the wind caught her and blew rain into her face. Outside, she gripped the raincoat tightly as it jumped and flapped around her. She was immediately chilled to the bone. In the west it was clearing, and she could see thick clouds, torn by the wind, revealing a moon that was almost full. Her nightdress, billowing below the raincoat, caught on a branch ripped from the apple tree. The loose shed door banged into her hand as she approached, but she didn't notice the pain. The hammer was there. She stared at it for a moment before picking it up and then examined it by the weak light of Jackie's bicycle torch. It was a Stanley 5lb claw hammer with a rubber handle, just as he'd always had. No. Didn't he used to have a hammer with a wooden handle, with a chip out of the handle? But surely that was at the old house? She couldn't remember! It was no use, it was no proof one way or the other! She hurled it across the shed. It scarred the wood and brought tins and plant pots clattering down. She wrapped her arms round herself, appalled, and stared out of the shed, half expecting lights to go on in the neighbouring houses, although nobody could possibly have heard anything above the gale.

She found a piece of wood to wedge the door of the shed shut, and ran back to the house, her wet hair blowing round her face. If anyone had seen her they'd think she was mad. She was. Or going mad. That kind doctor, Dr Seymour, was wrong. The episodes, what he called self-limiting episodes, weren't. She'd gone mad after each pregnancy, and, for some reason, she was going mad now. No, madness was nothing to do with reason, there didn't have to be a reason. That was the point of madness. Hadn't she seen Jackie as evil, as a little monster? Wasn't she doing exactly the same thing to Stephen?

It had been coming on for months. There was the nightmare, the sort of waking dream. There was her imagining Stephen staring at her in her sleep. Her hitting Stephen.

She sat at the kitchen table, her elbows planted on it, her fingers furrowing ceaselessly through her wet hair. There was some comfort in these thoughts. He was all right. She was the one who was sick. She had coped with it before, and she would cope with it again. She must ring Dr Seymour.

She got up and saw to her bewilderment it was only ten-to-four. It must be later than that! No, the second hand was moving in slow jerks, and it was still black outside. The rain had stopped but the wind was as ferocious as ever, whistling under the door and turning her feet to blocks of ice. Shivering uncontrollably, she changed her wet things, put on her dressing gown and crouched over the gas fire in the back room, her hands wrapped round a cup of tea.

Clearly she did not want to think herself mad, for now another thought occurred to her. At first she resisted it, but it grew more insistent as the warmth crept back into her body. She did know where he'd been, of course she did. The sales records that until recently she'd kept for him showed mileage, accommodation and meals, all covered by bills. They were locked in the bureau in the front room, away from the children. She knew he'd been in one place where there had been a murder – Manchester on Christmas Eve – because he'd told her. Why? Had he been trying to tell her . . . or was he more clever than she ever took him for, casually mentioning it, because it was exactly the sort of thing an innocent man would say?

If she checked his visits against the murders, then she could see if the two tallied. She would know, without any tortured doubts or imaginings, whether her suspicions were true. Curiously, now she was on the verge of knowing the truth, she felt reluctant to move away from the warmth of the fire. At long last, as the appearance of the bare branches of the apple tree rather than any lightening of the sky suggested dawn, drowsiness was stealing over her. Her head lolled several times, before she jerked it up and rose to her feet stiffly.

The key to the bureau was in a vase on the mantelpiece. The bottom two drawers contained all the household papers: birth certificates, guarantees, her building society book. She opened the top drawer which contained all his office records. There was nothing there from several months before Christmas. Her stomach lurched. She spread the papers out on the table and went through them carefully. There was nothing dated later than August the previous year.

At first she was bewildered, searching other drawers, in the kitchen, in the bedroom, but gradually a chill entered into her. She had taught him to keep a copy of records, so he could compare one journey, one year with another – that was how accounts caught people out. Why had he removed them? And where were the recent bills? It was the middle of the month, and his claims were not completed until the end of the month.

"Put them in drawer. Don't leave them in car where the kids can get at them."

She heard herself saying that. He was very good about it: one of his routines when he returned, the opening of the bureau drawer, the tinkling of the key falling back into the vase.

She was in the hall, staring at the phone. For the first time she thought: I must call the police. I must call the police. Her hand moved past the pink pig, which had part of the hall lampshade reflected in it, touched and then picked up the phone. She saw herself in the mirror, her long bony face with hair sticking out in spikes from it, and put down the phone. They would think she was mad.

She took down the kitchen calendar, and found last year's. Among the jumble of children's parties, and school pick-up arrangements, she tried to work out when he was away, and, as far as she could recall, where. On pieces of board that were kept for the children's drawings she tabulated the information in columns, just as if she was a top secretary back at Hallet's preparing a yearly sales forecast. The task absorbed her and calmed her. At first she was surprised about the amount of information she could extract and blessed her organised mind: within two arrows "SA" marked every day that Stephen was away. The problem was where! Just before Christmas, Manchester. February 14th to 17th – Sheffield, because he'd visited a cousin there. Leave that. When were the murders? One before Christmas. One in

November. That girl in Leeds ... when was that? Frantically she searched through old newspapers, now cursing her organised mind, for she'd had a clear-out recently, and could find nothing.

But, it struck her, he didn't have to be away, did he? Somehow she had got it into her head that he wouldn't, he couldn't do that, and then come back here to this house, park the car, put the chain on the door, undress and get into bed beside her ... But this girl was killed in Leeds, twenty miles away. Sometimes he went out and didn't come back until God knows what time! It could be just after she'd fallen asleep at half-past-eleven, or two o'clock in the morning, she wouldn't know. Why oh why had she always treated that so casually? It seemed incomprehensible to her now that she had never said anything about it. If the police asked her about that, what on earth would she say? That night ... the night when he'd thought she was asleep and had stood, just stood staring at her ... hadn't she known then that something terrible had happened?

Footsteps sounded on the stairs and she started up in terror, forgetting for a split second that Stephen was away. She stood on the trailing cord of her dressing gown, staggered, cannoned into the chair and gave a little sob as Matthew ran into the kitchen. It couldn't be morning, but it was light outside.

"Hi Mum, what are you doing? Here that's my paper!"

She snatched it from him, frightened that in some way he might decipher it. Then, fearing that if she made too much of a thing about it he might talk to Stephen about her mystery drawings, she tried to be casual about it, telling him she was just making plans, boring things like that.

"Plans for what?"

He was always at his most eager, his most energetic first thing in the morning, poking into things, asking questions about space rockets and why his letter from the Weetabix Club hadn't come. He grabbed one of the cards.

"S ..." he hissed, "t ... Stephen."

"Very good," she said, taking it from him.

His hair was rumpled and his pyjama trousers trailed

round his ankles. His eyes, as black as Stephen's, shone up at her from his grinning face. Sensing now that the cards were forbidden territory, he jumped up at her, trying to grab them.

"Stop it . . . stop it!"

She put them on the top shelf of the top cupboard, where the biscuits were kept, away from the children's prying fingers. He pulled a chair over to climb up to them.

"Now will you stop it! I mean it!"

She pulled the chair back to the table. He sulked for a moment, and then, with a cry of glee, jumped after her trailing dressing-gown cord, yanked it out and began to tie her foot to the chair. She whirled round, the momentum adding force to her hand as she cracked it to his head. He was stunned. Then tears came and with angry cries he flung himself at her, fists flailing.

"Don't hit me." She caught at his hands.

"You hit me!"

"I'm sorry but I told you! I warned you! Now stop it!"

He ran into the next room. Upstairs she could hear Jackie, disturbed, moving about. It was twenty-to-eight. She filled the kettle and stared muzzily out of the window. The sky beyond the bare apple tree branches was a pale wash of blue, bearing only a few tatters of cloud. On the garden path lay a broken tile with splinters, a brighter red, splayed from it. The tilted dustbin lid lying on the lawn scarcely rocked: the wind had practically blown itself out without her realising it.

She drank some water to try and refresh her stale mouth. Her aching limbs misjudged distances and she bumped into the chair Matthew had tried to tie her to as she went into the back room, finding him curled up on the settee, his knees touching his chin, his nails digging into a cushion.

When she touched his reddened cheek he jerked his head fiercely away.

"Sorry," she said.

He became an even tighter ball, burying his head in the cushion. She shrugged and began to return, with slow

132

dragging steps, to the kitchen. He sat up, his skinny frame taut and quivering as a thrown knife, his face screwed up with hatred. The transformation was so sudden she laughed.

"Don't laugh!" he screamed at her.

She caught him up and held him until he stopped struggling and started laughing with her, wriggling his warm body, his sharp bones against her, tightening his arms round her neck. She found herself thinking about Mrs Marsh and Stephen, their closeness; she imagined them like this, as she buried her lips in Matthew's spiky hair, stroking him and murmuring to him, and even that moment of happiness was infected by the thought: was he always at his mother's when he said he was?

Within minutes Matthew was leaping about the kitchen, teasing Jackie, who, unlike him, always took half-an-hour to wake up, chanting to her: "Happy birthday to you, squashed tomatoes and pooh, I saw a fat monkey, and I thought it was you!"

She was proud of her self-control. Whatever happened you did not give in, you went on. That was her one rule in life. While her mind was on the columns she had written, tucked between the biscuit tin and the cake-stand above her head, which she glanced at from time to time as if they might vanish, she got them dressed and tied shoes. Where could she get information on the women who had been killed, cornflakes, don't pour too much milk, did the library keep papers? . . . check they've cleaned their teeth, Matthew's reading folder . . .

In spite of her sleepless night, they were ready to leave with five minutes to spare. She took her car keys from the hook and, finding the milk had arrived, returned with it. As she did so, the phone rang. She knew what that meant: the only people who called at that time in the morning were neighbours in crisis: Mrs Norris, or Mrs Shepherd, wanting a child to be taken to school, and knowing they could rely on Annie. It was neither. It was Stephen. His flat, ordinary tones came as such a shock that at first she could not speak.

"This is a right job is this . . . I shan't be home tonight . . . Hello? . . . Annie?"

She swallowed. Matthew was tossing his reading folder in the air.

"Annie?"

"I'm here."

"I shan't be through till Friday. I thought I'd better tell you."

Her throat was dry. She had to ask him, she had to. "I wanted to speak to you."

"What about?"

What about! A pulse was hammering in her head. She was gripping the phone so tightly, she thought it must break. "I had nowt to do so I thought I'd bring your accounts up to date. I couldn't find them."

"They're at work."

"What are they doing there?"

The line crackled. Faintly, in the background, she could hear another phone ringing.

"A girl does them for me."

"Oh does she!"

She was aware of the tartness in her voice and could almost see the rather sheepish grin.

"Well you were allus grumbling . . . "

Wasn't she grabbing too eagerly at the explanation, wasn't there an edginess, a sudden nervousness in his voice?

"I thought you were doing it yourself."

"I am, practically . . . it's easier doing it there . . . "

His voice was injured, a little truculent, and she knew exactly what he meant: it was easier doing it without her criticisms: it was true she had gone on at him about it, grumbled . . . She suddenly wanted to tell him, to pour out all the fears that had built up in the night, to hear him laugh at them, to know that they were ridiculous . . . Through the open front door she could see the children

134

swinging on the gate, out of earshot. A few words and she would be out of the torment.

"Stephen."

"Yes."

Broken thoughts tumbled about in her head but wouldn't form into a coherent sentence: you know when I missed the hammer . . . that woman . . . that woman was a prostitute . . . I was looking for your records because . . .

Jackie was pushing the folder at Matthew and jerking it away before he could get it. At any moment there was going to be a fight.

"Sorry. It's the kids." She shouted at them. "Give it back to him! Jackie! It's the tiles," she said into the phone. "There were a right gale last night."

"Aye, it blew here."

"I told you we should have them seen to!"

"Front and back?"

She gave him the details and he told her the name of a roofer he knew, who was reliable and wouldn't charge the earth. It was a Leeds number and she wondered if the roofer drank at the Mucky Duck. She called the kids over to say hello to him.

"Hi Dad . . . What are you going to bring me . . .?"

There was an unwritten rule that if he was away more than three days he brought them a small something: a toy car, or a talking book. She'd stopped objecting: he enjoyed the kids jumping round him, and usually pretended he'd forgotten.

"What have you got? What have you got?"

"Got? What are you on about?"

As the kids chattered she turned away, close to tears. He was their father! He was no killer! Could he be talking to them now like this if he was?

It was five-to-nine. The necessity of getting them to school on time drove everything else from her head. She got them off the phone, picked up Matthew's reading folder and went to the hook for the car keys. They weren't there. This was impossible! They were always there. She had drilled it into them not to touch keys.

Had she taken them before he called? She couldn't remember. She'd brought in the milk. She searched near the fridge. The kids joined in, their unconcern at their increasing lateness, and their treating it as a game, first of all irritated and then infuriated her. It was five-past-nine. Never before had they been so late. She was almost crying with desperation and frustration. What was wrong with her, what was happening to her when she couldn't even find her bloody car keys?

At last the mystery was solved. As she had gone to the phone, she must have put the keys on the table next to Matthew's reading folder and gloves. He had taken them outside with him, put them on the gatepost, and promptly forgotten them. The part of her that recognised it wasn't his fault was submerged in a frightening burst of rage. How many times had he been told *never* to touch those keys! He flinched away, silent at first, then breaking into tears, amongst which was a jumble of words which became more and more confused and incoherent at the injustice of it all.

She was cut to the heart, but she couldn't stop her own rage. She pushed them into the car, trapping Jackie's coat, wrenching the door back open, shutting it again. Everything she did seemed to be thwarted!

"Mummy . . . "

"Shut up!"

His pale tear-stained face shrank back into the seat when she turned.

"We're late, don't you understand! Late late late!"

They had never seen her like this before, shouting, crashing the gears, jerking the clutch. A lorry driver hit his horn as she shot out into the main road in front of him. It only made her put her foot down more. In Church Street she did fifty, shooting the lights on amber. In the mirror she could see their white faces. Jackie was rigidly still, while Matthew, who had stopped crying, pulled a scrap of dirty tissue from his pocket.

The road outside the school was almost empty of cars. Always when she got there the air was full of the shrieks and yells of children: now there was an unearthly silence. Matthew turned to her apprehensively and she might then have comforted him, but she saw, walking through the playground on the path she must take, Norma.

She took them by the hand and walked swiftly, grimly, the children running and stumbling to keep up with her. When they had nearly reached Norma, who was with a couple of women who took children to the nursery, Matthew's reading folder slipped from his hand. Norma and the women chased after the booklet and leaflets.

"Are you all right?" Norma said.

"Yeah. Are you?"

She was off, half-running, before more could be said. It was nearly half-past-nine! The closed doors and the empty corridors stared at her accusingly. She dropped Jackie off and then Matthew created a scene.

"I don't want to go."

She was exhausted. Now her rage, like the wind, had blown itself out. She tried to comfort him but it was too late. They were in the classroom with the children staring and the teacher, Mrs Saville, holding the kicking screaming child. She couldn't leave him, not after what she'd said to him, but Mrs Saville was saying: "Be best if you went," and she knew it was true. His screams followed her down a long corridor until she was out in the playground again. Norma had gone, thank God. For a long time she sat in the car, trembling, unable to do anything but stare through the windscreen.

If only she could stop thinking about it for an hour, just half-an-hour, ten minutes, she would feel better. It was like a constant dull pain which would not go away. She drove, not knowing where she was going. She passed a policeman, and looked away, afraid that if he looked into her face he would know. She parked, intending to get some bread, but thought she saw a neighbour and, unable to face talking to anyone, drove off again. Aimlessly she wandered until, simply because she found herself near her own street, she went home.

The house bore a battle-scarred look. All the blooms

had been ripped from the magnolia and lay, in discoloured pockets, under the hedge and rosebushes. Twigs and even a complete branch were scattered on the lawn. And it looked as if the wind had swept through inside: the hall and kitchen were littered with things overturned in the search for the keys: books, letters, a scarf, he'd forgotten his scarf, a mug, the leaflet on the back of which she'd noted the roofer's telephone number.

She huddled at the bottom of the stairs, clutching the leaflet, not knowing whether to laugh or cry. Had they really talked about roof tiles? She began picking things up from the floor and then stood in the middle of the kitchen, forgetting what she was doing. Oh, if only it was one thing or the other! She could face up to her madness, she thought she might even be able to face up to the other; what she couldn't stand was the continual, aching uncertainty, interrupted only by short periods when she was sure he was the killer, or equally convinced that she was mad.

She was holding a Superman mug, a scarf and the leaflet. How long had she been standing there? She dumped them on a chair, then picked up the leaflet. Roof tiles. The way the children had laughed with him.

She got down her scrawled columns on the cardboard. The hieroglyphics spun in front of her eyes. She locked them in the bureau drawer and kept the key.

Now she drove slowly through Hillthorpe, past the school, to the hospital. Twigs snapped under the car wheels as she parked near an avenue of trees. They were beautiful in summer. She remembered staring down at them when she was coming through her episode after having Jackie; the leaves hypnotised her for hours, waves of green, light and dark, some like polished mirrors when the sun caught them.

She looked at the signs marked "Psychiatric Department", although she didn't need to. The familiar smell of carbolic came to her nostrils. A patient stared: a look of unabashed curiosity such as you only got in hospital. The custard yellow and green corridors did not seem to have been painted since she was last here.

In an overheated room marked "Appointments" an elderly woman was on the phone at a desk strewn with brown files labelled "Not to be seen by the patient". Annie had a weird feeling that one of them was hers. They were waiting for her. Ever since the last time, they had been waiting for her. She would be here perhaps until summer, when the leaves were fully out, rippling in glittering green waves beneath her window. She sat down, her hands plucking edgily at her skirt, while the phone conversation, which was about a lost file, went on and on.

"It was returned from the path lab and signed out . . . I can't decipher it . . ."

She must have dozed a little in the stuffy room, seeing the green waves beneath her closing eyelids, for the woman had put the phone down and was staring at her as if she'd asked her a question.

"Mrs Mulroy?" she said.

"No. Marsh. Annie Marsh."

The woman frowned at her from behind large spectacles which rested on the tip of her nose. "Which doctor are you?"

"I haven't an appointment – "

"You must have an appointment from your own doctor."

"Dr Seymour said I could see him at any time. Please. I've got to see him!"

"Dr Seymour isn't here."

"Then when can I see him?"

"You can't. He isn't – "

"Please, I must, he told me I could see him, please, I can't take any more."

Her hands were locked, twisted together, pleading. The phone rang. The woman told the caller she'd ring back. She took Annie's name and address and her patient number, which she had written in her diary, transferring it from year to year. The woman looked at a list and then removed her spectacles. Her eyes looked smaller, less

139

formidable without them. She told Annie to wait a moment and left the room.

Annie sat staring at the spectacles, which rested on top of the askew files. One end of the curling plastic stalk was chewed. The phone rang again and eventually stopped just before the woman returned.

"Dr Patel will see you in a little while."

"It's Dr Seymour I must see!"

"He isn't here any more!"

"I've got to see him!"

"Mrs Marsh." The voice had that patient, smiling, firmness that went in Annie's memory with the carbolic smell and the yellow walls. "He doesn't work here any more."

She couldn't take it in. "I must see him."

"He's in London. He hasn't been here for two years. Don't you understand? Dr Patel has taken his patients. He's very good."

As the woman advanced on her, smiling, Annie panicked. She shook her head, picked up her bag, and wrenched open the door, the woman's voice following her. She collided with a cleaner who dropped a bag of waste and shouted after her. She had a sudden, violent picture of being kept in, of being given shock treatment as they had tried to do last time before she'd seen Dr Seymour. The lift closed just as she got to it and she ran down the stone stairs, nearly falling when her shoe twisted off. In a mirror in the reception hall she caught sight of herself. Her hair, which had dried any old how after she'd been out in the rain last night, stuck from her head in tufts. Her eyes were wild.

No one was following her but she ran until she reached the car. If they kept her inside what would happen to the children? She might not be mad. They might still keep her in, looking like this and with her brown file. She might be quite right, he might be a killer but they wouldn't believe her. Then what would happen to the children? The thought was like a blow.

140

"I see, I see, but didn't you also think Jackie a monster, Mrs Marsh?"

The car wouldn't fire. Sobbing, she pressed the accelerator to the floor and turned the key again. The engine roared and revved, scaring birds which rose and wheeled as she careered off down the drive. She didn't want to go back into Hillthorpe and took the Leeds Road. She found herself, she didn't know why, heading towards Birchgate. Perhaps it was because she was thinking of Jan, the prostitute. For the first time she felt some sympathy for her: she had had her children torn away from her. Annie now realised she would have fought too: she would have scratched and bit. In the Mucky Duck that night hadn't Jan been at the end of her tether, as she was now?

She left the main road just past the Pavilion and entered the back terraces of Birchgate. When she smelt the fish and chip shop she stopped. She hadn't come here just for fish and chips, had she? Well, she was ravenous. She bought rock and large chips, swishing the pungent vinegar on it to kill the smell of grease. She ate as she walked, finishing every flake of fish, every crumb of batter. All around her was poverty. A woman slopped by in slippers, her bare legs scratched and dirty. At the Heath, a small patch of green, a group of winos with patchy red faces passing round a bottle of Strongbow shouted to her.

"Give us a chip."

"Give us a kiss."

"How about a kiss and a chip?"

"How about a kiss and a chip and f – f – ish?"

She didn't mind. In fact she nearly smiled at them. Nor did she mind the crumbling terraces, the litter blown everywhere by last night's wind, the heap of furniture and second-hand clothes in the window of Jacks's Store (DHSS vouchers taken). Was it because she was reaching a decision?

Or just that she had eaten for the first time since last night and was regaining some composure?

For the first time she had looked at people like those winos, without hurrying past; people with only the clothes they stood up in and the next swallow of Strongbow. Wasn't she wandering like them? She was even clutching at a plastic cup of tea she'd bought from a carry-out. The man had shovelled in two spoonfuls of sugar. Although she didn't take it, she had let him do so without protest. She must be looking poor. The poor took everything they were offered. Now she sipped the stewed, sweet liquid and dropped the plastic lid in the gutter like the winos. No. It wasn't the first time she had looked at people like that. She used to look at people like that when she was ill, when the drugs insulated her senses and slurred her movements. Moving through the world was like moving through cotton wool. Like now.

It was some time before she realised it was raining, steadily and softly. The wind had dropped completely. A woman strapped a struggling toddler into a buggy, yelling at her: "We'll be late for your brother."

She looked at her watch. It was half-past-three. The kids. Even then she didn't move quickly, reluctant to leave this aimless, drifting cocoon and return home. Only when she was caught in the traffic, building up towards the evening rush hour, did panic set in. She'd never get there! This was worse, far worse than getting your children there late! The teacher would have to stay with them. And Matthew, Matthew had been so upset! What the hell had she been doing!

It was ten-to-four. They'd been out five minutes. She could see the children's faces, expectant, then bewildered. It would be like the end of the world, their mother not turning up. It was the end of the world.

"Come on come on come on," she yelled at the traffic, which was moving agonisingly slowly through lights.

She turned left and, knowing there was right-turning traffic coming up, was in the inside lane when the driver in front put his winkers on and parked. She swore and pulled out. Horns blared, forcing her to stop. There was a gap but she was in such a hurry she stalled the engine. She could still make it. Shaking, she turned the key and shot forward, just misjudging the distance of the parked car.

142

Her bumper caught and smashed the tail-light. The driver of the parked car was returning, open-mouthed, with the paper he had bought. Traffic bent round her, faces staring, the occasional horn going. She folded her arms on the steering wheel and dropped her forehead on them. Somebody had gone into her once on Hillthorpe Rise, but she had never done anything as stupid as this.

There was a tapping at the window. The driver's mouth was a moving O, like that of a goldfish. She wound down the window.

"In a hurry?"

"You shouldn't park here!"

"You shouldn't be driving that bloody car, love."

She was still trembling when she got to the school, half-an-hour late. Her hair, wet from walking in Birchgate, clung round her face. The school playground was as silent as when she'd left that morning. It was totally bewildering; she never saw these buildings, this yard, without people; to see it twice in one day like this made it seem as if all the order which she had carefully built up over the years had suddenly, without warning, collapsed.

She was not even hurrying now, in fact she was slowing down. The asphalt gleamed with rain and a tiny lacework of water ran from a broken drainpipe. As she turned the corner of the nursery, by the red climbing frame and slide, she saw in the distance a small group of figures; at first indistinguishable through the gloom and rain, they seemed like one person with many arms and legs – like the goddess they had pinned in the school corridors when it was an Indian festival. Then, approaching, she deciphered them as Matthew, Jackie and Susan playing hopscotch. With them was Norma.

Matthew saw her first. His legs pounding, his face breaking into joy, he flung himself up at her.

"Mummy Mummy Mummy!"

"Where've you been? Errr . . . you're all wet!"

Now she had both of them in her arms, jumping, wriggling, pushing their wet faces at her, the morning's scene completely forgotten. She hugged them and kissed

143

them till they squealed: it seemed weeks, months since she had seen them.

11

Norma asked her back to tea because she was in such a state, which Norma put down to the car accident.

There turned out to be another reason: John was there, and he had told his wife about Norma. Not only that, he was leaving her shortly and moving in with Norma. Assuming that was still all right, he said. Well, said Norma, she'd think about it.

They sat there laughing nervously and exchanging glances like a couple of teenagers. Normally Annie would have been shocked; now she could barely pay attention to what they were saying.

"I feel so much better now I've told her." John twisted his hands together nervously. "Of course it's not over . . . but I feel the worst is . . . Thanks to you, Annie."

"Me? I've done nothing."

"You have. You did. You went on at me to say something. Spurred me into action. At our . . . chaotic dinner."

There was silence. No doubt they were all thinking about Stephen getting drunk, being sick. She had helped him? It seemed improbable. But perhaps she had. Perhaps the talking had helped. Perhaps she should talk, as he had done . . . She dismissed the thought. How could she? How could she talk about *that*?

They were in the front room, drinking tea, while the children listened to Susan's new cassette recorder upstairs. The black storm clouds outside made it gloomy but no one switched on the light.

Norma refilled her cup. "What's been happening to you?"

She sat up tensely in the chair. "Nothing."

"We've been worried about you."

John's quiet voice made her even more nervous. She laughed. "Oh. Have you? I've only been going mad, that's all."

She expected them to laugh, but it was incredible. When she said things that weren't at all funny, people laughed. Now she'd made a joke, and they didn't even smile, but just stared at her waiting for her to go on. She had an urge to spill everything out but was suddenly frightened. Their eyes were still on her. To cover her confusion she reached for a biscuit and had bitten it before she realised it was a Garibaldi. She detested Garibaldis, but she would have to finish it now.

She washed away the taste of the biscuit with tea, and had a sudden inspiration. John was clever. He lived in the world that Dr Seymour inhabited. He would know where to find him. In a curt, matter-of-fact way she told them about her pregnancies, about the way she had to give birth twice: first to monsters, then to children. It was happening again.

"But you're not pregnant . . . are you?" Norma said, with a puzzled expression.

Somehow she had not expected the conversation to lead to this. It was obvious, but totally unexpected. She floundered out words, then petered out.

"But what gives you this feeling?" John asked.

He didn't look at her, but kept his head low over his cupped hands. Huddled low on the settee she could see big bruised-looking clouds hanging over the houses opposite. She began to shiver uncontrollably.

"Are you cold? . . . Come nearer the fire . . . "

"I'm all right."

The children were screaming upstairs. Someone ought to go up to them. No one moved. The electric fire had a faulty element which sparked from time to time. Wasn't John like Dr Seymour in some ways? In the way he sounded uncertain about everything he said, the way his voice trailed, even in the way he kept fiddling? He was picking now at a loose thread in his sweater which she could swear was the same one he'd worn at the dinner, only dirtier, more out-at-elbows.

She did not decide to tell the story, it just came out, piece by piece, as his sweater would unravel into an untidy heap of wool if he pulled that thread long enough.

In the gloom she could not see their expressions, and they kept perfectly still, except for that finger and thumb plucking at the thread, and said nothing.

When she had finished there was a long pause, punctuated only by the yells of the children, who had been silent for a while.

"Of course I'll help you to find Dr Seymour," John said. "If that's what you want."

"What do you mean, if that's what I want?"

"If that's what you want," John repeated.

Annie's voice burst out, "Do you think I should go to the police?"

"Yes," Norma said. She moved to Annie as if she was going to squeeze her shoulder, but didn't touch her. "I mean, it's most probably nothing but . . . "

"But . . . "

"It could be anyone, and Stephen . . . "

"Stephen what?"

"I don't know, love, I don't know. He keeps himself to himself doesn't he, and if you think . . ."

Annie felt a rush of hatred for Norma, but before she could retort, the children thundered in demanding food. Norma took them away to have tea in the kitchen, leaving John and Annie alone. The fire's faulty element crackled, and John kicked it.

"Of course it's all circumstantial," he said.

"What does that mean?"

"It's all indirect . . . a number of things which point to the possibility . . . but that's all . . . you mustn't think it's true until, unless . . . "

She sat up taut, her tea spilling, hot on her knee,

ignoring it. "Of course it's not true! You don't think I really believe he's the killer, do you? Stephen? Of course he's not! I know he's not! You think you and Norma, you think you're in love, well Stephen and I, well I don't know what you'd call it, I don't have the words you have, but we're married, we have these two lovely children, we're together, I know him, you don't think I believe it's him, do you?"

He stood over her, arms hanging by his sides, head bowed. When she stopped he wandered round the room, touching the tops of furniture, giving the fire a rap, although it wasn't sparking now.

"I don't believe it's true for one minute, Annie."

"I can't stop thinking about it."

"Go to the hospital. Seymour's replacement is probably very good."

"Suppose they keep me in." She stood up, her fists clenched. "Suppose it's true?"

"Then go to the police. Go now."

"Now?"

"It'll put your mind at rest."

Now. That was something she had not bargained for. The word made her aware they were talking about something real, not some fancy of her imagination. She was going to go into the police station and say she thought her husband was a murderer. No, she didn't, she couldn't think that! As she got up, one of her legs had gone to sleep and she staggered. He caught hold of her.

"I'll take you."

"I'll go on my own, thank you."

"You can't."

"I can. I can manage."

"You can't manage, Annie!"

"Let me go, please."

"Are you going to take the children?"

She sat down on the edge of a chair. The tea had soaked into her skirt and tights. She rubbed a hand ineffectually at it.

"They can sleep here," he said.

"No."

"Why not?"

"Because what do you think they would think?"

She had shouted and they both heard the chatter stop in the kitchen. Then came Norma's voice, unnaturally loud, asking if anyone was interested in choc ices. She suddenly realised how exhausted she was. She kept rubbing at the spot of tea. The room was blurring and her head kept dropping on her chest.

"How much sleep did you get last night? . . . Annie, you've already had one accident!"

She levered herself up and, with an immense effort, focussed on the room, on him. "All right," she said, "but I'm taking them home and putting them to bed first."

She wouldn't leave before Matthew had fallen asleep. She wanted him asleep. The trouble was he sensed something was up, suspected she was going out.

"I want to come with you!"

John paced in the hall where he gazed at the pink pig. She heard him switch on the television news, and her heart thumped when she heard the word "killed" and she rushed to the banisters, but it was someone shot in Northern Ireland. While Matthew settled she tidied up, conscious that John had not been in the house before, apologising for the state of the place. She searched for the little white embroidered cloth that she had picked up in a jumble, it was supposed to be very old, and put it on a tray with a bottle of sherry and a glass.

"Please don't bother."

"It's no bother."

In the end, with Matthew, she had to resort to what she used to sing to him as a baby: "Wee Willie Winkie, runs through the town, upstairs and downstairs in his night-gown . . ." Just as he was falling asleep, she felt tears coming. She stopped, bit her lip so hard it bled, and continued, "Rapping at the window, crying through the lock . . . are the children all in bed . . . "

She couldn't finish. She hurried to the bathroom, locked

herself in, and sat on the bath while great racking sobs shook her. They were uncontrollable until, refusing to give way to them, she levered herself up and scooped handful after handful of cold water on her face. When she returned to Matthew's bedroom, he was asleep.

There was one awkward moment when they had left Mrs Crowther reading to Jackie. She shouted downstairs: "You haven't left me where you'll be."

Recently she had always left a note on the tray with tea and biscuits. She stood, staring up at Mrs Crowther, struck dumb. Behind her came John's voice: "They're not on the phone. We'll ring if we're going to be late."

As if they were just going round to the pub. As if they were having an affair. She should have invented something. But what could she say? What could she tell the children? If the police came round to the house? If they questioned Stephen?

John had an old Austin Maxi, as shabby as his pullover. The back was full of books and files, and she saw among them a couple of cartons of rose fertiliser.

"Are you a gardener?"

"A bit . . . I shall be sorry to lose my garden."

"Norma's will keep you busy."

"Yes."

"You should have fed them by now."

"What?"

"The roses."

He grinned at her and started the car. She felt a little better with the cold air and the activity of getting the children to bed.

She looked at John's silent profile as he drove, slowly and carefully, along Stanningley Road towards Leeds. It was his idea to go to the central police station, where there was an Incident Room. What would she say? She had worked out nothing, nothing! She should have confronted Stephen, said something on the phone, she should wait until Friday, when he came home. She suspected, but she didn't, no couldn't, no didn't, believe he was the killer. If there were police cars in Hillthorpe Drive, and she was wrong, what would it do to their marriage, to the children?

"Stop."

He glanced in the mirror before pulling in to the kerb.

"I'll talk to Stephen."

"Can you?"

"Yes."

"About this?"

She clenched her hands. They were in Armley Road, not far from the canal. She thought of Stephen's silences, of his secrets, of his knowing prostitutes, of his returning late at night, of the hammer, of the records.

John spoke very quietly, diffidently, probably as he spoke about a student's work. "The killer will have two personalities. One at home. The other on the streets. You know him only at home."

"I can talk to him! He's not the killer!"

"But if he is . . . is he going to say he is?"

So obvious, but she seemed unable to see the obvious. A few drops of rain splashed on the windscreen. The threatened storm had passed over without materialising.

"Why don't you let me take you to the hospital?"

"You think I'm mad?"

"Overwrought. I don't know what to think."

"If I talk to Stephen I'll know."

"I suppose, well . . . "

"Well what?"

He made a deprecating gesture as if he knew that what he was saying was completely foolish. "There's a risk."

She stared at him, her mouth falling open. Again the obvious, and the totally unexpected. A picture filled her mind of Stephen standing in the bedroom staring fixedly at her while he thought she was asleep. She voiced what, up to now, she had been avoiding thinking.

"He wouldn't kill me."

"This is a silly conversation . . . " He smiled at her, but a moment after added: "Christie killed his wife. At the end."

"Who?"

"He killed prostitutes. An innocent man, Evans, was hanged for the murders."

"Oh yes. It was a film."

"Yes."

"I thought it was . . . just a film. Was he . . . ?" she fumbled for a better word, but couldn't find it, " . . . respectable?"

Neither of them was aware of the traffic, of a passing heavy lorry shaking the car. His head, half in shadow, was sunk in his chest. "Yes. An ex-policeman. Special constable."

Without her knowing how it happened, her head was on his shoulder and his arms round her. She burrowed her face in the pullover, which had a mouldy, earthy smell. Once he rubbed her shoulder, once he stroked her hair. She was dimly aware of the flicker of passing headlights. The drivers, she thought, would not think twice about them being lovers. Nothing was what it seemed.

She sat up.

"I don't want the police at the house."

"If it's nothing—"

"It is nothing!"

"Then they won't come."

"You don't know that!"

"Annie, it's in confidence! They wouldn't get anyone talking to them if they trampled over people's lives!"

"They'll interview him."

"But he won't know it's because of you. They won't tell him."

"Won't they?"

"I don't think so."

"You're not sure."

"Of course I'm not sure." His voice was edged with exasperation.

"He'll know."

"How will he?"

"He will! Don't touch me!"

She broke out of his encircling arms. Her mind was such a whirlpool of confused emotions she just wanted to be taken there, wanted him to take the decision for her, but he made no attempt to move. She began to resent his patience, his concern, and in the end it was simply the thought of spending another night alone that decided her. She couldn't face that.

"Go on."

"Home?"

"To Leeds."

Now, perhaps, he began to have doubts about what they were doing, the responsibility he was taking. He didn't start the car.

"Do you sleep together?"

"What?"

"You and Stephen."

"That's got nothing to do with you."

"I'm trying to help."

"No you're not! You've got a dirty mind, I think it's disgusting . . . disgusting the way you and Norma . . ."

"What?"

"Go on." She was screaming at him, as she'd screamed at Matthew, was that only this morning, and, like then, a scrap of herself was appalled at what she was saying, but couldn't stop. "You think it's something to do with me, don't you?"

"I didn't say that."

"That's what you mean. You think I've known all the time, don't you? You think I've been protecting him don't you?"

"Annie – "

She wrenched at the door handle, and it came off in her hand. "Your bloody car's falling to pieces. Your pullover smells." She stared at the handle, then began to laugh and sob at the same time.

He took the handle from her.

"Let me out," she cried, "I'll walk."

He seized her by the shoulders and shouted: "Don't be bloody silly." He released her and fitted the handle back. "Walk if you like."

Her legs wouldn't move. Now she simply wanted to get it

over with and, above all, to sleep. He drove her down Westgate, below the motorway which bisected Leeds, and into Grace Street. There was nowhere to park near the grimy Victorian building which contained the police station. He trickled past it, and round a double-parked police car. She opened the door.

"I'll come in with you," he said.

"No. They'll wonder who you are."

"I'll tell them."

"Please."

He looked exasperated, but gave in. "I'll wait."

"You don't have to."

"I know I don't have to!"

As she got out of the car he said: "Annie." When she turned, he simply squeezed her hand.

Now she felt terribly alone. She wished he was coming in with her. She'd refused because, well, wouldn't the police be curious about their relationship? She'd seen the look in Mrs Crowther's eyes.

She walked up the steps. In the glass case, next to a poster about an armed robbery with drawings of two men, was the poster you saw everywhere. She knew it off by heart. There were the pictures of the four women, staring, smiling, one so out-of-focus it was difficult to work out her expression. Under the faces, one word in red capitals: MURDER. "We believe these crimes have been committed by the same person, who will strike again if he is not caught. He may appear to be leading a normal life. If you have any information about these crimes, or have suspicions about any person in connection with them, contact Leeds City Police, at Grace Street, LS1 and ask for the Incident Room."

The words echoed in her head as she pushed at the worn wooden frame of the glass-panelled door, through which she could see a policeman in shirt sleeves writing at the desk. Warm air hit her. Further down the counter a man was protesting in slurred tones to a sergeant about his overcoat, which apparently he'd hung up in a pub, only to find the sleeve slashed on his return.

"I know the man who did it!"

"Did you see him do it?"

"No, but I can tell you his name . . . you wouldn't replace a coat of that quality for fifty pounds . . . seventy . . . feel that . . . "

The policeman in shirt sleeves glanced up at Annie, smiled briefly, and finished his writing, which he did slowly and precisely, as if she, too, had called about a torn coat, or a missing dog.

WPS Clarke

Woman Police Sergeant Clarke felt a quiver of excitement run through her after she had spent a few minutes with the woman. So much so, that she had to calm herself down by reminding herself how often it had happened before. They came in, eyes avid with excitement – so this was the murder room, this was where they'd bring him – their suspicions pouring out even before they'd sat down.

"I think I know the killer . . . "

"He was covered with blood . . . "

"I see him go out at night . . . at all kinds of odd hours . . . "

All that had unearthed had been a printer on the *Yorkshire Post* whose face had been horribly scarred in a machine room accident, a butcher, and a night security worker. But you had to listen to everyone, record and file every interview.

This woman was different. She was so nervous she dropped her bag twice while she was sitting down. As Clarke took down her details on the yellow card they used for all initial interviews with informants, she saw across the plain wooden table a woman in her early thirties who, she judged, was close to breakdown. Her brown hair, in which you could just see the first grey streaks, straggled round her square-jawed face. Her large, bony hands were red and rough from work, and with a finger and thumb she twisted round her plain gold wedding ring, clicking it constantly against her engagement ring, so that Clarke suspected what was coming long before she said: "It's my husband."

Clarke waited, but there was a silence, apart from the clicks of the ring, so she said, neutrally: "His name?"

"Stephen."

More details. Age. Place of work. How long married. Clarke jotted these down on a separate card and when she went out to ask for tea, passed it to the desk for an immediate computer check. The West Yorkshire Police, who had faced many criticisms for not using a computer in the Yorkshire Ripper case, now had a "Major Incident Facilities Computer" which already contained details of nearly ten thousand interviews carried out on the killings.

When she returned, Mrs Marsh was standing by her chair. "He's not the killer," she said.

Clarke merely nodded reassuringly. She waited until the tea came, asking more neutral questions, trying to relax her, win her confidence, and then, when the tea was warming her hands, said in the same conversational voice: "He's not the killer? . . . "

The woman's head dipped, but she steadied herself and told her story, slowly at first, but then so fast that Clarke, who did not want to stop her, took only the occasional brief note.

When Mrs Marsh told her that her husband had been in Manchester for the Christmas murder, and she was sure he had been out late on the night of the Bradford one, Clarke had a struggle to keep calm.

But Mrs Marsh was confused about where her husband was on the night of Maureen Nelson's murder. That Saturday, Mrs Marsh suddenly exclaimed, was Jackie's birthday. He was at her party! Why hadn't she thought of that before!

"Did he go out in the evening?"

"No. He helped me clear up."

"You're sure?"

"Yes. I'm sure . . . well I think so . . . wait a minute . . . there is something . . . "

The woman shook her head as she couldn't remember and stopped in a state of some distress and asked to use the lavatory. Clarke got a policewoman to take her and indicated she must not let Mrs Marsh out of her sight: she didn't think she was the type to kill herself, but she was taking no risks.

Clarke was now in a high state of tension. Most of the informants who came were friends of the people they suspected – or had been friends and bore them a grudge – or neighbours. There were some brothers and sisters, no mothers and fathers and she knew of a number of wives, although she had not interviewed any herself.

The evidence was jumbled and certainly not hard, but the woman struck Clarke as honest – honest to a fault, she thought – and she would be, Clarke surmised, in normal circumstances level-headed. The couple were not at the point of divorce or separation; she didn't hate or even seem particularly to dislike her husband; indeed she was constantly denying the conclusions of her own evidence, and the struggle she had in giving it was painful to see.

Clarke, like many police officers, followed what she called her gut instinct and looked for evidence to fit it. It was the only way to deal with professional crime. Any armed robbery would have a style, a pattern that pointed to a number of known criminals. They would automatically have alibis. You pulled them in, used your gut instinct, and then tried to make a case that would stick. This crime was different. One man unknown to other criminals, who were the normal informants. But the gut instinct still applied about the members of the public who came in, and she had a strong one about Mrs Marsh.

While the informant was at the lavatory she was on the edge of phoning Chief Inspector Daybury. She picked up the phone and put it down several times. What stopped her was that two months ago she'd done a similar thing late at night. She had been taking a statement from a prostitute, who had been attacked by a coloured man with a knife in Leopold Street, Chapeltown. He had run away when another prostitute had shouted, and she identified him as Winston Place, a thirty-four year-old electrician from the Binder Estate. It was shortly after the murder of Maureen Nelson, who had whispered "Black . . ." as she died in Leeds Infirmary, and half the West Yorkshire Police believed they were looking for a coloured man.

Clarke had alerted Daybury, and the full team came out.

The knife turned out to be a pocket screwdriver. The quarrel with the prostitute had been about money. Winston Place had a record for GBH – but he was still serving part of the sentence in Armley Jail when three of the women were killed.

Daybury hadn't minded – he said. Better safe than sorry. But it was such obvious routine to check Place's form before jumping the gun that she couldn't imagine how she'd been so stupid, and the look on Daybury's face still rankled.

She was still in a state of indecision when a computer print-out was handed to her. Stephen Marsh was one of nearly ten thousand men who had been interviewed by the murder squad. Her heart jumped as she scanned the torn-off pages, although the classification was not encouraging: the lowest: no further follow-up.

What was on the print-out decisively altered everything. This is what she read:

MARSH, Stephen. d.o.b. 10/9/53. 5 Hillthorpe View, Hillthorpe, Leeds 28. 747 8280.
Employment: Hallet's, Ring Road, Rothwell. Since 1980. Service Engineer.
Reason for interview: company has fleet Escort cars. Marsh is one of twelve Hallet's representatives and service engineers to have an Escort car. Some are A, and the majority B registration. Marsh stated that he had driven a B registration car, but not at the material time (the death of Maureen Nelson) when he had an A registration car. Checked Transport Department, and the record cards confirm this. Tyres are Michelin.

Clarke knew they were looking for a B registration car with Pirelli tyres. She read on.

Marsh was quiet and cooperative, volunteering that he had driven a B registration car at one time. Maude, the Technical Services Manager, told me that, although he does not write well, he is a model employee and one of the

158

company's best engineers. He has been married for nine years and has two small children. He has one conviction for, with others, stealing a car, but that dates back thirteen years, when he was twenty. He has no record of violence, although when I saw him he had a black eye – caused, he said, by a car door.

Clarke could see the last triviality being put down by a . . . DC Saunders it was, to lighten the boredom of a long day of dead-end interviews. Quite clearly, he'd had no gut feeling about Marsh.

"Black . . . "

Because she'd just been thinking about it, it rang in her memory.

"Black . . . "

Had the driver who picked up Maureen Nelson on the A58 that night had a black eye? She thought about it for perhaps a second, then dismissed it as too fanciful – she was clutching at straws. She could see Daybury's face if she brought that one up! She read on.

Marsh was concerned as to whether I intended to interview his wife and when I asked him about this concern he said it was because his wife had been in a mental hospital and it might "set her off again".

The meticulous DC Saunders had recorded Marsh's statement that his wife had been in Hillthorpe Hospital on two occasions.

At this point Mrs Marsh returned from the toilet, looking white and exhausted. Clarke excused herself and phoned Hillthorpe Hospital and spoke to the night superintendent who, while refusing to give any details, confirmed that Mrs Annie Marsh had been an in-patient twice: for several months in 1977, and for the same period in 1981. After a small hesitation, the night superintendent asked if she was in trouble.

"No," Clarke replied.

159

"Only she was in here today. Very distressed."

"Why?"

"I don't know. There's a note on the changeover sheet."

Clarke was more pleased than disappointed – pleased she hadn't called Daybury. She could see it all now – Stephen Marsh must have mentioned the police interviews at work, his wife worried about it, and with her history, anxiety had turned into illness. There had been similar reactions. She went back to the interview, concerned now only to get rid of her as politely as possible. But when she saw her again she had a nagging doubt. The woman was in a bad state, but she was holding on to herself, in a way most nutters didn't. She looked at her notes, at the print-out, which she'd slipped into a file, and, for the want of anything better to say, asked: "How did he get the black eye?"

The effect on the woman was extraordinary. Her white face reddened and she gripped the edge of the table. "How did you know that?"

"He told us."

"When?"

"When we interviewed him."

"You've interviewed him?"

Clarke cursed her assumption that Mrs Marsh knew this, but it was too late to go back now. She told her that a lot of the men at Hallet's had been interviewed. It was pure routine, that was all.

"He didn't tell you?"

"No."

"He probably didn't want to worry you."

"It doesn't worry me." The woman was leaning eagerly across the table, her face transformed. "You mean you didn't find anything?"

Her eyes, her whole frame was quivering with hope and energy, and Clarke suddenly felt very sorry for her. All she needed was a bit of support, of reassurance. She closed the file.

"Go home and have a good rest, Mrs Marsh. And stop thinking about it."

"I will. You know . . . I am positive he didn't go out that Saturday evening. Not at all. We cleared up after the party and his brother stayed. They drank at home. Why oh why didn't I think of that before?"

As the woman got up, she slipped and fell against the table. Clarke moved fast to catch her and steered her back into the chair. Another few minutes, another cup of tea and she looked a new woman. Clarke had been on a course on Criminal Psychology. Wasn't this woman a manic-depressive?

On the way out she asked: "How did he get his black eye?"

"I hit him."

Clarke sighed. The car was wrong. His wife had a mental history. And she hit him, not the other way about. A few minutes after she'd recorded the interview she forgot about Mrs Marsh. And a week after, she would have found it hard to put a face to the name.

Part III

TERROR

terror n. 1. great fear, panic, or
dread. 2. a person or thing that
inspires great dread.

12

Annie loved rhododendrons, although they fought a
losing battle in the chalky soil of the hill. Shortly after they
had come to the house she had dug a pit opposite the
apple tree, virtually replacing the soil with peat and
manure. There she grew an evergreen Japanese variety
and a Cilipinese – a little bush which flowered in late April,
which it now was.

They had just finished tea and Stephen washed the
dishes while she dried. She gazed anxiously out of the
window. The Cilipinese was beginning to flower – it
usually started a week after the apple tree. It had been a
day when she could go out in the garden without her
anorak, but the cool westerly wind had dropped, and the
sky was a sharp, milky blue. There was going to be a frost.

He knew what she was going to do before she did it, and
when she got the tablecloth from the drawer and went out
into the garden, she heard him call the children. She
draped the cloth gently over the white blooms tipped with
red, which were beginning to close in the evening cold. As
she weighted the end of the cloth with stones, she heard
the rattle of crockery. Every year there was the let's-have-
tea-on-the-rhododendron joke. Stephen and the children
never tired of it: in its way, it was the beginning of spring.

"In't it a bit bumpy for a table?"

"Shall I lay table Mum?"

"If you break just one of those blooms! Now stop it!"

She chased Matthew, who cannoned into Stephen. She
couldn't stop herself, and Stephen's arm went round her
as they all fell in a heap laughing. His eyes were close to
hers, and she could feel his chest rising and falling against
her. For a moment, as they rolled over, she buried her face
in his jumper: a cricket-style one with a blue V, smelling of

washing powder, unlike John's mouldy pullover. She scrambled to get up, but he held her for a moment, squeezing her arms. His tongue ran over his lips, and his eyes looked darker than ever in the fading light.

"What is it?"

He helped her up, and brushed the back of her skirt. Now he was in the shade of the apple tree, and she couldn't see his eyes. It must have been her imagination that his hands were shaking, for when he moved into the light she could see he was grinning.

"We soon will be having tea out here."

"Aye. Soon be warm enough."

There was nothing more to say. While he took the children in, she pottered, pulling a weed, checking the emerging apple blossom for pests.

It was impossible to think that this wouldn't happen next year, or the year after that. It was impossible to imagine the nightmare only a month ago; and almost as impossible to imagine why it had gone – if not completely.

She had decided, after the night at the police station, to confront Stephen with her fears, now that they were groundless. After all, he had been wonderful when she'd been in hospital after having the children.

So why hadn't she told him?

There was the prostitute, Jan Stephenson. Did he go to prostitutes? Did he have other women? She ought to have been in a rage about it, but she was so full of relief it was not the other thing that she – well, she didn't dismiss it, but she put it to the back of her mind, wanting to enjoy her relief. And, as the days passed, it was such bliss to return to normal, to her garden, to getting Matthew first in the line at school again, that she continued to say nothing. After all, what had it amounted to? He had taken her to a pub where there were prostitutes. Or at least one. That was all. The mysterious business of the money bothered her more, but she was keeping a sharper eye on him.

He went out less. Once she said: "Are you going to Mucky Duck?"

166

He looked uncomfortable and shook his head. "I don't use it now."

It was true that they got through to one another without words, like many Yorkshire people. You could say too much; as one of the cleaners at the home used to say to her, almost every day: "Least said, soonest mended."

So life gradually returned to normal. Not quite. They were still not sleeping together. But that would come back too. They were both so tired when they got into bed that after a mumbled "Night night" they would be instantly asleep. What was wrong with that, if that was what they both wanted?

She weighted the tablecloth on the Cilipinese with another stone and looked towards the house where, through the lighted window, she could see Matthew grinning all over his face as he rode on Stephen's back. Birds suddenly chattered, deepening the evening silence. Yes, she could feel the chill on her cheeks now. There was going to be a frost tonight.

It was only when the fear reappeared that she realised it had never gone at all. It had dived to the bottom of her mind, like the fish boys at the home used to catch in the canal. Most of the time you could not believe there were any fish in the still, oily waters, before which fishermen sat hunched for hours. And hadn't she been waiting, just like them, knowing, no matter what things looked like on the surface, that there was something there?

She was in Leeds shopping. Stephen had taken the kids to his mother's so she could have a good wander on her own. She'd come in by bus, so there was no hassle with parking. The main purpose was to get a summer sweater for Mrs Marsh's birthday in May. This was soon done as Annie knew that whatever was bought would be met with "Oh yes, that is nice . . . Marks, is it? I allus say you can't beat Marks, my mother used to shop on their first stall in Leeds . . . wool, you can't beat sheep . . . nice shaping round the . . . lovely, I wonder if it's quite me, though . . . ?"

She would wear it for an hour with the labels on, refusing tea in case some got spilt on it, then fold it carefully back in the plastic bag, getting Stephen to risk a ticket while he parked outside Marks and helped her into the shop to exchange it.

It was cold but bright enough for the chess players to attract a small crowd outside the Town Hall. The chess boards were made out of giant tiles set into the pavement and one of the players, a wizened old man who leant on a stick, got a boy who was only just bigger than the pieces to move his black castle. He rapped triumphantly with his stick on the square it was to go on.

"Mate! Get out of that, then!"

His opponent, a middle-aged man with an open shirt and a dead pipe clenched between his teeth, conceded defeat. Annie knew nothing about the game but she enjoyed the spectacle and, for once, enjoyed doing nothing. Two days ago a woman had been found stabbed to death in Liverpool, which had brought out a rash of headlines and television speculations that the killer was back. The police dismissed these; it was a one-off crime, they said, and they had reinforced that only this morning by arresting the woman's lover for the murder.

What a state she would have been in a month ago! It was luxurious to think of that, to feel that things were slowly returning to normal, just as the sun was growing a little warmer each day, and to feel that she had little more to worry about than a sweater that was going to be rejected. That was why she lingered, sat on a bench, while the pieces were reset and the players argued.

Near the Art Gallery a policeman stood by a parked car and wrote out a ticket.

The man who had lost, looking for something on which he could turn his resentment, said: "Bastard would be better off catching the Hawk."

The old man, the victor, broke off from watching the game, which had started with different opponents. He said, with absolute certainty: "They'll not catch him."

The other man's pipe slid to the corner of his mouth. "Oh, you know, do you, Arthur?"

"I reckon, Ted," said Arthur, who then turned to one of the players to say: "You've buggered your defence. Pawn to King Bishop's Three is superior."

Ted squirted a lighter flame into his pipe, bringing out a shower of sparks. "What do you reckon?"

Arthur kept his eyes on the pieces. The player dithered between two pieces, glancing once at Arthur, who kept his face expressionless until the player moved, when he shook his head sadly.

"Stands to reason," he said.

"What reason?"

"There's been no murder for three months. They said they were close after last one. Well, they must have been wrong, mustn't they? Couldn't catch a cold, this lot."

Arthur was so close to her that when the wind blew, it flapped the edge of his raincoat against her knees. She was getting cold, in spite of the sun which was so bright she had to half close her eyes. Shadows slid over the pavement as the players moved the chess pieces. Ted bit on his pipe, evidently searching for a fresh argument with which to beat Arthur.

"They caught the Ripper," he said.

Arthur laughed. "Fluke. Two coppers on the beat find him on the job with this woman in Chapeltown. He says, can I go for a pee, officer? Certainly, said the officer. I'm surprised he didn't offer to do up his fly-buttons. Sutcliffe chucks his knife over wall, while he's having his pee. They don't find it till later, and they nearly let him go."

"They didn't though."

"Took 'em how long? Eight years?"

Ted knocked out his pipe and moved his last argument into position. "They have a computer now."

The old man drew himself up as straight as his stick, his voice full of scorn. "Computer! That's just a bloody great adding machine! They've interviewed thousands! They've probably interviewed him. D'you know how many times they interviewed Sutcliffe? Three bloody times. They joked about it to his wife – if you want to get rid of him, Mrs Sutcliffe, now's your chance." He poked his stick at one of the players. "You can't castle, Henry, he's covering that square."

At first she wouldn't let the thought get in. She hurried down the Headrow as if, by escaping from Arthur's insufferably knowledgeable voice, she could escape from the thought. She tried to wander, but found herself in Briggate, with a bus for Bramley coming, and ran for it. She didn't have the right change for the driver and dropped coins when scooping them out of the metal bowl. She stopped pretending to be calm. She could no longer keep the thoughts out. The bus journey seemed to take hours.

In Bramley she ran up the sloping terraced street where Stephen had been born, where the windows of the small black stone houses looked directly out onto the cracked pavement, most containing a plant, or a pottery ornament. In Mrs Marsh's it was a horse pulling a plough. She rang the bell, then knocked on the door. Jackie answered.

Matthew did not look up as she came, straight from the street, into the room. Stephen barely glanced at her. He was absorbed in making a spaceship from Lego, a complicated model with a launching platform which drove her mad searching for the right pieces, but Stephen was putting it together with unerring precision; his fingers seemed to see, fitting in the rocket launcher while he studied the diagram. Matthew, at his father's elbow, watched with a rapt, silent face.

Mrs Marsh eyed the green Marks and Spencer's bag. "I'm not looking," she said.

Annie went through the rest of the day mechanically. Sometimes they had to talk to her twice before she heard what they said. It wasn't going to start again, she told herself, building up inside her; she didn't know what she was going to say, but that Saturday evening she had got to say something.

13

He was planning to go out, she sensed that. He said nothing, but he was extra sharp in getting the kids off to bed, and didn't linger over his meal. The clinching thing was that he didn't take a beer from the fridge before he sat down. Was he going to ask her?

No. He clipped out his Spot the Ball entry and put it into the envelope on which he'd already written the address in his sprawling block capitals, underlining it with a thick squiggle. He folded the paper on the arm of his chair and did his usual little yawn and a stretch.

"Well . . ."

They had their language, although words played little part in it.

He was half-way out of his chair now. It was just like it used to be. Things had returned to normal. He was about to say: "Just going round corner . . ." when she spoke.

"I want to talk to you."

He stopped exactly where he was, one hand resting on the arm of his chair, knees slightly bent, as if he was something paused on the video – Matthew's favourite trick at the moment.

Now the words were out of her mouth, she had no idea what to follow them with. Why was it so frightening when he wasn't there, and so ridiculous when he stood opposite her in his V-necked sweater and jeans – an ordinary husband who had put his children to bed and was going out for a pint?

He was waiting, as only he could wait. The silence lengthened. She was holding a shirt, and searching for a button in her workbasket. She looked up to find his eyes on her, waiting. Stupid that she hadn't worked out what to say.

But what could she say? "Are you . . .?"

Her hands were beginning to tremble. She found a button, but couldn't thread the needle with his eyes on her. The end of the cotton grew frayed and she had to lick it again. Was he smiling? She couldn't look, but she felt he was.

She rammed the needle into the chair arm and said: "That woman's a prostitute."

"You what?"

"Jan. Jan Stephenson. Ken's friend in The Swan. The Mucky Duck."

"Get on."

He looked at her in such bewilderment that for a moment she thought the newspaper clipping was part of her fantasy, until she drew it from her workbasket. He read it slowly, with deep concentration, spreading it out on the arm of the chair, a finger following the words.

"Bloody hell," he said.

"You didn't know?"

"'Course I didn't know!" He gave her back the clipping and grinned. "Papers! They allus make more of it."

"How do you mean? Make more of it?"

"Some fellers might have given her money while her bloke's in prison."

She jabbed her elbow on the forgotten needle, and pulled it out of the chair arm. "Have you?"

He got up, the clipping fluttering to the floor. She expected a joke, a grin, and was startled to see his face set and his hands thrust into his jeans, as he did when he was worried.

"You have."

"I haven't!"

"You're lying!"

"Do you think I'd go with a rotten slag like that?"

His eyes blazed for a moment in his taut face. She got up and followed him into the kitchen. When he moved away round the table, she stood in front of him. They bumped into chairs, oblivious of them. Now, from no words, there was suddenly a confused mass of them.

172

"Ken goes wi' her."

"Do you?"

"I've told you!"

"I don't know what you do half the time."

"You do."

"I don't, Stephen. I've been worried, worried sick."

"What about?"

"You."

"What about?"

"Don't keep saying what about! Ever since we went to that pub . . ."

"That was weeks . . . two months ago . . . "

She was getting hopelessly confused. "Since I saw her name in paper . . . They were laughing at me!"

"Who?"

"The people in the pub! Bahnu, Bernie, that Pakistani. Dry cleaner."

He grinned. She went for him, all that she'd been through coming out in her flailing fists. He caught them, the grin stuck on his face, which enraged her even more.

"You'll wak' the kids."

She didn't care. In a moment she would tell him everything, about the hospital, the visit to the police station . . . the fear that had come back that day . . . it would all come out. Now she kept on about the money she had seen in the pub. Where had that come from?

"Our Ken won on the dogs."

"You're lying."

The grin began to look permanent. "How d'you think he could afford all those snowballs?"

"What did he put in them?"

"Vodka!"

The grin suddenly went and he released her. The bones of her wrists stuck out from the reddened flesh. His tone of voice was still jocular.

"Ken were so pleased to see you he wanted you to enjoy yourself."

"I'm not bloody daft, Stephen Marsh! He didn't want me to see what was going on."

"Nothing's going on!"

"It is it is it is and you're going to tell me!"

"I wouldn't have taken you there if there was summat, would I?"

"Yes you would." She had a sudden shaft of perception. "You want me to know, sometimes you want me to know, don't you?"

He turned towards the back door. "I'm going out."

She got there before him, locked the door and put the key in her apron pocket. Then she ran to the front door and did the same thing.

His knees seemed to sag beneath him. He drew out a chair and sat at the kitchen table, planting his elbows on it. The keys clinked in her pocket as she leant over to him, her voice calmer, quieter. She could see his face only through the bars of his linked fingers. He wasn't a killer! This man crouched over the table? He'd got caught up in something, been duped by the others.

"You're in trouble, aren't you . . . ? Tell me . . . "

He would never admit to things being wrong. It had driven her up the wall at first. When she'd first got him the job at Hallet's he'd said he didn't want it, it didn't suit him, when the problem was he couldn't fill out the application form. He was on the point of losing the job before she realised that. She could still see the sweat on his face as he painfully followed the letters she had drawn on a separate sheet of paper.

Then she said: "It's the school's fault . . . " Now she said: "Ken's got you into something."

"Happen . . . "

The words came out as slowly as his writing. Bahnu was a bookmaker. Because of his background – principally because he was a Pakistani – he couldn't get a licence. So he worked illegally through a network of runners, which included him and Ken.

"Why do people bet with him, when they can bet legally?"

"Because he gives them better odds."

"D'you get paid for this?"

"Aye."

"How much?"

"Fifty. Now and then."

"What do you spend it on?"

He hesitated. He knew she knew every item on his pay packet, and kept a note of everything they bought. "Booze. Car parts. Tools."

"Women?"

"No!"

There was more, a great deal more, and she suddenly saw what it was. It was obvious, obvious what he had been up to, obvious where this money went. Her hand was shaking, and she steadied it by gripping the table. He had so little go in him, look at him now, locked in, crouched over the table, so little go it had never occurred to her; it had been her own monstrous fears and fantasies that had sidetracked her, and prevented her from seeing what was going on under her own nose.

"I know, Stephen," she said, "I know."

He remained crouched, so still it was as if he had stopped breathing. The refrigerator whirred and shook a little. She clicked her wedding ring against the engagement ring and thought of the police station, where she had been crouched over a table like this.

"You're going with other women, aren't you?"

Although he remained in the same position, he seemed to collapse. His hands lowered slightly, and she saw that his eyes were closed.

"That's why you've taken your records away, isn't it? You've given them to another woman because ... I watched you writing the Spot the Ball envelope. You're no better, are you? I know you're no better!"

A sigh came out of him, seeming to bring his silent shape to life, like a wind passing through a tree.

"Who's doing it?"

"I told you!"

"You did not! You never tell me anything! Who is she?"

"Mrs Harris!"

"That cow. Have you slept with her?"

175

She wrenched his hands from his face.

"No . . . Annie . . . " The grin was coming back. "She's married."

"That stops no one. Why have you got her doing it?"

He got up abruptly. "Because I'm fed up of you doing it! I'm fed up! I'm fed up! I'm . . ." He walked about the kitchen as if he was in a cage, blundering into things. "I never get no further. She helps me."

"So do I."

"She doesn't make me feel . . . "

"What?"

"Thick."

"I don't make you feel thick. You're not thick." Now she was blundering about. If this was what John meant by talking to each other, she wanted no more of it, it was worse than dealing with her own fears, it was as if not she but the whole world was going mad, falling apart. They were both walking about the kitchen, clenching their hands, turning to each other, turning away. "I've been through hell," she got out. "I've made you what you are, Stephen."

"Aye, aye, I know, I know . . . "

"Tell me everything . . . "

"Everything?"

"Don't repeat everything I say! It's so stupid! Is there more?"

"More?"

"There you go again! More! Now say more again! Go on! More more more more more more more more more more. You haven't said more!"

"I'm going to bed."

"Oh no you're not."

She stood in front of the kitchen door, barring his way. Then, abruptly, she made a hopeless gesture, opening the door, flinging it wider and moving out of his way. He stayed where he was. She moved about, shaking her head. The man next door was putting his car into the garage; the engine throbbed and died, and the doors creaked to. She went up close to him.

"We've had a good marriage, Stephen . . . Stephen, look at me, please look at me . . . we've had a good marriage . . . "

"Aye."

"We've done all this. We have two lovely children."

"They are. They are lovely children. They are."

There was such a harsh, terrible agony in his voice that her arms went round him.

"What is it? What is it?"

He was muttering something incoherently.

"I can't hear you."

"Annie . . . "

"Tell me, tell me."

His features were breaking up; there was something coming from his black eyes like a terrified animal emerging from its hole, needing, wanting, pleading; his whole body was trembling; he was going to say something but perhaps because she was so frightened of what that was going to be, she interrupted him with a banality.

"It is her, isn't it . . . Jan Stephenson?"

The terrified creature ran back. The black eyes closed and he lurched away from her.

"I told you! A slag like that! They're disgusting! They . . . "

At the same time as he shouted, they both heard Matthew calling out. She stayed, waiting, but Stephen had turned away from her.

Matthew was standing at the top of the stairs, and the act of comforting and settling him calmed her. He was quickly asleep. She tucked him in, checked Jackie and then stood on the landing listening. What was Stephen doing? The house was so quiet that she could hear the slight trickle of water into the tank in the loft.

While she had been putting Matthew to sleep, she thought she had heard the back door. Had he gone out? Locking the door had been more a gesture than anything else; he had his own mortice keys. She opened her mouth to call out but stopped, afraid of waking up Matthew again.

"Stephen?" she whispered, gripping the banisters as she

went down the stairs. Half-way she stopped. The kitchen light had been switched off, and from the light in the hall she could see he was not in there, nor in the back room.

"Stephen?"

What was she doing whispering, creeping down the stairs? Oh, this was ridiculous! She cleared her throat and walked normally. As she passed the front room door, which was partly open, she clapped a hand over her mouth to stop herself from crying out.

There was a man in the front room.

It was like that time in the middle of the night when he had been watching her when he thought she was asleep; and, like then, something silenced her, stopped her where she was.

He was standing near the bureau which she had desperately searched for the records that weren't there. The room was in darkness, except for light spilling into it from the hall. Stephen had his back to her, his hands bulging out of his jeans pockets. He seemed to be staring across to the mirror over the mantelpiece where she could see a reflection of his face so dim that it seemed to be another person's, the cheeks hollowed out in a strange way, the eyes black pools. She became aware of her own breath, hissing in her nostrils. He must have known she was there; now her reflection joined his in the mirror, but still he didn't move.

"Stephen?"

There was no movement. It was as if he was in a trance. She swallowed. Her mouth was dry and her tongue stuck to the roof when she tried to speak.

"Stephen?"

The fear came, as strong as a smell, the fear of him, urging her to run, but she forced it away: she would not believe it, she would not; this was her madness, not his, and if she faced him she would face it and break it for good.

"Stephen . . ."

As she touched him he whirled round and grabbed her, his hands going round her throat, and it was another man, or another creature, eyes enlarged, mouth open, who was

178

strangling her; and as the room spun round, the irrelevant thought that reverberated in her head was that they were wrong wrong wrong, those kindly liberal people, Norma and John. He was, he was a monster . . .

Her ears thundered as if she was drowning in the sea and black spots throbbed across her vision as if his eyes had left his face and multiplied and were dancing in front of her, filling the room.

I'm going to die.

Curious how matter-of-factly she was accepting it, with about the same level of disappointment she felt when she missed a bus.

Amongst all the thundering and the flashing there was a tiny pinprick of sound that ought to have been drowned in it.

Matthew's voice.

She struggled with a sudden violence. His grip slipped. In another moment it would tighten again. She was sprawled against something, it was the easy chair, half on that, and half on the floor. He had snatched up a cushion, while the other hand still pinned her down by her throat. Her hands scrabbled, found the seat of the chair, and she pushed up with all her strength. As his hand left her throat she kicked at his balls. He rolled over in a little scream of agony.

She ran, snatching up the phone in the hall, and dropped it immediately as he moved. The front door. The key. She scrabbled it out of her apron and was fitting it in the wrong way round as he came into the hall. With a little whimper of despair she shoved it in the lock. There was a noise behind her. She turned to protect herself, then saw he was still by the stairs. She opened the door and ran into the garden, opening her mouth to shout for help. Nothing came out of her bruised throat.

He was standing in the doorway, not moving, the hall light behind him.

"Are you all right, Mrs Marsh?"

It was Jack Scholes, Mrs Crowther's next-door neighbour,

on his way to his Saturday evening pool game at the Working Men's.

"Yes."

"Nice night."

"Yes."

He was walking away, whistling, no doubt already tasting that first pint of Tetley's.

Did she prefer them all to be dead, rather than that the neighbours should know? Really it was that she had seen that the monster had gone.

Stephen was wandering on the front lawn towards her. It was as if he had been hit on the head; he shook it and shook it in a dazed fashion, and then, incredibly, as slowly it seemed to her as ice melting, the old familiar sheepish grin appeared on his face.

The grin chilled and horrified her even more than his other face. She ran past him, into the house, and locked and bolted the door. Then she ran up to her children. Both were curled up: Matthew must have cried out in his sleep. She dropped to her knees, head bowed, as if she believed in God.

He might break in. She went to the phone, then to the front bedroom window. He was standing in the same position she had left him in. She got his leather jacket from the wardrobe and his car keys from the kitchen and opened the bedroom window. He looked up as she dropped them in front of him. As she slammed the window shut, she caught a glimpse in the window opposite of Mrs Tate's face, before the net curtains dropped back.

She watched him pick up the jacket, and disappear under the porch below her. He tried the door. She picked up the bedside phone, dialled 99 and was half-way through the third 9 when her finger stopped. Pictures flashed into her head: police cars outside, police in the front room, questioning her.

"He tried to strangle me. He's the killer. The Hawk."

Mrs Tate's net curtains wouldn't drop back then. She would be at her gate. So would the rest of the street. She put the phone down. What was he doing? She went to the head of the stairs, but couldn't see his shadow in the panes at the top of the door. She ran into the kitchen and snatched down from the wall a large Sabatier kitchen knife. Her breath rasped painfully in her swollen throat, and she could hardly swallow. He wasn't in the back garden, but when she returned to the front room she saw him in the blackness.

He was standing by his car, head bowed, his jacket slung over his shoulder. As she watched, he got in, and he must have sat in the car without moving for ten minutes before he started it and drove away. From the top window, she saw him turn left at the bottom of the road, which probably meant he was going in the direction of Leeds. Spread below her in the growing dark was the view she always loved but now found hideous: the network of lights split by the neon-lit snaking motorway. It was where he was going. To pick someone up? To kill someone?

She picked up the phone. And put it down again. It would be best to phone the Incident Room at Quay Street. She opened her phone book and then something happened that made her so dizzy and sick that she had to sit at the bottom of the stairs holding her head in her hands, the phone book falling to the carpet, spilling out several pieces of paper tucked in it.

It was one of those pieces that had produced the nausea: a list of people Jackie had invited to her birthday party. Stephen had been there. That had been quite true. And he hadn't gone out that evening, because there'd been the whole place to clear up and they'd eaten late. And Ken had been there. And they'd all stayed in. That was quite true.

The day the girl in Leeds had been killed had been Jackie's birthday.

She remembered herself saying to the policewoman: "He was in all evening. I'm positive."

There was only one thing she had forgotten. Jackie's birthday party had not been held on her birthday. She'd refused to miss her swimming on Saturday afternoon. The party had been held on the next day. Sunday. On Saturday . . . yes, he had been out, because she'd had all the work to do for the party and she'd grumbled because Jackie had had her other presents but not the bike they'd bought her because he hadn't checked it – Mrs Crowther had wheeled it over so it would be a surprise, that's right – and he'd had to check it on Sunday morning. After . . .

She was shuddering so violently she couldn't dial the police, let alone speak to them. After killing that girl, the next day he had checked Jackie's bike, lowered the saddle, taken her down the street for a ride, been disc jockey at the party for all those eight-year-old girls . . . it was beyond imagination.

And what about her part in all this? Hadn't she really known, all the time? What sort of tricks had her mind been playing on her? She had gone along to the police station to tell them he was a killer, and had ended up giving him an alibi! It was Jackie's birthday! He couldn't have done it! That's what she'd said! And she *must* have known! How could she have not known! It was obvious, so glaringly obvious! Vomit rushed up from her stomach and spurted through her fingers as she clapped them to her mouth.

She hung over the kitchen sink, sobbing in agony; every time she retched, it tore at her bruised throat. After washing away the gobbets of half-digested food, she let the tap run on, playing on her forehead, lips and throat. Now all the pieces were remorselessly coming into place. Wasn't that the week that they'd had the argument about the overalls? That week, or the week after?

She could hear his casual reply when she'd remarked on his new overalls.

"What? Oh. Yeah. Others were ruined at work."

Ruined at work? Or covered in blood?

She'd known. She'd known really, all the time.

She saw the police notices, the police announcements: someone is protecting him.

The top of her dress was soaked, but she scarcely noticed it. She heard the neighbours' voices in her head as she went to the phone: "I reckon she must have known all the time . . . Aye, it were only when he went for her . . . "

She didn't care about that. What stopped her as she

reached out for the phone was the pink pig. The children. Vividly, all the feelings she had had in the police station crowded back into her mind; it was as if that had been a rehearsal for this; what would she tell them? They would know. The police would be here. His picture would be on the front pages. She couldn't hide every newspaper from them. Every time the television was switched on he would be jumping into the room. They would see it with their friends'. Friends! She could hear some mothers.

"You don't play wi' them . . . "

Could she blame them? Isn't that what she would say?

And school. The other children would be merciless. She could hear their taunts in the playground, see Matthew's white bewildered face . . .

Even if they moved, would it make any difference?

"What does your dad do?"

"I can't phone, I can't," she said out loud.

She walked from the hall to the kitchen and back again. If he killed again, she would never forgive herself! But he wouldn't now he knew she knew . . . he would imagine she'd already phoned the police! He would be on the run, getting away from her as fast as possible!

Would he? Throwing his coat, his car keys out of the window, was that the gesture of someone phoning for the police, or helping him to escape? Or the action of a wife whose husband had just assaulted her during a row?

Might he not think that? For didn't he have a split mind, like Jekyll and Hyde? When he stood there at the front door, with that foolish grin on his face, how much did he remember about the assault? If he remembered nothing, then why had he picked up his jacket and gone off, just like that? He knew, of course he knew. He would go off. He would not dare do it again. He would go away. Get another job somewhere. Disappear.

Her mind grew more confused as the night wore on. She did not sleep, or dare to. At every sound she got up, and her hand then hovered over the phone, but she made no call. Confusion turned to exhaustion, and exhaustion to anger. If he did kill, it would be a prostitute, and why should she worry about them? They asked for it, every time they went out. He'd gone. That was the main thing. He'd gone. He was probably miles away by now, but, just in case, the first thing in the morning she would have the locks changed.

Stephen

When Stephen had stood in the front porch grinning at his wife, he did not know who he was, or what he was supposed to do. He knew he had attacked her, he could still feel her neck between his fingers, but how had it happened? He was Stephen, not the other person, and the other person was always left behind in the night, in the streets.

That was not quite true. Sometimes, rarely, never after a murder, but sometimes when he had been close to but frustrated in a kill, the other person came back with him, up to the room where she was sleeping, and he could feel him breathing at his shoulder, like the bird whose name he had been given, but the bird could do nothing without him, he was in control, and after a while he would feel it go, rising, soaring, vanishing into the darkness.

He had nearly told her about the bird, and the bird had been angry, is that what it was?

As he stood in the porch, he could have wept. He hated the bird, he hated it! For a long time things had been separate. The killings had been separate from his normal life. They took part in another country to which he travelled at night – the red-light districts of Yorkshire and Lancashire. Impossible to say how they had begun. He started going to the pubs and clubs because the other lads went. Women were both desirable, but strange and frightening; warm and soft but also hard with red nails and white glittering teeth between which laughter could come, sharp as breaking glass.

Stephen didn't know how to talk to them, how to handle them at all. He didn't know what they were thinking, what world they lived in; they would say one thing, and look another.

At nineteen, with his pale skin and black hair and eyes, and the coloured T-shirt he wore inside his black jacket he attracted plenty of them.

For a tortured minute.

"Hello handsome."

"Hello."

"I'm Dot."

Or Stevie or Janey or Marilyn or . . .

"Have you got a name, or did your mum forget?"

During which sparkling interchange another lad would have pushed his way in, with the instinct that Stephen was no rival, and say to the girl: "Hello beautiful."

"Hello ugly."

"Who are you calling ugly?"

"I don't know, 'cos I don't know your name."

At which the newcomer would grab her arm and twist it behind her back. She would swear at him viciously and try and clock him with her handbag. Ten minutes later he would have bought her a drink and have his arm round her. It was all totally confusing to Stephen. Teeth could be bared one minute and lips pursed the next. Some people pick up this kind of sexual sparring as easily as they breathe, and as unconsciously, so that they can never understand the complete isolation of those who do not.

When, on the fringe of the crowd as usual, he saw Annie, in her outlandish sweater, gripping her drink with one hand and her bicycle basket with the other, her lips a compressed, closed line, it was not attraction that drew him to her, or sympathy, but recognition. They could talk without speaking. So they came together, but remained isolated. He didn't think of her as a woman; he had scarcely

ever seen her naked; and during sex he had to move her legs apart to penetrate her; it was as if she was dead.

He became closest to her when she was mad after having the children. She let the food dry round her mouth like a child and he washed her face and held her hand hour after hour. Sometimes she hit him, or threw things; he didn't mind; he bore the bruises; cleaned the mess, looked after Jackie when Matthew was born, and when he helped her, fatter and slower, out of hospital into the car, he felt a secret sadness he did not understand.

She wouldn't let him sleep with her, for fear of another child.

One lunchtime he'd gone with a mate to the Gaiety in Roundhay Road, where they did a lunchtime strip – 60p it was then, OAPs half price. In the darkness, among the standing men – one leant on a stick – all holding straight pints, he saw her. She had a cheeky face and a turned-up nose, and was dressed as a schoolgirl, in gymslip and tie. The compère announced that she had been late for school and had to have her bottom spanked, no volunteers please.

The men watched in silence, one chewing a sandwich, some supping from their pints, while the gymslip came off, and she pushed her bottom, clad only in a G-string, towards their vacant faces. Although he was at the back, Stephen was sure she smiled towards him. She removed her tie and sawed it between her legs, writhing and turning her white face up to the lights with a moan of ecstasy. He began to get an erection. At the end he had rapidly to drop his applause to the perfunctory level of the others when people turned and stared.

He returned next day. She wasn't there. The next two times he saw her he had seated himself in the inner ring of tables, within the pool of light where she performed. Now she definitely acknowledged him, treated him like a regular. When she had stripped to her G-string, she leant over to him, murmuring into his ear and asking where he came from.

"D'you like fucking?"

"Yeah."

She grinned and danced away, her tiny breasts an inch from his face.

The next time the girl, whose name was Selina, was supposedly getting out of a bath. After placing a shaker of talc between her legs and panting over it, she held it aloft, kissed it, and said she didn't suppose anyone would want to powder her, looking at Stephen. She padded over to him in the silence. Not a pint moved. The lights were hot and there was a little glitter of sweat, like sequins, running along the top of her breasts. Sweat was trickling down his back, as she held out the shaker of talc. There were purple and white flowers running down it. As he shifted in his seat and put out his hand, she flung a cloud of talc into his face and darted away.

There was a great shout of laughter and a roar of applause as he coughed and dashed at his clothes. He was enraged and humiliated. The sickly sweet smell of the powder clung in his nostrils when he waited for her afterwards. He was told she'd gone. That night he threw a stone in the back window of the pub and ran to his car. He hunted her everywhere. What he was going to do to her when he found her, he was not sure, but he had to find her. He searched for her among the younger prostitutes and one night – it was about six months later – he saw her in Lumb Lane, Bradford.

He had had a bit to drink, rather more than usual, when he approached her. She was wearing a black leather jacket and a tight orange skirt. Her face was as cheeky and chalk-white as ever. She said her name was Terry, but he knew she was lying. However, he was nice to her, he had got a bit of the chat now, it was easier when you were paying for it, and she agreed to do business for ten.

She told him to go to Armitage Street, where there was a deserted cul-de-sac, and he asked: was it dry?

She said if he wanted it dry it was five extra, what did he fucking expect, a fucking mattress? She was sullen because she had been thrown out of her flat in Horton and was faced with sharing with an Irish girl who brought punters home. If she could turn four tricks in an hour and a quarter she might pay her rent and get her room back.

The cul-de-sac ended in an alley which was damp and dripping with water. There was another prostitute she knew with a punter at the dry end.

He went on about her being Selina until she told him to give her the money or drive her back. He gave her ten pounds and as she handed him a rubber, a drop of water fell down his neck. He wanted to do it in the back of the car but she said what did he think she was: a fucking acrobat? Really, it was because if they got too comfortable they took too long; she'd been ten minutes on this bugger already. She put a dab of jelly on her cunt and lifted her skirt.

When he tried to kiss her she said: "Just fuck me, darling. I want to feel you inside me."

"I can't do it just like that," he said.

She smiled, unzipped him and worked at his cock while she breathed a mixture of obscenities and compliments in his ear, and told him how she was longing to come with him.

It was fifteen minutes by the Mickey Mouse watch on her wrist; with any luck she'd have wanked most punters off by now, but he was still too limp to get the rubber on, let alone fuck her, as limp as a piece of wet cod. She told him so, laughing.

"You'd better run me back," she added.

"I haven't done it."

"You can't do it, love. You're not in the mood, are you? I'll bet you've just had someone, haven't you? Eyes bigger than your belly?"

She zipped him and patted him sympathetically. Funnily enough, as she did so, she felt it grow.

"I can do it now," he said.

"Sorry, love. I have to go."

"I want my money back."

Her smile went. "You've had your money's worth, love."

"I want my money back!"

She pulled her arm away from him. "Sod off."

He picked a stone up from the gutter. At first she thought he was going to hurl it at her, but he gripped it like a knuckleduster and punched at her face. Later in the evening she would have been too drunk to avoid the blow hitting her full in the face; as it was, she just managed to jerk her head so that the fist, and the edge of the stone clamped in it, caught her at the side of the mouth and cut open her cheek. Blood smeared her teeth and trickled down her chin. For a moment they stood there looking at one another, and then she ran for it.

She had three stitches in her cheek, and lost a tooth. For a week afterwards Stephen was afraid she would go to the police, but evidently she did not, for there were no consequences.

He thought the Selina business was over. In fact it was just beginning. A few months later, at the onset of winter, he began going to illegal dog fights run by Bahnu, the Pakistani, at the Mucky Duck. These were held in isolated spots: a barn near a Pennine village, a swimming-pool attached to a large house. Nobody would know the venue until the last minute, when the "faces" would be collected from several pubs. Ken was one "collector", Stephen another.

The dogs were Staffordshire bull terriers, or pit bulls, savage dogs bred for fighting, imported from America. A great deal of money changed hands – Stephen had once seen a bet of £25,000.

As soon as the dogs were released they ripped and tore at one another, going for the face and the jaw, egged on by the cheering crowd, one of whom took a video for later consumption. Stephen never cheered. He sat on the edge of the pit, as near as he could to the blood-spattered carpet which was laid on the wooden floor so the dogs would get more purchase. Sometimes Ken would have to shake him after the fight was over. Then he would become alive, eyes shining, arguing and shouting with the rest of them.

"I told you big bugger was too slow! When little one got his ear! Did you see that? Play that back!"

When a man who had been for the first time was sick round the back of the barn, and criticised the sport, it was Stephen who said: "It's in their nature. That's what they're bred for. They're not happy when they're not fighting."

There were strong murmurs of agreement. Stephen swelled visibly. He had never been the centre of a crowd before. He got to know more about the dogs than anyone else. He betted and usually won. After the fights and drinking at a nearby house or pub he would still find himself shivering with tension and would get in his car and head for the nearest red-light district. One night he thought he glimpsed Selina's white face again among the trees lining Spencer Place in Chapeltown. It was actually Debbie Bright, doing her last trick before going home to Back Molton Terrace, but he was not to know that until he read about it in the papers.

He got an erection but he was so high and excited he forgot the rubber and when she insisted he put it on he started to lose his erection and he hit her. There was blood over her white face and he wanted more blood so he hit her again and she was screaming and so he picked up an old pillow, they were near a dump by some condemned houses, and he put the pillow over her mouth and then as her legs kicked he got more and more excited until he ejaculated and lay exhausted on her. Someone passed along the end of the street. A dog barked. He lay there until there was silence. When he pulled the pillow from her face it was covered in blood. He knew she was dead. He felt nothing – only exhaustion and the need to get away. Selina was dead at last. He dragged the body into the middle of the dump and pulled the legs apart. Remembering the tin of talcum powder she had squirmed and wriggled over, he found a piece of wood among the junk and rammed it between her legs.

There was surprisingly little blood on him, some on his hands, some on his shirt. He washed his hands and face under the garden tap at the back of the house, as he was to do in a kind of ritual after each subsequent murder. The shirt he soaked in a bowl of Ariel while he had a cup of tea, thinking it was fortunate that Annie slept so soundly. He felt no regret, no remorse, only anxiety that she would find him there without a shirt on, with that incriminating bowl in front of him. Before going to bed he rinsed the shirt and put it under the pile of clothes in the washing machine. As the kitchen and house closed round him, it was already as if the murder had been done by another person.

He became calm, slow again. The shivering tension had

gone. Already the details of the murder were going from his mind. When he switched out the lights in the kitchen, he peered out of the dark windows for a moment, as if the murderer might be outside, waiting to be let in. No. He was quite safe. He was Stephen. Whatever, whoever it was had been left behind in the streets. Annie did not stir when he got into bed beside her.

When the press christened the killer the Hawk, in a curious way it fitted in with what he had come to feel about the other person. It was as silent, as unmoving as a bird a long way off, a remote fixture in the sky. He could talk about it to other people just as if it was nothing to do with him, while he held the secret inside him.

At home and with his mother he agreed it was terrible. In the pubs it was different. The main concern was that the police were not doing anything. There wasn't much sympathy expressed for the women.

"Aye well, they're asking for it."

"They don't have to go out."

"Wish he'd get the one that gave me my dose."

Stephen sat with his half-pint, which he'd barely sipped from, and joined in the laughter. Just as at the dog fights, he felt the centre of things.

When he picked up his jacket and car keys from the lawn, he was bewildered. Was she not going to let him back in then? He lived there. He belonged with her and the children. Had he really attacked her? He'd been angry . . . or the bird had been angry . . . but what had the bird been doing there? He could sense its shadow and he shouted at it to go away, to leave him alone as he wandered into the back garden. He leant against the wall near the garden tap, his jacket slung over his shoulder. He needed Annie, he couldn't do without her, he would tell her, he would tell her everything, she would understand, she would know what to do, she always did . . . The path was suddenly dark and he jumped, thinking it was the bird behind him, but it was the clouds going over the moon.

He didn't want to be outside, he mustn't be, he wanted light, he wanted her . . . He hammered at the back door.

He heard her coming, running, then a crash from the kitchen and a long silence. He walked slowly to the front of the house and stood by his car. He mustn't get in his car, he knew that. He struggled against himself. Clouds unpeeled from the moon, which lit them from inside as if they were thin paper.

He knew she was watching him from one of the windows, but he couldn't see her.

"Annie," he cried, "Annie . . . "

He flung the car keys away from him.

Without being conscious of it, his hand had closed round the door handle. The door was unlocked. He was sitting in the car. The mirror. The driving mirror. It always started with that. Is that what had happened in the front room, with the mirror there? His black eyes stared back at him, and he touched his lips, his nose, his cheeks with his fingertips, which abruptly had a tremendous sensitivity. It was someone else touching them, stroking them. He grew quieter and quieter, stiller and stiller until his fingertips stopped, and then the bird looked at him; he could feel its great talons, its great soaring strength, and he could see everything, everything seemed minute and insignificant under his gaze.

He could see inside the house. She was in the top room, staring down at him. She knew. She knew something. She had known something for a long time, but she had sheltered him, it had been all right. Now he would have to kill her.

As he took his eyes from the mirror he felt it was such a pity, such a shame, but really, hadn't he known it was bound to happen? He moved to start the car, but the key wasn't in the lock. Dimly he remembered flinging it away. Why on earth had he done that? He knew he would find it straightaway, and in fact his hand went straight to it, half-buried in the fertiliser she had spread round a rosebush.

She might go to the police – but she had no proof. Even if she had, he didn't think she would. He knew Annie. The

bird was infinitely cunning. One night he would release it
... and to the outside world it would be one of those
random, pointless killings, just like the rest.

Part IV

MURDER

murder n. 1. the unlawful premeditated killing of one human being by another. 2. *informal* something dangerous, difficult or unpleasant. 3. get away with murder. *informal* to escape censure; do as one pleases.

14

Two days after he had tried to kill her, she found Stephen and his mother on the front doorstep, when she returned with the children from school.

She was so stunned that at first she could not speak. The children were overjoyed to see Stephen: they were used to him being away, and she had simply told them, for the moment, that he was going to be away much longer than usual. Now he was here, with toys and sweets, and she could only watch helplessly while they swept him inside.

One of Mrs Marsh's gnarled old hands leant on her stick, the other gripped the edge of the porch, almost the same colour as the purply red bricks. "I'm sorry we had to wait in front of the neighbours," she said, pointedly. "But his key won't work."

"I've changed the lock," Annie said.

"Have you?" The old woman's breath came in short sharp bursts. "What was wrong with the old one?"

"I don't want you here," Annie said.

It was as if the old lady hadn't heard. She thumped her stick into the hall, levered herself inside, lowered herself into the chair next to the television and put her tablets on it. Stephen had gone into the garden with the children.

"What's happened between you two?" Mrs Marsh said.

Annie turned away to stare into the garden. "It's nothing to do with you."

"Don't upset me."

Annie heard the snap-snap of the child-proof pill container as Mrs Marsh fumbled with it. Eventually it got on her nerves and she unscrewed the cap. Mrs Marsh put a small white tablet under her tongue.

"There's two cases of his things upstairs," Annie said. "You can unpack them."

"He's not coming back."

"This is his house."

"It's my house!"

"What's wrong with you?"

"There's nothing wrong with me!"

She was standing over the old woman, the hatred that had been bottled up for years coming out in her glaring eyes and clenched fists.

"Calm down. You want to take one of my tablets, love. What do you mean – there's nothing wrong with you? There's something wrong with him?"

"Yes."

"What?"

She jumped, knocking over the container of tablets. He was standing at the door, leaning against the jamb. She could hear her heart hammering.

Mrs Marsh sighed. She shifted the tablet, now the tiniest white speck in her mouth. "I expect it's six of one and half-a-dozen of the other."

Annie picked up the container. In the garden, the children were shouting for their father. Stephen was looking at the carpet, his hands thrust into his jeans, which were bleached nearly white. His newly ironed check shirt was open at the neck.

Mrs Marsh's head was cocked like a bird's; her eyes darted from one to the other. "Is there any tea in this house?"

As Stephen moved, Annie said: "I'll do it."

"He can put a kettle on," said Mrs Marsh. She was settling back now, adjusting the cushion for her head. "I've allus said, the trouble with you Annie is you won't –"

"He has other women," Annie said.

Stephen stopped at the door. The children ran in from the kitchen, Matthew yelling that he'd got a big fat worm.

"Out," Annie said. "We are talking."

"Daddy, come and see! It's this big!"

"Will you get out!" she shouted at them.

Matthew seemed to shrink, pressing himself against the

wall as he slunk out of the room. Jackie stared back at her, white-faced, then followed him. Annie closed the door.

"Women?" said Mrs Marsh.

Stephen played with the keys that dangled from his belt and shook his head with a slight smile, as if to say he wished he had.

Annie sat down, her head in her hands, her eyes closed. "Prostitutes." Her heart was hammering again so much, and the blood was roaring in her ears.

The cushion dropped down as Mrs Marsh sat forward. "Mind your language."

"Prostitutes! He goes with prostitutes!"

"Don't talk daft."

"He does. He . . . "

The slight smile was fixed to Stephen's face.

"I know my son."

"You don't, you don't know your son at all."

"I ought to. I brought him into the world."

She was leaning forward now, almost pleading with the old woman to listen to her. "He attacked me."

"Attacked you?"

She got up, hands clenched as if Stephen would go for her again, although nothing looked more unlikely; he was staring at her, mouth slightly open, a look of astonishment on his face.

"He tried to kill me."

Now the old woman was smiling. Annie tore down the collar of the high-necked blouse she was wearing, exposing the ring of livid bruises on her neck, where his nails had bitten into the flesh. She thrust her face into the old woman's and gripped her by the shoulders.

"How do you think I got those?"

There was a long pause. The old woman's eyes went from the bruises to Annie's eyes, to her son's.

"Nay, I don't know," she said. "You tell me."

"D'you think I did them myself?"

"I've no idea."

The children were staring in the window and they ran

away to the bottom of the garden as she turned round. "Stephen," she whispered, "Stephen, you know what you did, don't you?"

For an instant a slight tremor ran across his expressionless face and she remembered the moment in the kitchen when he had seemed to want to tell her, when she had suddenly been so frightened at what he would say she had interrupted him. Now it was different: in the daylight, with someone else. Perhaps if he would give himself up . . . it was impossible for her to keep silent any longer, to shut herself off as if it would all go away. She had sought to protect the children, but what was this doing to them?

"Stephen," she said. "I'll help you. I'll stick by you . . . I will . . . I will." She went up to him. "Tell me. You want to tell me, don't you?"

The tremor became a little ripple, as the wind makes when it disturbs the surface of a lake. His eyes seemed less black, more translucent than usual.

"You killed them," she said. "You killed all those women."

The tremor broke into a smile, a smile of complete, of pure sympathy and understanding. His hands were warm and slightly damp as they took hers.

She pulled away from his grip as if his hands were white hot.

Mrs Marsh's face cleared and she manoeuvred the cushion into the small of her back: a shifting and settling that suggested it was all right: she understood everything now.

"You've had one of your turns," she said. "Haven't you, love?"

At last Annie got them out of the house, but at the cost of agreeing that Stephen could visit the children at weekends. It was as if it was an ordinary separation. Every day Annie argued with herself about phoning the police; every day the thought of the children stopped her. Every other day Mrs Marsh phoned.

Annie tried to keep calm, but when the old woman said the children were in danger, she lost her temper.

"Danger? What the hell are you talking about?"

"You might do something."

"What? What do you mean?"

"You're ill, Annie."

"I'm not ill!"

"You are, love. You don't know what you might do."

"I'm not the one who's ill!" She slammed the phone down.

She began to feel even more isolated when, one day in the supermarket, she heard a familiar voice on the other side of the shelves. It was Mrs Crowther, and Annie was about to wheel her trolley round when she realised she was the subject of the conversation.

"She's just chucked him out," Mrs Crowther was saying.

"Why?"

"Nay, don't ask me. I don't know how he puts up with it . . . the way she goes on, she'd try patience of a saint. You know, when he left, she chucked all sheets in house out . . . right good sheets, flannelette, well I would have took them, but she just stuffed them in the bin. Said they were done . . ."

It was true. She had stripped the double bed of the sheets, and then thrown away too the others he had slept between. She couldn't bear the sight or smell of them.

She had removed everything she could of his, including his tools. Among them, a box on a high shelf where she never normally went, was something curious: a pair of chisels, but pointed, sharpened like surgical instruments. One pricked her, drawing blood instantly from her finger. She hadn't thrown them out with the blankets. She'd taken them to Quarry Wood and flung them down Matthew's Well. Were they evidence? She didn't know. They were simply sharpened chisels. They were ugly, obscene; but that was to her; perhaps they had an innocent purpose. Perhaps she should have kept them, but at the time she thought it was over. Finished. And in any case, what did they prove?

She abandoned her trolley of groceries, crept out of the supermarket, and did her shopping elsewhere. It was a great pity, because she now needed help with the children more than ever before, but now she couldn't – wouldn't – ask for it from Mrs Crowther.

Nights were the worst, although she felt more secure when she had an alarm system installed – an action which confirmed her oddity among the neighbours, for there had not been a burglary in the street for years. It cost her three hundred pounds, and brought her savings down to fourteen hundred pounds, but it was worth it, for she had the first full night's sleep since he had left.

She continued to sleep well until one night when she switched on the nine o'clock news to hear the first reports coming in of another murder.

15

The murder had been committed at around seven o'clock that evening, near Didsbury, Manchester. The police said it bore all the signs of a murder by the Hawk; it was unusual only in that he had struck in broad daylight in a middle-class, not a red-light district; the victim was an ordinary housewife (who was not at the moment being named), not a prostitute. The body had been found by children in a copse not far from a path across a common. The police were anxious to question a man seen running to a white car parked on a road near the copse. He was about thirty-five, had black hair and wore a blue and white jogging suit.

Annie was totally bewildered. This couldn't be Stephen. Not now she knew. It couldn't be him. Not this diffident, good father who visited his children every Saturday.

Then she remembered. He was in Hull! He'd told her

on his last visit he would be in Hull all week! If this woman had been killed by the Hawk, she must have got it all wrong! Had he really tried to kill her, or was that in her imagination? Had his attack been that of a killer, or just the blind reaction of a man at the end of his tether, in trouble and in a corner after her questioning? If he'd really wanted to kill her, could she possibly have stopped him?

She remembered where he stayed in Hull from doing his records: a small hotel near the Marina. Feverishly she dialled directory enquiries. Yes, the woman at the Marina Park Hotel told her, Mr Marsh was staying there. He wasn't in; did she want to leave a message?

"No. No message."

She put the phone down, a sickness in the pit of her stomach. Why did she continue to hope? Hull might be on the other side of the Pennines to Manchester, but she had forgotten about the M62. She found it on a road map. It was what, two hours, two-and-a-half between the cities. Didsbury, she saw, was very near the motorway.

He was driving a white Cavalier.

Was he still on his way back?

She picked up the phone and put it down again, sure that the police wouldn't believe her. She could hear them saying it.

"Mrs Marsh? She's tried to get rid of her husband before."

She would make an anonymous call, but not from here, where it might be traced. She checked the children and went down the road to Jack Scholes. He'd just returned from the club and was unlacing his shoes. She told him her phone was out of order.

"Use mine," he said.

No, she said, she fancied getting out for a few minutes.

"I wouldn't. There's been another murder."

"Not here."

"Not far off."

"I can look after myself."

She got him to lock the doors when she left, and drove down the hill. The good weather was breaking up. It had been sultry all day, and in the town it was still warm and close. There were mutters of thunder while she parked near the swimming baths. The first box she tried had a coin stuck in it and she had to go to Church Street to find one that worked. The Leeds bus picked up the few passengers waiting, and that left the street deserted, apart from a man looking, with important interest, in the gas showroom window.

She knew the number off by heart.

"Incident Room."

"I know who killed the woman in Manchester."

"Who's speaking please?"

"His name is Stephen Marsh."

"Stephen Marsh. Who's speaking please?"

Chisels, she ought to say something about the chisels. What? That she had buried them in Quarry Wood? Then it was driven from her mind when she realised that the man looking in the gas showroom window had gone, and she couldn't see him anywhere in the street. Had he been watching her? She craned her neck one way, then the other. He was nowhere in sight. It was stifling in the box. She panicked.

"You've got to help me."

"Give me the box where you are."

If the card giving the location of the box had been in place she would have read it straight out, but the glass was broken and the card missing, and, as she hesitated, with the abruptness of a tap being turned on, the rain hissed down.

They wouldn't believe her if she told them her name. Nobody believed her. She forced herself to speak slowly and clearly.

"He's staying at the Marina Park Hotel, Hull. He's driving a white Cavalier."

She gave the man the registration number and told him he may be returning on the M62. As she put down the phone she thought: unless he's here. Waiting for me to come out of this box. She could see little through the windows, the rain already smearing the dust that had accumulated during the hot weather. A couple ran by, shrieking with laughter, the girl jamming a coat down over her head.

The back of Annie's dress was sticking to her. She looked up and down the street, pushed the heavy door and ran. The rain hammered on the black gleaming road and sprayed from tyres. She saw the man as soon as she passed the gas showroom – the door was set into a kind of passageway into which he had disappeared: an old man sheltering from the rain. She sobbed. She had been a fool to come out, a fool to park off the main street, near the baths where it was badly lit and deserted now the rain had driven everyone off the streets.

The road leading to the car park was potholed, and rain was already forming small, muddy pools. In jumping to avoid one of these, she wrenched her foot, but ran on without stopping, ignoring the stabbing pain. It seemed to take forever for her fumbling fingers to get her keys from her bag and open the car door. Then, once she was safe in the car, she cursed herself for leaving the children; Jack Scholes would let him in, why shouldn't he?

Jack Scholes was drinking tea, placidly watching the BBC weather forecast. Had she been away only half-an-hour?

"They've just been forecasting storms," he said. "I could do better looking out of window."

While she took off her wet clothes and put on her dressing gown, he insisted on making her a cup of tea. She felt his eyes on her while she drank it. Her mind was on the M62, on a police car flagging him down.

"Mr Marsh?"

Or they might pick him up at the hotel.

"Stephen Marsh?"

They would come here. She could see the children's white faces. Well, there was no help for it now. She had done all she could. She had drained the last of the tea and still felt thirsty.

"What's wrong?" Jack Scholes asked.

Before he retired he had been a man from the Pru for

thirty-five years. Years of listening to people's problems in between skilfully extracting or augmenting their weekly premiums had implanted turned-up crinkles at the corners of his eyes and mouth. She was so tired, finished, that she would have spoken to him, but the last thing she wanted was sympathy and kindness. All she wanted was someone to believe her.

As she stared at him, he added: "Your foot."

"Oh. Twisted it. In one of those potholes near the baths."

"What on earth did you go down there for?"

"I fancied a run."

He stared at the curtained windows, on which the rain was drumming. She got up to get more tea, but winced when she stood on her swollen ankle. He took her cup, and when he returned said: "Oh. Lady called Norma rang. About the school run."

"Oh. Yes." She swallowed half the second cup. She would have to visit Stephen. She'd said she'd stick by him. Well, she would, she would. But what about the children? How could they visit him? How could they not?

"Seems to work all right now."

"What?"

"The phone."

She stared at him, her mind paralysed for a long second. He was a kind man, but a bit of a gossip; this was another story which would go round the street.

"It goes on and off," she said.

"Like me," he grinned.

"And me," she said.

They laughed together.

The murder was on the front page of the morning paper, but there was nothing about any arrest, or even about anyone being questioned. There was a photograph of the copse, roped off where the body had been found. There was little more on television that day. Her ankle was swollen, and so Norma took the children to school and brought them back, giving Annie the evening paper she'd asked for.

On the front page was a picture of the dead woman, now identified as Joan Driverton, a schoolteacher from Lestringham. She was twenty-nine, married, and had a six-year-old son called Matthew.

Annie couldn't believe it. She stared and stared at the picture, which showed a woman with a rather long nose and bubbly hair, holding a BMX bike while her son clambered on it. The story included an interview with her husband who said: "Please, please, if anyone knows who this maniac is, please come forward, and stop other people suffering as we are suffering."

Annie sat at the kitchen table, holding the paper rigidly in front of her, looking from the picture to the husband's plea again and again, until her eyes swam. If only she'd acted sooner! If only she hadn't persuaded herself it would go away, told the right story at the police station . . . Selfishly, she'd thought only of her own children.

At least she'd told them now. They must have picked him up by now. Why wasn't there anything in the paper, why wasn't someone, in that terribly oblique phrase, helping them with their enquiries?

There was a sound behind her, and Norma put a hand on her shoulder.

"She had a boy called Matthew," Annie said.

Norma said how terrible, awful it was and then when Annie still did not move, or put down the paper, lit a cigarette and said: "You're not still thinking that, are you?"

All she had told Norma was that there had been a fight and he had walked out. That had been when she had thought, so naively, he would run for it, disappear.

Norma took the paper from her and folded it up. "You are, aren't you? Nay Annie, you proved to yourself it couldn't be him!"

And to Norma. And to John. And to the police. Would Norma believe her? Or would she think she was mad? Why hadn't she shown her the bruises? She was afraid to talk. Wait wait wait, she told herself, there would be something on the six o'clock news.

"Why don't you go away for a bit?" Norma said.

She described a cottage near Whitby which belonged to a lecturer friend of John. He rented it out for seventy pounds a week. It was so impracticable Annie scarcely listened; how could she go away – their money was dwindling, the kids were at school, and she wouldn't trust the car to run further than to Leeds and back.

There was nothing on the news that night, and the murder story had dwindled to a few lines on an inside page the next morning. There was nothing until the afternoon, when Mrs Marsh phoned. Her voice was harsh, like the vengeful rasp of a crow.

"He's had the police round, Annie. Was that you?"

Pain shot up her leg as she forgot her bad foot. Dizzily she leant against the wall, gripping the receiver tightly. "Have they arrested him?"

The old woman's voice rose so high she lost it for a moment. "Of course they haven't arrested him! He were in Hull. Hull! That was you, wasn't it? Wasn't it? I've had enough. We've both had enough! You ought to be in hospital."

"Is he there?" Annie whispered.

"No. He's back tomorrow. The police came here. Here! My house! When they couldn't find him first at hotel!"

Annie went back into the kitchen and looked at Joan Driverton's picture in the paper, as she did several times a day. He was too clever for them, and far too clever for her. He would get rid of the evidence, and always have an alibi: he could merge into the background of a pub so easily he could have a drink or two and say he'd been there all evening. And a crazy woman, phoning up from a call box, how seriously would they treat that?

He would be here tomorrow. And she was virtually crippled.

When Norma came in with the kids she said: "That cottage. Is it available?"

"When?"

"Tomorrow."

Norma's jaw dropped. "You can't walk!"

Annie walked across the kitchen, ignoring the pain stabbing in her ankle. "It's much better now," she said.

16

She did not expect it to be a holiday, or even to do them any good: they were running away. But from the moment she took the decision, and walked on her bad foot, she found new energy.

Norma was astonished to see the careful and cautious Annie acting as *she* usually did. She found herself in the unaccustomed role of telling her she must be sensible. It was great to do things on the spur of the moment, she knew the feeling, but leaving a week before the school holidays were due to start, with a dodgy car, a lame foot, and rain forecast . . . she wanted her head testing!

The children had no such doubts: they were ecstatic with excitement; could they pack the tent; could they pack the frying pan; could they cook breakfast outside; was it Scarborough; was it a smuggler's cottage; was there a lighthouse flashing signals to smugglers out at sea; could they go now; why not; they'd never sleep; were there bunk beds; was it hundreds of miles away; where was the *Observer Book of the Sea-Shore*, the buckets, the spades, the fishing nets, the torches, Matthew's knife that would open everything, Jackie's swimming goggles? And soon Norma was swept away in the tide of enthusiasm. While she helped with the packing, Annie just got to the building society before it closed, and drew out two hundred and fifty pounds.

It seemed an enormous sum but she didn't believe in credit cards and had no bank account, so there had to be enough to cope with emergencies.

There seemed something disapproving in the way the clerk asked her to sign the withdrawal form; her balance had rocketed down in the past month. She didn't care. She folded the wad of notes into her bag and hobbled out. Her foot was hurting so much she broke into a sweat and had to rest on a seat. Could she go to her doctor? Normally she wouldn't dream of doing so; Dr Gregory worked strictly by appointment.

Perhaps her demand to see him took them all by surprise; at any rate there was a broken appointment and she got in to see him almost straightaway.

He was brusque, like Dr Seymour – perhaps she chose brusque doctors – but unlike Seymour, seemed uninterested in people; in fact, uninterested in anything. He prodded at her ankle; she gasped; he made no comment, but wrote out a prescription. Only when she asked him if it was a sprain did he say "Yes" and when she followed that with "Nothing broken?" he said, after a pause, "I doubt it." Since the nurse was not there, he bandaged the ankle himself. As he did so, she realised that he was staring at her neck. She was wearing a dress with a low collar, and had thought the bruises had disappeared, but they must have been just visible under the strong neon light, for he said: "How did that happen?"

"I fell," she said.

His head bent over her foot as he cut and tied the bandage. His hair was short, and parted exactly in the centre, like that of a man in a pre-war film.

"Try and walk on it as little as possible for the next twenty-four hours."

He pushed her notes to one side dismissively. She had no idea why she spoke then; it was not premeditated; it was part of a process which she was vaguely aware had started, but could not describe or control, any more than she could her food digesting or her heart beating.

"He tried to strangle me," she said.

He removed his hand from the buzzer he had been about to press. His face was impassive.

"Who did?"

"My husband."

He examined her neck, her tongue, and looked down her throat.

"Is it still sore?"

"A little."

"When was this?"

"Three, four weeks ago."

"Did you tell the police?"

She shook her head. "We're separated."

"Ah." And, as if that solved the problem, he pressed the buzzer.

She woke at five and thought they would be away by seven, but it took so long to do things with her foot, and if it hadn't been for the milkman lugging the cases out to the car, they'd never have made it.

He asked where they were going and before she could intervene Jackie said: "Whitby."

"Well we're going touring," she put in quickly. "We don't know where we're going really."

The children looked up at her with puzzled eyes, and she pulled Matthew away as he started to say: "I thought we were going to Whitby –"

As she checked for the fourth time that all the taps were off, she had a dreadful moment of doubt. Her foot stabbed, and Whitby seemed on another planet. The cottage had been described as picturesque, which probably meant damp. All the old cautious side of her came flooding back, and if it hadn't been the thought of him arriving at nine she'd have given up the whole crazy idea.

Nine! In just over an hour. She locked the back door and limped down the path. She had not phoned him – Norma was due to phone him at half-past eight. Norma was going to tell him they were touring, so she couldn't give him an address.

That only gave her half-an-hour. Suppose he turned up early? The car didn't fire first time or second. She gave it full choke and thank God it burst into life, the children cheering wildly.

My home, she thought, my garden, I might never see it again.

Don't be daft, Annie Marsh, said a sterner voice inside her, get on with it, get on the road!

She eased her bad foot from the clutch and the car bumped off, passing Mrs Crowther, who was paying the milkman, and some of her earlier spirit returned as she saw Mrs Crowther's face gawping in amazement at the loaded car, and she joined the children in waving to her.

"This is a real adventure," said Matthew.

"Aye love," she said. "Tha's got the right word there."

She took the road to Horsforth, aiming to pick up the ring road there. It would take longer, but she didn't want to risk passing him on the direct route through Leeds. She couldn't work out whether the clutch was stiff, or whether it was her foot, but the car was running well, the children were singing "We're walking on the air!" and they were soon on the York Road.

It was cloudy and spitting with rain when they drew in at a Happy Eater on the bypass, but their spirits were still high. Annie had a coffee and gave in to their pleas for milk shakes and doughnuts. Why not? They were on holiday. Holiday! Up to that moment she had not thought of it as that, but it was wonderful, luxurious, to sit in the warmth, enjoying her coffee without looking over her shoulder, watching the children blow the remains of their milk shakes into a pink froth, in a competition to see who could produce the biggest bubble.

The problems began as they left the restaurant. Matthew picked up a brochure with a picture of the Flying Scotsman. He wanted to know immediately what it said and when he found out it was the Railway Museum in York passionately demanded to go there. Annie looked at the map. It was right on the other side of York. She was worried about her foot, the clutch, getting there . . . she tried to bargain with him; they would go on the way back but he became hysterical; his dad had promised him and it was the place he wanted to go to more than anywhere else in the world, not stupid Whitby!

Eventually she started the car. Was he coming with them, or did he want to stay at the Happy Eater? He began to cry and she tried to comfort him, but when he started to hit her she caught his hands and bundled him in the back of the car.

"When's my dad coming?" he sobbed.

"He's not coming," said Annie tightly.

Her stomach lurched as if she was going down in a lift. She had assumed they realised that.

Jackie leant forward. "Not coming?"

"No," said Annie, "sit back in your seat."

A mood descended on them as black as the clouds that were beginning to fill the sky. The children quarrelled bitterly. As Annie went up hills the engine revved as she accelerated, but the car was sluggish, labouring. The clutch seemed stiffer than ever, and made a whirring, grinding noise as she changed down. Was that smell the countryside or the car?

Just before Malton she pulled into a small garage with three pumps and a faded, cracked sign which read: A. Richards, REPAIRS, all makes. The youth who filled up her tank had spiky hair, tinted blue and red, a gold earring and acne. The children stared at him in silent wonder. Annie asked if Mr Richards could look at the car.

"You'll be lucky." The youth chewed gum with one corner of his mouth, and spoke out of the other. "He's dead." He gave her her change, picked gum off his tooth and said, as if there were very little prospect of it: "I'll see if Sam can help you."

Sam was about fifty and had torn overalls, black with dirt and grease, and a face like the weather. At first he said even less than Dr Gregory. He listened to the engine and tried the clutch, his face growing longer and longer.

"Well, you'll not get far on this, love, will you?"

"Won't I?"

"You'll be very fortunate if it's only your clutch release bearing that's gone."

He was despondent about doing anything. He hadn't the parts, he was up to his eyes and it was Saturday. She could try Anstruther's in Malton. He gave her complicated directions to get there, and walked off.

"Dad would have fixed it in a minute," said Jackie, as she started the car.

She pushed the clutch down viciously. There was a sickening whine like a circular saw, pain flooded up her leg, making her pull her foot away, and the car jerked forward and stalled. Matthew laughed. She turned round, only just biting back a yell at him, and got out of the car. She felt the first raindrops on her cheek.

"Please," she said, "you've got to help me."

He stopped and turned. She walked towards him deliberately so he would see her limp.

"It's a two-, three-hour job," he said. "Box has to come out."

"I'll pay you extra. Cash," she pleaded.

"I haven't got the parts."

She felt sick and giddy but, for the first time in her life, she played up her symptoms instead of trying to conceal them. She dipped her head and clutched at the petrol pump.

The youth pulled at his earring and unexpectedly said: "I could go for parts."

It had been raining steadily for three hours. She couldn't keep the children out of the wet. There was nowhere for them to go except the small cabin where Andy, the youth with the earring, kept the till, and the rusting tin toilet which Matthew insisted on visiting frequently. It was exhausting trying to keep him out of the garage where she had heard Sam mutter to Andy, as he wrenched at a bolt on the swinging gearbox, "Niver do no one a favour."

It seemed as if she would never see anything again but the same strip of road, shining black in the rain, the same dead tree with creepers growing up it, or hear anything but the creak of the Castrol sign and the occasional ting of the bell as a car drove over the wire to draw up for petrol.

All the drivers might be the same for the conversation they had.

214

"Wet."

"Aye."

"Set in."

"Aye."

The worst thing was that the interminable wait gave her time to reflect on how stupid she had been. The milkman would undoubtedly tell Mrs Crowther that they were on their way to Whitby, or at any rate touring in the Whitby area. How long would it be before Stephen bumped into Mrs Crowther? And here they were, stuck on the main road to the coast! Every time a white car came into sight she tensed, and tried to keep the children in the cabin. They would treat it as a game, running from her as she hobbled towards them, until her nerves were at breaking point.

Sam was as reluctant to finish the job as he had been to start it; although it was his own obsessionalism that was now driving him on, he grumbled about "customers" and "Saturday afternoon" while he checked everything, replacing the fan belt and changing the oil. The bill came to seventy pounds, plus VAT.

He saw her face and said: "If it's cash I'll forget VAT."

Numbly she watched the folded notes disappear into his dirty brown overalls. When the rent had been taken, she would have about fifty pounds left. And the one thing she had forgotten, she who normally made lists and remembered everything, was the most important thing of all, the thing she'd never been parted from in her adult life: her building society book.

She offered two pounds to Andy. Again, unexpectedly, he refused it and winked at her. "I enjoyed watching the old sod work."

"Are we going home?" Matthew said, when they were in the car, which was cold and smelt of wet clothes.

"No. We're going on holiday," she said brightly.

"I want to go home."

So do I, thought Annie, so do I. His nose was running and, after a search, she found tissues. The car was an absolute tip, just like Norma's.

She became still, her eyes fixed on the driving mirror, in which she could see a white car approaching, slowing down, turning in towards them. She shut her eyes and swallowed. It was a Sierra, not a Cavalier, with a woman at the wheel, drawing in to the pumps. She looked at the map. It would be sensible not to go to the coast, but to turn inland at Malton, and make for Helmsley or Kirbymoorside, where there were bound to be bed-and-breakfasts. But it was quarter-to-five. She couldn't face trying to find a place with two tired children. And they'd paid, booked . . . and Whitby was a big place, wasn't it?

The rain was relentless as they went through Malton, where the market stalls were being cleared by hurrying men, hooded in soaked anoraks; they crossed the River Derwent, and passed between mile after mile of flat fields and dripping hedges.

"Look," she said, pointing ahead. "It's brightening up over there."

"It's not," Jackie said, "it looks horrible."

She was right. Beyond Pickering the moors began. If anything, the rain increased, and it was difficult to see where the clouds ended and the moors started. Sheep scrambled away from the road, their coats lank with rain. Annie was not a traveller. Their holidays were spent generally at Pontins in Morecambe or Scarborough; they had been to London once. Although she liked the West Riding moors round Bradford, that was home; this was a bleak and alien place. There was little traffic, only the sheep and, occasionally, through the drifting rain, a wheeling bird.

A chill settled into her. Adventure! This was a mad thing to do! And what was the point of it all, they would have to go back. What for God's sake was she doing here? Half-a-dozen times she slowed, with the thought of turning back, only the thought of meeting him on this desolate road making her press her foot down again. Jackie was slumped down with her knees in the driver's seat; occasionally she would give it a vicious nudge. By a minor miracle Matthew had fallen asleep, wedged between a suitcase and his bucket and spade.

He awoke, his cheek marked red by the side of the suitcase, fratchy and calling for a drink she couldn't get at, as they began the long winding descent from the tops into the dale at Sleights. At half-past-six they caught a tantalising glimpse of the sea, which gave her fresh heart, but then Norma's incomprehensible map led them up a wrong turning and it was nearly seven before they found Denholme Cottage, Eastcote. Her heart sank.

Just off the road, down a rutted, muddy track were a number of small cottages surrounded by trees. As she got out of the car she smelt woodsmoke, but it was evidently not from the cottage whose broken sign on the gate said it was: DENHOLME COTT. The children joined her, Matthew still sleepy, and stared at the neglected building in front of them. The red, pantiled roof was green with moss. The windows were hung with brown, faded nets except one, which was whitewashed.

"Is this Whitby?" Matthew said.

His voice was so full of shattered illusions that, incredibly, she found herself laughing. She hugged him. "Wait until we get a fire going."

"A fire!" He ran down the overgrown path. "I'll find the flowerpot."

According to Norma's instructions, the key would be under a flowerpot near the front door. There was no flowerpot near the front door, or on the path; there were flowerpots in a rickety shed, but no keys under them. It had stopped raining, but every time a breeze rocked trees it splashed drops over them. Her foot was now so painful she could scarcely bear to stand on it. She searched through her pockets. There was an emergency phone number on Norma's instructions, but where on earth had she put that vital piece of paper? The children looked at her, but she who always knew what to do had come to a complete halt. All she wanted to do was to sit on the step, take the shoe off her swollen foot and close her eyes.

Matthew suddenly ran to her, clutching at her jeans.

Her heart quickened as she heard what he had heard: a footstep ringing on stone. A blue blur seen between the green leaves became a sweater worn by a woman of about fifty, whose grey hair was tied in a scarf.

"Mrs Marsh? I were expecting you after lunch."

"We got held up. I can't find the key."

"Tha'll have a job finding it there. You're in number three."

"Three? This is Denholme Cottage?"

"Cottages. Nobody lives there except mice. Didn't she explain?"

Number three also looked gloomy and a little desolate from the outside; flakes of whitewash were peeling from it and a tree overhung it; but the chimney was smoking, and a purple clematis grew up some lattice near the door. And inside was a huge log fire burning in a stone fireplace, warming a poky but comfortable room. In the small kitchen, on a scrubbed wooden table, was a list of instructions, a large loaf of bread, some ham, milk and a carton of eggs.

The woman, Mrs Plater, who said she cleaned the place for John's friend, added, apologetically: "I niver know what people'll bring. You don't have to buy it, but there's bill if you want it."

At the end of a day like this Annie was prepared for anything, except warmth and kindness. Tears pricked her eyes alarmingly, and she turned away so Mrs Plater wouldn't see them.

"You sit down," Mrs Plater said.

Annie looked longingly at the logs in the hearth, wrapped in flame, and hesitated while Mrs Plater put the kettle on, but when she proposed to unload the car Annie protested and limped over to the door.

"I can't afford to pay you."

"You'll pay me if you just sit down and gerrout of way. The kids'll help me."

"I can lift the cases," said Matthew.

Mrs Plater unloaded the car and fussed round Matthew and Jackie in the way only someone whose own children

218

have just left home can do. She showed them their room and Matthew yelled down that it was a terrific bunk bed while Annie drank tea by the fire, and gazed out of the small window at the banked trees which were beginning to disappear in the gathering darkness.

She dozed and when she awoke, stiff and muzzy, the room was dark except for the fire and a small standard lamp. Laid out on a coffee table was the ham, a salad of egg, tomatoes and lettuce and a pile of bread and butter.

Annie struggled up guiltily. "Oh my God! You shouldn't have done all this."

"I did nowt," said Mrs Plater. "I supervised. I'm good at that."

"I cut the bread," said Jackie proudly.

Normally Annie would moan on at her hacking door-steps, and these were doorsteps, topped with blobs of butter, but she hugged her daughter, and then Matthew when, with a jealous push, he broke in with: "I cracked the eggs *and* sliced them!"

Mrs Plater left them to their meal. Annie was strict about mealtimes, even on holidays, so this was unprecedented, an amazing treat, tea by the fireside, eaten largely with the fingers in the mysterious semi-darkness, at the unknown hour of quarter-to-nine, in the middle of a strange forest near the sea.

Annie was too tired, too sleepy, too full to brush the crumbs from them, or wipe away the butter that glistened round Matthew's mouth when the firelight caught his face. No one wanted to move, although it was approaching half-past-nine, and the children's heads were sagging on their chests. At last Jackie, whose job it was to clear the dishes, began to stack them.

"Leave them," Annie said.

That had never happened before, and neither had the moment when Matthew was tottering round the bath-room, unable to find his toothbrush.

"Leave it," said Annie. "Have a good rinse."

They were asleep in seconds. At the back of her mind she had been dreading that, dreading the sudden silence and the blackness like a wall outside, without the comfort of street lamps and houses opposite. But as she wandered round, picking up one of the well-thumbed mystery stories other visitors had left, staring at a map of the North York Moors pinned to the wall, far from being scared, she had a great sense of peace. He would not find them here. They had come over the moors, as travellers did, and found another world.

The next day wasn't easy. The rain was in place when they got up, a permanent grey curtain. Her foot was so swollen she could scarcely get her shoes on. Just when she was starting to scream at them, Mrs Plater arrived. Would the children like to see her cottage, just up the road? It was impossible for Annie to keep them cooped up; and equally impossible for her to go out. So she had the most delicious rest, and fell asleep over a mystery book in bed where the children found her, shocked beyond measure to see their mother, who was never ill, in bed during the day. They were soaked, but both speaking at once from excitement; they had been hunting through the forest, and Mrs Plater had shown them the mystery trail, which led up through the forest to the ridge; and from there they could see the sea.

"And Mum," gabbled Matthew, "it's *enormous*! I've never seen a bigger sea!"

It was the turning point of the holiday – for it had become that. On Monday her foot, although still painful, was a good deal better, and the rain cleared by lunchtime. In the patchy, sunny days that followed they went to the beach, collecting shells, rocks and seaweed, and Matthew, with a boy he palled up with, built the Great Dam of Whitby, and was mortified when it was not there the next morning. They drove up to Staithes to see the fishing boats come in and above all, for Annie, they went up onto the moors, where the heather was beginning to purple, stopping to walk, or stare at one of the stone crosses which marked the old paths across the moor.

Had she been told before going away she would forget

about him and the murders she would have laughed at the suggestion. But she did, almost completely — at any rate for the first week. She had taken so much her mind could take no more and she drank in the constant wind on the moor and the sharp cry of the curlew as if it was a transfusion, giving her new life. As the time they'd got at the cottage — and her money — began to run out, a curious thing happened.

The old Annie and the nightmare slowly returned, but she was somehow detached from it, as if she was thinking about the problems of another person. This person was still helping him, wasn't she? Helping him to stay free, to kill, to kill people like that teacher, the other Matthew's mother. Now she'd run away, just as before she'd refused to believe it, refused to say anything to protect the children, hoping against hope it would all stop, go away.

Well, it wouldn't.

And she was the only person who could do something.

But what?

Each afternoon, after tea, a habit had formed. She would leave the children with Mrs Plater and go up Matthew's mystery trail. She still limped a little — she wondered if Dr Gregory had got it right, and it was only a sprain — but she wouldn't miss walking between the fir trees, skirting a clearing where logs were piled, although they never saw anybody cutting them, and reaching, in a last scrambled ascent, the ridge, where the sea suddenly appeared, crashing silently below and she smelt — or imagined she could — the salt among the pines.

Each afternoon she felt nearer an answer, although nothing came into her head. When it did come, it was obvious.

Why should she go back? She would not be running away from the situation: on the contrary, she would be able to face things without the constant fear of his visits. Wasn't she thinking much more clearly after ten days away? She could see how stupid she had been. Of course the police would disregard an anonymous call, or at least not treat it seriously. They got them all the time. People getting their own back, nutters, practical jokers; she could see that now. But if she went to them in her present state of mind, calm, detached . . . she could tell them how he had tried to kill her.

Then there were the chisels. The sharpened chisels. Why would anyone want to sharpen chisels . . . ? They could recover them from Matthew's Well.

Yes. She was getting there. When she had gone to the Incident Room and said he had been with her when the Leeds girl had been killed — wasn't that a perfectly understandable mistake? She had confused a birthday with a birthday party.

It was the school holidays. If they couldn't extend their stay here, they could find somewhere else. All they needed was money. She could copy her house keys and send them to Norma, who could post her building society book to the cottage. Yes, it was all falling into place.

The next day she sent the keys off to Norma and then, feeling a great lift in her spirits, as usual she left the children with Mrs Plater and went for her afternoon walk. The weather, in Mrs Plater's words, didn't know what to do with itself. The sun shone for ten minutes, brilliantly warm before it was extinguished by swelling clouds which might spatter a sudden, heavy shower, before being blown away by a nippy east wind. From the cliff she could see the gaunt ruin of the abbey above the old town. She sat on a rock, turning her face to the sun, reluctant to go back. At her feet she found a rock with black and cream swirls in it. Was it jet? She slipped it in her pocket. She'd ask Matthew, who had become the great expert on rocks during the holiday.

"Jet?" he'd say, contemptuously. "That's not jet!"

She enjoyed the thought of his scorn, and forgot to look, as she always did, from the one point on the cliff where she could just see the cottage through the trees. She returned a few steps. She liked to see the plume of smoke rising from the chimney and think of the evening meal: tonight it was already cooking: a rabbit casserole.

The wind was blowing the trees so much that she almost

missed it, and it only registered in her mind when she had started to move again down the path. Beyond the blue of her car was a patch of white. She had to wait agonising seconds while the wind blew the trees in a green whirl in front of her eyes. When the movement stopped she could see, beyond doubt, that there was a white car there next to hers.

The path was muddy, the grass wet, and it was a miracle she didn't slip as she ran down. Now she was amongst the trees. A branch stung her face. She was near the clearing, on the last part of the steep descent, when a hidden root caught her foot. The top part of her body was falling forward; she fought to keep her balance but her feet skidded on the wet ground and she crashed down, knocking all the breath from her lungs. She was unable to move for a moment. Then a picture of him putting the children into his car rose up in her mind, and she scrambled up onto her knees. She was about to get onto her feet when she saw a movement on the other side of the clearing.

She froze. She was imagining it. No. There was someone behind a pine tree, in the long grass. She dropped behind a pile of cut wood. Her foot was throbbing but she scarcely felt it. She was what, a good five minutes away from the cottage? Behind her was the older part of the forest, before they had replanted it with pines. There was a path which went back to the cottage, if she could get to it. She edged away from the pile of wood. Where was he? There was nothing, no movement on the other side of the clearing. A blackbird chattered suddenly. She jumped and looked round wildly. When the blackbird stopped the silence seemed to deepen. Her hand knocked against something: it was the stone in her pocket. She pulled it out and held it in her clenched fist. She slipped to a tree, looked round, slipped to another. She was on the path. The sun went in like a light going out. Behind her she heard a crash in the undergrowth and a yell, and before she could turn he was on her. "Got you, Mum," Matthew cried, "I hunted you! I hunted you!"

223

The words were all tumbling out at once as he danced with glee around her.

"Hey Mum! You didn't tell us Dad was coming! He's here! In't it great! He's found our secret place!"

17

The great shock was that she found herself faced, not with a violent murderer, but a distraught father, almost sick with worry about his missing children.

When he raised his hands to her, she backed away, but he was raising them pleadingly, or so it seemed. There was not a glimpse of the detached, mocking Stephen. He paced about, saying: "I didn't know what to do, I didn't know whether to go t'police . . . "

"Police?" She was astonished, unable to reply.

"I thought you might kill them," he said.

Her jaw dropped, by slow degrees, until suddenly she began to laugh, which brought the children, who were with Mrs Plater, running over.

When they had gone back to their game he said: "You would have done. Those times. If you hadn't been in hospital."

She would have yelled, gone for him if it hadn't been for the children.

"You don't know what you were like!" he went on. "You didn't know what you were doing, Annie!"

How much did he know what he was doing?

So they returned home, all the careful plans she had made on the cliff disappearing, as if she'd lost them on the mad descent down it. A week later the letter arrived.

It was a summons to appear at the County Court on the twenty-fifth of July at eleven o'clock, as the defendant in a case brought by Mr Stephen Marsh, who was seeking care and custody of Jacqueline Mary Marsh and Matthew Stephen Marsh, because of the inability of the aforesaid Annie Jane Marsh to provide such care and custody.

Inability to provide care and custody! This was his mother! He would never have thought of this! She rang the court and after an interminable delay got through to the clerk's office. Yes, it was on the list for a hearing. List, what list? What hearing? She listened in total bewilderment and disbelief as the clerk's voice droned on over her interruptions. He began to sound like a recorded message. Had she a solicitor? She would be well advised to get one. The Citizens' Advice Bureau could provide her with a list of solicitors in the Legal Aid Scheme.

Another list.

It was Monday, and she knew John worked at home in the morning, preparing a tutorial for the afternoon. Norma brought lemonade shandies out onto the overgrown back lawn; it was hot, and John's old pullover, discarded at last, was draped over the back of a canvas chair.

Annie expected him to dismiss the letter for the nonsense it was. But he did nothing of the kind. He told her she must treat it seriously and go to a solicitor.

"Why?"

"Stephen may take the children away from you."

"He can't do that."

"The court can."

"How?"

"If they decide that you're incapable, that you're an unsuitable parent."

"How can they do that?"

"On the evidence."

"What evidence?"

"You won't know what the case is until your solicitor finds out. Has Stephen said anything?"

"Stupid things. Lies."

"What lies?"

"I'll kill them, he says . . . It's ridiculous! Because we ran away he thinks . . . he thinks I've gone like I went in hospital . . But that's a pretence . . . I think it's a pretence . . . he's saying that because he wants to get rid of me, because he wants to . . ."

The words tumbled out incoherently. It was all such a muddle, such a mess she couldn't put it together properly. She walked about the lawn, kicked over her shandy, refused another glass, and when John said he was sorry, he had to go soon, she knew she would have to tell them. Well, wasn't that what she'd decided to do, on the cliff? Wearily she sat down. John poured the last of the beer, and kept cracking the can between his fingers. Norma had kicked off her shoes and dug her toes in the grass.

"He is the killer."

John stopped cracking the can. Norma stared at her, her mouth slightly open, a little spike of saliva between her tongue and lip.

"He tried to kill me. The night he left."

They were quite still, giving her no response at all, and so she unbuttoned her dress to show her neck. They peered at it.

"The marks were there . . . Can't you see? The doctor saw them . . . it was six weeks ago . . ."

Norma moved close to her. "Why didn't you tell us?"

Annie's brain stopped. She had gone over things so many times that she was totally confused; why hadn't she told them; told Jack Scholes, the police? Just beyond Norma's head a bee hovered, settled on a petal, and crept into the flower. She ought to think, answer the question, but all she could do was look at the bee in the shaking flower.

Was that a glance between Norma and John?

The bee wriggled backwards, its legs yellow with pollen, and hesitated before another flower.

She caught the tail end of what John was saying. "Annie, I know what you're going through. You're trying to build up a case —"

"Build a case?" she whispered.

"Against him. So he doesn't get custody of the children."

"Is that what I'm doing?" she said. The sun was so bright

she had to half-close her eyes, so that John and Norma seemed to shimmer in front of her, but still she didn't move into the shade.

"Well no, I'm putting it crudely, very baldly, the mind works in funny ways . . . "

"Does it?"

"You *believe* what you're saying because you're so upset about the children and – let's say unconsciously – you think this is the best way to make sure he doesn't succeed, but it's not."

"It's not," she repeated helplessly.

"No. You're making things worse, in fact. You've told me Stephen said he was frightened for the children, because of what happened when you were in hospital? . . . Yes. He may claim you're unsuitable to look after the children because you're mentally ill."

"That's rubbish!"

"Of course it's rubbish! But if you go on calling him a killer his lawyers will say: 'Look, you hear what this woman's accusing him of, is this the behaviour of a sane and sensible woman?'"

He was standing in front of her, in imitation of a lawyer in court, one arm flung out triumphantly. The glare was making her dizzy.

"But it's true," she persisted.

"Oh Annie," Norma got up with a frustrated gesture. "You haven't been listening! You mustn't get paranoid, that's what John's trying to say."

Paranoid? Boiling hot as it was she felt cold, very cold; in fact she was shivering.

"I've got to go, I'm very late, I'm sorry," John said. He went in and returned with a bundle of papers which he stuffed into his briefcase. "Look, it'll be all right."

"Will it?"

"Of course it'll be all right. The woman gets the children. Much more often than not. But you must get a good solicitor right away!"

Norma booked an appointment for Annie to see the

solicitor that afternoon, arranging to take the children swimming. After leaving Norma, Annie stopped by an ice-cream van to buy an orange drink. The wall was almost too hot to lean against.

The solicitor would say the same as John. If she saw him she would have to stop saying Stephen was the killer. How could she do that and live with herself? Yet if she didn't go to the solicitor, what would happen to the children? Several times she got in the car to go to Bradford, only to get out again. In the end, it was too late to go. She went to the park, where she had arranged to meet Norma and the children at the tea house at half-past-three.

Surely it would rain soon? There was a dull, coppery-coloured sky now, and not a breath of wind.

The park was full. People sprawled on the grass or walked slowly, their red faces glistening with sweat. Paper cups and plates littered the tables and the grass round the tea house. Norma and the children weren't there, but it was only twenty-five past. She bought tea while all around her small children were clamouring for ice creams, trying to see over the counter. She lifted up a little girl whose mother's hands were full.

"Ninety-nine vanilla."

"Space lolly banana."

Ice cream smeared mouths, dribbled down T-shirts, splashed on the pavement outside. At twenty-to-four she began to worry. It was unlike them to be late for their ice cream. At quarter-to she began to look for them, walking round the lake where, at intervals, people were feeding a mixture of gulls, ducks and pigeons. She went to the adventure playground, and then, in a rising panic, back to the lake.

She felt a trap was closing round her. It was absurd, but it was happening. If she denounced Stephen they would say she was mad, she was having another attack, and she would lose the children like that prostitute, Jan Stephenson, who had fought so wildly for her children. She knew this was going to happen, perhaps she had always known it, from the time she had cried in her secret place near the canal because she could not have children because her face was like the back of a bus.

But she had had children! She *had* children! They were her children, hers!

It was difficult to say what happened next, perhaps it was the stifling heat, but the colours of the world changed, and the people became remote, as if a glass shutter had suddenly come down between her and them, but the birds became sharper, definitely sharper as they flew and swooped, and the cries of the gulls more piercing and raucous, and perhaps one of them had spoken to her, it was difficult to say.

And in this changed world, inhabited by silent people and crying birds, she knew she was in communication with that man in front of the mirror, who had tried to kill her. He was telling her he was the Hawk, he flew immensely high and he could see all things and make quite sure of his prey before dropping, silently, swiftly, from the sky. She learnt that the bird was infinitely cunning and knew of the dangers of killing her; but why should he when she could be disposed of so easily because she was mad?

Yes, she was mad, because she could hear the bird, that was quite right. It might be disguised as any bird, she would never know; a thrush, a blackbird, that shrieking gull catching a crust in midair in its pointed, yellow beak. Another gull flew straight towards her and when she ducked away she collided into someone who swore at her silently.

If only she could believe in God, that would save her, but the only thing she believed in was the bird. God was dead. God was only the stone crosses on the moor. She thought the moor, the crosses, the silences had helped her but they had not. Nothing could help her now.

Except the bird.

"Where have you been?"

"We've been looking all over for you."

"All over park, Mum!"

Matthew flung himself at her, smearing her with chocolate

ice cream. He and Jackie and Norma had found her feeding the birds from a screwed-up bread wrapper, which she had found in the bin next to the bench she was sitting on.

"I looked for you," she said.

She didn't get up, but continued rubbing bread into crumbs in the palm of her hand.

"Sorry," Norma said, "Matthew wouldn't leave adventure playground."

"I would!"

"You wouldn't!" Jackie put in.

Matthew knocked a ball from Jackie's hand and they chased after it. Annie laid a thin line of crumbs along the arm of the bench. Sparrows perched, pecked, not at all afraid. Annie leant forward a little, staring at them intently. Norma watched her as one bird eyed them, cocked its head, pecked and flew away. Annie's eyes followed it.

"Are you OK?"

"Yes," Annie said.

"Did you find the solicitor all right?"

"Yes."

"What did he say?"

"The same as John."

"There you are! I told you you would feel a lot calmer, once you knew where you were."

Annie shook out the last of the crumbs, crumpled the waxed paper, and smiled at her.

That evening she phoned Stephen. She told him she had got the letter from the court and she wanted to talk about it as soon as possible. Well, he said, in that slow hesitant voice, he didn't rightly know about that. He didn't rightly know, she said? When he said things had gone too far she said far enough, and there was a comfortable familiarity about the conversation that followed, with her nagging on at him and his voice sliding away into silence. In the background she could hear his mother's voice, going on and on. No doubt her ear was close to the receiver, straining to pick up what she was saying.

"I don't want her here."

"All right," he said.

She heard Mrs Marsh clearly: "What are you saying? What's she said? What's going on?"

He must have covered the phone and said something, or made some gesture, for from that moment the old woman was silent. They fixed on the next day, at three o'clock, at her house.

"Our house," he said, and she could almost see the mocking smile on his face.

"Our house," she said.

She slept well that night, but woke up early. A thin mist blurred the valley, and the motorway lights were still on. It was six o'clock. She did a big wash, cramming the machine full, mostly with the children's clothes, and had it out on the carousel by just after seven, when the sun was beginning to appear. If the day was the pattern of recent ones it would be baking hot by midday, then cloud over. There would be mutterings of thunder, but it would not come to anything.

There were warnings about saving water, and prohibitions on hoses and sprinklers; nevertheless she had given the lawn a good hosing by the time the children were up.

For lunch, to their surprise, she took them to Macdonald's, where she continued to wear the paper hat that Matthew put on her head and again surprised them by buying an extra milk shake and splitting it between them.

When Jackie asked what "this" was for, she said, well they were on holiday, weren't they?

Then came the real treat. She told them that Norma was taking them to see *Back to the Future*, which was coming round again.

"Why aren't you coming?"

"Because I'm busy."

"You're allus busy, Mum, these days!"

She laughed at Matthew and gave him a hug, as Norma's car arrived. "Gerrin car, will you?"

She waved to them, but they were chattering to Susan and too excited to wave back. She stood there watching the car drive away, and it was only when someone grinned at her that she realised she still had the paper hat on her head.

At home she ironed the children's clothes, and left them in neat piles in their rooms. She made an orange layer cake, which was a favourite of Stephen's and then unusually – for she never fed the birds in summer, because they took her raspberries – she spread crumbs on the path. Watching from the kitchen, she saw only one blackbird come hopping, fanning its tail. Once she thought it looked towards her.

She put a skewer through the cake, and left it to cool. Again there was no wind, not even on the hill, and her dress stuck where it touched her. She had a bath, changed and was piping cream on the cake when the bell rang.

There was no silhouette in the panes of the front door and when she opened it she saw Stephen was helping his mother from the car. When he had set her on her feet and given her her stick, he moved behind her and raised his hands to Annie in a helpless gesture.

"I wasn't expecting you," Annie said.

The old woman did not reply until she had clambered up the steps. She paused for breath, one hand leant against the wall, the other knotted on her stick.

"I know you weren't," she said.

She was wearing her best summer dress, a shiny silk-like one, decorated with roses. Over her shoulders, like a small cloak, was her cardigan. She sat in her usual chair, facing the garden, and snapped off the cap of her tablets.

When she had put one on her tongue, she said: "What is it you want to say?"

The only sound in the room was the click of the old woman's tongue as she shifted the tablet to the right position in her mouth. Stephen was staring at her. He twisted his fingers together above the crease of his cream slacks. His T-shirt, which Annie had not seen before, was monogrammed "Hi-Tech". She went up to him.

"I'll say what I have to say to Steve."

232

Steve! It was the first time for a long while she'd called him that, and his glance showed he noticed it.

"You'll say it to me."

"Mother –"

"It's all right, Stephen."

"I just want to –"

"You know what the solicitor said," the old woman interrupted.

He wandered behind his mother's chair and gave Annie a helpless grin. Annie looked at the carpet. Although the French doors were open, the curtains were quite still. She felt sweat trickle slowly down her back.

"I don't want to go to a solicitor," she said.

"Oh, don't you? Well that's your affair."

Annie continued to look at Stephen. "Will you stop the court case?"

"It's gone too far for that," Mrs Marsh said. "It has! You are mentally ill! You stood in this room, I'll never forget it, and said he was the killer! In this room! And you phoned the police, it was you, don't say it wasn't you, you phoned the police after that dreadful, that horrible murder . . . "

Their faces were bent forward at the same angle, and she could see how alike their eyes were, black and shining. He was still. Not a muscle of his face moved; he might have stopped breathing.

Nor did Annie move. Her dress clung to her back. There was the faintest muttering of thunder, and in the following silence the birds in the apple tree began to whistle and call.

Mrs Marsh shifted, and dislodged her stick. As Stephen picked it up she said: "Get me some water, since nobody's going to give me any tea. Tea seems to be a thing of the past in this house."

When he returned, she drank thirstily, her fingers smearing the fog on the outside of the glass. She dabbed at her lips, which seemed to be shrinking, disappearing into her mouth, and looked at Annie.

"You should be in hospital."

"All right."

233

"All right what?"

"I'll go."

"Into hospital?"

"Yes."

The old woman's eyes blinked suspiciously at her. She handed the empty glass to Stephen.

"You're not just saying that?"

"I went before. I can go again."

"Then you'll get better."

"Yes. I expect so."

Mrs Marsh gripped the arms of her chair and shook her head. "Why on earth didn't you say that before?"

"I'll get the tea," Annie said. "Help me get the tea, Steve."

Steve again! On the way to the kitchen she knocked into Mrs Marsh's stick, and took it into the hall. Stephen followed her into the kitchen, where the cake was on a tray, half-piped with cream.

"Is it an orange cake then?" he asked.

"Yes," she said. "Will you fill the kettle?"

As he turned the tap on to do so, she picked up the Sabatier knife and stabbed him in the back.

The blade must have struck bone, for it did not go in very far, and he couldn't have realised what had hit him, for he turned round with an almost puzzled expression and as he did so the blade came out and he stared at it. There was some blood on it, not much, and his face in that instant was pleading, but for what she did not know, for he did not move, and she thought I can't kill him, I can't, I don't know how to, and then the glass shutter came down and the only sound was the chattering of the birds, swollen to an immense vibrating chorus and he too was vibrating between the man in the mirror and the pleading face and she struck again and again, and it was soft and easy, the blood spurting, washing over everything and then the sound came back, the birds fading to a shivering echo as she fell on him, crying and weeping, Steve, Steve, oh, Steve, oh Steve, oh Steve oh Steve.

The tap was still running. As she moved off his body her

elbow touched the fallen kettle, and it rocked gently on the floor. There was a sound behind her. Mrs Marsh was at the door, holding onto the jamb.

Annie got up. She still had the knife in her hand.

"There's been an accident," she said.

Mrs Marsh ran. She ran without her stick, without even thinking of it, wrenching and wrenching at the knob of the front door before managing to open it. She fell on the step, scrambled up, and ran down the path, screaming and shouting for help.

18

John drove her out of the hospital and through Hill-thorpe. Neither of them said anything. She had been in prison and mental hospital for two months. Now they said she was better: if she had ever been ill. It was confusing. Before the stabbing people thought she was mad; now they – or at least the police and their doctors – thought she was sane. A very sensible woman, she heard one doctor say. They were going to try her for murder, believing she had faked her illness. Perhaps she had; but if it had grown too complicated for her to follow, how could they hope to unravel it? To her bewilderment – hadn't she killed someone? – bail had been granted, but she did not have custody of the children, who were staying with Norma and John.

It was a cloudy day, with a bit of a breeze, and she knew it would be windy on the hill. It caught her as she got out of the car in the driveway, whipping her hair past her ears, and flapping her coat. Mrs Crowther scuttled by on the other side of the road, pretending not to see her.

"Are you going to move?" he asked.

"Why should I?" she replied. "It's my home."

"What about the neighbours?"

"They can move if they like."

Next day the children came to lunch. They had visited her in hospital at first, but not when she was bad. Norma suggested Annie came over, but Annie had insisted that they came to her house.

Matthew went to his mother strangely and quietly, but quickly turned to Norma for reassurance. Jackie ran straight upstairs into her room and refused to come down. When she was eventually persuaded to do so by Norma, she wouldn't look at her mother, and scarcely ate anything.

Norma's unending flow of cheerfulness depressed the atmosphere even further.

"My goodness! What's this? Chocolate mousse! Who wants chocolate mousse?"

Jackie pushed her spoon into it, and then repeatedly stabbed at it.

"If you're going to eat it, eat it," Annie said. "Don't play with it."

Jackie shoved the bowl so that it skidded violently across the table and fell on the floor. She stared defiantly at Annie, who said nothing. Abruptly, Jackie got up, her chair going over, and ran from the room.

The next morning Temple, her solicitor, rang her. He sounded very excited: could she come in to see him now? There had been an important development and the police wanted to see her.

Not again! She was due to visit the children. There was so much to do in the garden. She said as much. There was a moment's silence, and then a sigh on the other end of the line. She could picture him dragging his handkerchief from his pocket, for he always seemed to have one in his hands, wiping them, or his nose or glasses. He was the solicitor John and Norma had tried to get her to see that stifling hot afternoon, when she had phoned Stephen instead.

"Mrs Marsh, your trial is in three weeks' time. The

236

police want to talk to you about allegations you made about your husband . . . concerning the murder of Mrs Driverton . . . the Lestringham schoolteacher. I don't want you to pin any hopes on this but the very fact that they're looking at this seriously . . . Hello? Are you there?"

"Yes. I'm here."

After putting down the phone, she sat at the bottom of the stairs without moving for some time. She had a curious, very definite feeling that Stephen was here. She swivelled her head round to look at the kitchen door, thinking she had heard the knob turn. The phone rang, making her jump. It was only Norma, but her heart was still pounding as she replaced the receiver, down which she had half-expected to hear Stephen's slow tones, calling from Manchester, Derby or Hull.

Temple's office in Bradford was organised chaos. Mountains of files looked about to collapse; and there were trays of papers tied with red tape. On the walls were pictures painted by his children, various certificates and a picture of the sixth form at Bradford Grammar School, in which she picked out Temple, looking not that much younger. She waited while he finished a phone call.

A girl brought in coffee in a mug instead of the tea she'd asked for, but she didn't say anything. At last Temple put down the phone, and immediately jumped up.

"They think they've got him."

"Got him?"

"The Hawk."

He went on talking about something, something about a sharpened chisel, but the room was spinning round her, desk blending into red-taped papers, until she felt about to topple, like one of the mountains of files around her.

"Are you all right?"

Her coffee was dribbling onto the worn carpet. He eased the mug from her fingers, and put it on the desk.

"Sorry. That was terribly thoughtless of me."

"Who . . . " Her voice caught in her throat. "Who do they think . . . he is?"

"What?" He had his handkerchief out, twisted between

his fingers, and, for a moment, she thought he was going to mop her brow. "Sorry. Jesus Christ, I'm being terribly clumsy! I thought I told you. They think it was your husband." He held her by the shoulders. "Are you going to faint?"

She pulled herself together. "If you think I'm going to faint now . . . "

In spite of everything, had she still not really believed it, until that moment? No, it wasn't that that had shocked her; it was hearing it on someone else's lips.

"Could I have some tea?" she asked. "The girl brought me coffee by mistake."

Temple told her that, in the last fortnight, the murder weapon had turned up on the other side of the common from the copse where Joan Driverton had been killed, not far from where it was thought the killer had parked his car. Children had found it, and it had been some time before the father of one of them, suspecting its significance, had taken it to the police.

So far as Temple understood, it was a type of chisel fairly commonly used in the engineering industry. What identified it was that it had been sharpened on a machine at Hallet Engineering, Rothwell, Leeds; the machine left characteristic score marks on the blade, just as the barrel of a gun scored a bullet.

"It was a routine check that some meticulous policeman did, not expecting a result . . . "

The tea arrived in the same mug, a faint line of scum on the inside betraying that it had been made with a tea-bag. It was sugared. Still she swallowed it, and felt a little better.

"Of course," Temple was saying, "on its own it proves nothing, but with your evidence . . . "

"No one listened to my evidence," she said.

"They will now. It's incredible! An incredible stroke of luck! I know they've checked on you at the hospital."

"Why?"

"Well . . . to see if you're back to normal."

"You mean sane."

"Yes."

238

"And am I?"

He looked uncomfortable. His handkerchief flapped as he cleaned his glasses. "Yes, of course you are."

He pulled over a pink file which she had seen in prison many times before, and snapped away the elastic closures. The cardboard was already dirty and furred, and someone had doodled on the spine, just above the label which said R v Marsh.

"It could put the whole of your evidence in a different light."

"Could it?"

"Of course it could! We might well alter the plea to one of self-defence . . . if he's shown to be a murderer, particularly that murderer . . . well my God!"

He was like Matthew with a new enthusiasm, bubbling away. In fact he was really enjoying himself.

"And if self-defence holds up, you'll get away scot-free."

Back to the children. Back to the house. But also, back to the house where the Hawk had lived. As everyone would know. The hot tea had made her sweat a little, and for periods she couldn't concentrate on what he was saying.

"You're willing to go over your statement with the police?"

She was silent. She thought of the two chisels lying at the bottom of Matthew's Well. All the police would have to do would be to see if they matched the one found near Mrs Driverton's body. Then Stephen would be the Hawk, and she would be free.

"I'll see the police," she said.

"This afternoon?"

"Yes."

He phoned his secretary to make the appointment and swivelled round in his chair closer to her. "I'll go with you. Don't worry, Mrs Marsh, lots of hurdles but I have a feeling . . . " He smiled at her. "We'd better go over your statement now again, if you can bear it."

She wrapped her arms tightly round herself and rocked

backwards and forwards in her chair. "I found two chisels . . . " she began.

They drove in convoy back to Hillthorpe, and then Temple took her in his car to Bramley Police Station.

"Why Bramley?" she asked.

"I don't know."

They were immediately taken inside and, while Annie waited, Temple spoke to a man in a dark grey suit who kept glancing at her while he talked in low tones, like a conspirator. Finally, the man smiled at her, introduced himself as Detective Inspector Hill, and Temple took her arm. To her bewilderment, she found herself being led outside to a police car.

"Are you arresting me again?" she said.

Hill grinned. "We ought to arrest your solicitor. He's on a yellow line."

The driver who was holding the door open for her laughed. As he got in beside her Temple said: "We're going to Quay Street. They're taking precautions."

"Precautions?"

"They don't want the press on to it yet."

She huddled in a corner as the car turned into the main Leeds road. The press! She could see the headlines, the television, everywhere she went, everywhere the children went.

The radio crackled. "Fox 23."

"Fox go ahead."

"I have my passengers."

"Fox, check prior arrival."

"Do you want the blinds down?" Hill asked.

"No," she said, "I want to see where I'm going."

Again, everyone laughed. Clearly it was going to be one of those occasions when people found the slightest thing she said funny, as had happened at that awful dinner at Norma's. Had it really seemed like the end of the world then, when Stephen had got drunk and disgraced himself? She stared out. It was getting colder now, and most people were wearing topcoats. The car stopped at lights and a youth in a bomber jacket peered at her and said something to his girlfriend, who turned to look at her.

"Better have the blinds," said Hill.

It was even stranger speeding along in the darkened car. Once or twice Temple smiled at her, but nobody spoke until Hill lifted the RT.

"Fox 23 Kirkstall Road."

"Fox 23 proceed."

The car bumped along cobbles and when Annie was helped out, blinking in the light, she found herself in a small yard, overlooked by tall black walls and barred windows. They hurried her past a pile of rubbish bags and along warm cream-coloured corridors to a large carpeted office where a big man, whose stomach bulged out over his trousers, immediately rose and held out his hand. She had seen his face many times in the papers and on television, and it was rather a shock to see it fitted to the bulging stomach and ill-fitting, crumpled trousers.

"Chief Superintendent Daybury," he said. "Do sit down, Mrs Marsh."

He waved her into a large comfortable chair, into which she sank several inches. She might, she thought, more bewildered second by second, be visiting royalty rather than a woman charged with murder.

If Temple had been excited, then his excitement was multiplied many times in the atmosphere of that room. Hill came in with two other people, a secretary appeared and Daybury signed something and said to her, "No one, but no one, not even the Chief Constable."

He turned to Annie. "Would you like some tea, Mrs Marsh?"

"Only if it's from a pot," she said.

What was so funny in that? Again she seemed to have cracked a huge joke without realising it. Daybury's stomach shook. "From a pot with real tea? You're a woman after my own heart, Mrs Marsh." He smiled at her, and handed her some typewritten sheets. "This is your statement to Mr Temple?"

"Yes."

Daybury took back the sheets and sat behind his desk. The atmosphere instantly changed, from excitement and hilarity to silence and tension. He studied the pages carefully, seemingly unaware of anyone else in the room, or of the tea when it arrived, in a fat brown pot, accompanied by a plate of biscuits. She wondered, nervously, if she was expected to pour it, but Hill did it, and offered her a biscuit.

The crumbs stuck in her dry mouth, and she had to swallow them down with tea. She had expected them to start with the chisels, but they hadn't. She wanted to get that over with. She felt guilty, because she had not been able to tell Temple she had taken the chisels from the house and thrown them down the well. It sounded terrible, as if she had known exactly what she was doing, what she was concealing. She was screwing herself up to confess that, and several times nearly blurted it out.

Daybury licked his thumb in order to turn a page. His hands were thick, and his nails cut very short. He went back over a paragraph and stared at her, and for the first time he looked like a policeman and she felt like a criminal.

"When did you sign this?"

"This afternoon," Temple said.

Daybury looked at Hill. He rubbed his forehead and his eyes closed briefly. He suddenly seemed old and tired; as if he could curl up where he was and have a long sleep. Then he straightened up. She supposed it was a smile on his face; he folded his hands together and spoke quietly, almost indifferently.

"When did you first suspect your husband was the Hawk?"

"Christmas Eve."

"Last Christmas?"

"Yes. He told me . . . he was in Manchester . . . "

"When Karen Jones was killed?"

"Yes . . . I didn't suspect him . . . I mean, later I began to wonder . . . it seems obvious now but I couldn't . . . I couldn't . . . "

He came round from the back of his desk and took the tea from her shaking hands. He sat in the chair next to her. "Take your time. Take your time. We've all the time in the world."

She stumbled on with her story until they got to Jackie's birthday.

"What car was he driving then?" Daybury asked.

"An Escort."

"Colour?"

"Blue. No, red. We had a row about it . . . "

She tried to explain about him swopping cars with the London rep. It all sounded so insignificant and trivial, but Daybury and Hill exchanged glances.

"Can we know the relevance of this?" Temple asked.

"Well . . . since we are cooperating," Daybury said. "The Leeds murder was done by a man in a red Escort. The car left a distinctive tyreprint at the scene of the crime. We've traced the red Escort Stephen Marsh had."

"If Mrs Marsh says he went out in it, that's pretty conclusive," Temple said.

Daybury shook his head. "We've traced the car, but you know the mileage reps do. It's been reshod."

Annie could almost see the faint, mocking smile on Stephen's face. She felt sick. Daybury's face was larger, blurred, bobbing in front of her.

"Are you all right, Mrs Marsh? . . . Ask Nell for some water. And more tea."

When Hill returned, he beckoned Daybury to the door. They went into the corridor and spoke in whispers. Daybury closed the door but not before she had heard him explode: "*Yorkshire Post!* Who tells them these things? Charging someone! We're not even interviewing a bloody suspect!"

She strained to hear more, but caught nothing. Temple said something reassuring. She wasn't listening. She was thinking that she had killed him, she had done that dreadful thing, and this was making it all happen again, making him live again; she might not have killed him at all; it was as bad as what she'd been through, these words, whispers, cars, corridors, tea, smiles, and questions questions questions.

"Do they know?" she asked Temple. "The papers?"

"They know something's up," said Daybury, returning. "But that's all. Don't worry about it."

"They'll write about it?" said Annie, feeling foolish. Of course they would write about it.

Daybury hitched his shirt inside his trousers and leant against the desk, close to her. "They'll get nothing from us before the trial. Don't worry about it."

"They can't print anything before the trial," Temple said.

"And after . . . ? They'll ask me questions . . . ?"

"Which you don't have to answer," Temple said.

But that would not stop the questions! Panic filled her. It was not merely starting again, once the press got hold of it, it would go on for ever.

Somewhere she felt the bird, waiting.

A hand held out water. Her fingers smeared the mist on the glass, as Stephen's mother's had done on that afternoon. It was stifling. She was near a radiator which was almost too hot to touch.

"Better?" Daybury smiled and picked up her statement. "On Saturday, April 26th, you say he went out at –"

"No. He was in that night," Annie said.

"Saturday? The 26th?"

"Yes. It was Jackie's birthday."

"You got mixed up," interjected Temple. "She had her party on the Sunday –"

"He was there on her birthday," Annie cried. "I know when her birthday is!"

They were all round her. Temple was leaning towards her. There was a silver cup on the bookcase behind Daybury, awarded in the Police Federation Cricket Tournament. Every so often, when Daybury moved, he uncovered it and it glinted in the light from the desk lamp. It was doing so now, as Daybury stood over her.

"You've said here he went out on that Saturday and did not return until –"

"That's wrong, that's all wrong, that's what I thought when I was mad!"

"You signed this today."

Annie looked wildly about her. "It's not true. I want to go now. I would like to go now."

"The chisels," Daybury said. "Tell us where the chisels are, Mrs Marsh."

"What chisels?"

"The chisels in your statement."

"I made them up." Temple was standing now, his face shocked. "I'm sorry," she said. "When you told me they'd found a chisel I made it up. I'm sorry, I'm sorry."

Daybury's stomach was on a level with her face. One of his shirt buttons was undone, and she could see an inch of his vest. He spoke soothingly.

"Mrs Marsh. We're on the same side. We want to help you. I know what you must have been through . . . "

"How can you know?" she whispered.

"No. Of course I can't. That was a silly thing to say."

He sat down, ruffling his hair, looking older, greyer and very tired, and turned the pages of the statement slowly, his mouth opening several times before he eventually spoke. "He's dead, Mrs Marsh. You can't harm him now by telling the truth. We suspect he was the Hawk, but we cannot prove it unless you cooperate with us."

She got up, almost colliding with him. "He wasn't, he wasn't, how can you say that? He was my husband!"

19

The trial opened on a bright, cold day. Temple picked up Annie and drove her into Leeds. When they got to City Square the traffic slowed. People, mainly women, were walking in the road, waving banners. Annie thought they were against the bomb, or protesting about unemployment, until she read one of the banners: ALL MEN ARE HAWKS. Another said: HOPE YOU WERE RIGHT, ANNIE.

She slid down in her seat as a group of women on the pavement broke through a police cordon. Temple had to brake as a woman with multi-coloured strands of hair ran in front of the car.

"It's her!" she shouted.

Bodies surged round the car and hands drummed on the roof.

"Lock your door," said Temple.

He was too late. A hand pulled it open. Others grabbed at Annie. She was half-way out of the car before the police pulled the women off. A policeman went down on top of a woman, his helmet rolling. Temple slammed the door shut and, as the police cleared a way, drove slowly through the crowd to the court. Policemen surrounded her as she got out of the car. One held each arm as she passed between lines of staring people, some of whom leant forward to touch her. Then she was inside the huge entrance hall, being hurried over the coloured marble floor, into a wood-panelled room, whose door shut out the noise of the crowd.

"Well," said Norman Henshaw, "they seem aware of something."

Henshaw was her counsel. He had a shiny, slightly olive skin and springy, corrugated black hair. Over the past two weeks he had repeatedly questioned her about the statement she had made, and then retracted. She had thought that was over, but now he tried again, echoing Daybury.

"There's no point in protecting him, Mrs Marsh. He's dead."

She said nothing. The wall clock showed that in less than an hour, the trial would begin. Then they could all talk to one another and leave her alone.

"Perhaps you think you'll get off?" Henshaw persisted.

Wasn't that true? It was amazing how a few weeks at home had diminished the memory of that prison hospital.

Still she said nothing, staring at her hands, which had begun to harden again. Yesterday, she had pruned shrubs and lifted dead plants and had what she always thought of as the great bonfire of the year at the bottom of the garden. She had felt calm and peaceful as the flames crackled and the smoke stung her eyes and, in spite of the shock of the demonstrating women, some of that feeling was still with her.

Henshaw was leaning forward earnestly, almost pleadingly. "If you're thinking of the man in Bradford who killed his nagging wife and walked out of the court scotfree, then don't. There was huge provocation over years and it was a spontaneous act."

He had got this from Temple, who had got it from John. He remembered her fascinated interest in the case when they had discussed it at the awful dinner party. Wasn't she relying on that? She often thought about it.

Skilfully Henshaw undermined her confidence. She was on trial for murder. The plea to have it reduced to manslaughter on the grounds of diminished responsibility might work, depending on how the court reacted to the medical evidence, but she was taking a great risk, even of an indefinite sentence . . .

It was too complicated. She couldn't follow what he was saying.

"Think of your children, Mrs Marsh."

"I think of nothing else," she whispered, just stopping herself from calling him "sir", because Temple had told her it embarrassed him.

He smiled encouragingly. "They need you."

"They need him as well," she said, trying to still the panic that was rising inside her, for the court, the smell of the waxed marble and the corridors reminded her of the hospital.

"Yes, yes, I see, I do see that. But he's gone, he's dead. And aren't you putting them in danger of losing both parents?"

He made her feel stupid. Well, wasn't she? All she had to do was tell them where the chisels were and they would release her. What was she playing at, she who had always been so sensible? It was not her fault she had been married to him, or Matthew and Jackie's that they were his children.

They were waiting for her to speak. Henshaw glanced at his watch. They must have left it deliberately until this moment, knowing she would see sense. She licked her dry lips, and tried to put into words what she was afraid of. "The newspapers . . . " she began.

Henshaw looked at Temple, and Temple misunderstood her so completely that in a few words he wrecked Henshaw's gentle arguments which had drawn her so close to changing her mind. "I didn't want this to influence you before Mr Henshaw had spoken," he said. "But I'm bound to tell you that the *Daily Post* has offered you £50,000 for . . . your story."

Henshaw gave a little gesture which conveyed both how dubious such a transaction would be, and how stupid she would be to refuse it.

She felt sick. What would they headline her story? I LIVED WITH THE HAWK . . . HE KILLED ON HIS DAUGHTER'S BIRTHDAY . . . ? They would have to move, but where? Wherever they went, people would find out. They would say she had protected him and now she was making money out of it! It would be a hundred times worse than the gawping women outside, and the thought terrified her even more than the court.

They couldn't convict her! How could they? She had been nearly killed by Stephen! Dr Gregory was giving evidence. That man in Bradford had got off. She clung to these thoughts as she struggled to get the words out.

"I've . . . I've told you the truth."

Henshaw sighed. He gathered together his papers. "I'll do my very best, Mrs Marsh," he said. "On the evidence you've given me."

The worst moment was when the last thing she expected came into court. Mrs Marsh. She had been reduced to a thing, but even now Annie felt no sympathy for her, only a grim satisfaction when she thought of the old woman, who had moved at only a snail's pace for fifteen years, running down the garden path.

She had suffered a stroke, paralysing her down her left side. When they wheeled her in, Annie thought that what she had seen must be sealed for ever inside that withered frame. Her head was cocked on one side, and the only movement came from her black darting eyes, which fixed immediately on Annie.

David Parsons, the prosecuting counsel, a spare man of about sixty, whose hair was as grey as his wig, spoke movingly and gently about "this courageous old lady". Her speech was severely impaired, he told them, but not her mind, nor her memory. She took so long to answer questions that each time Annie thought her tongue had finally stopped. But then her right arm would jerk, and her fist clench and unclench spasmodically.

"After Annie Marsh had agreed to go to hospital what did she say?" Parsons asked.

The silence. The jerk, the fist clenching. "I'll . . . get tea."

"And then?"

"She said . . . "

"To you?"

"Stephen. Come on . . . "

"He was to go with her to the kitchen?"

"Yes."

"Did she do anything before she left the room?"

The old woman's eyes flickered in her motionless face, white and dead as uncooked pastry.

"Was there any object –"

Norman Henshaw rose to his feet, but before he could speak the judge said that, even in these difficult circumstances, counsel must not lead the witness. But the old lady had understood. There was a spasmodic and, thought Annie, triumphant jerking of her right side, as the word came out, sharp and barbed.

"Stick."

"Yes, Mrs Marsh, your stick?"

"Took it . . . so I couldn't walk!"

Her voice rose in a scream. Far from failing her, it seemed to be gathering strength. The jury, which kept quite still while she struggled for words, leant forward staring. A woman with large, light-grey spectacles, whose blonde hair was perfectly waved each day, stared coldly at Annie.

When the prosecution case was completed Henshaw said: "You can still change your mind."

She shook her head stubbornly, although she was now trembling and could not eat: she was due to give evidence after lunch. The press box was full. In fact there was an argument about places, quickly stilled. She saw the stolid, bulging face of Chief Inspector Daybury, and dropped the Bible. A murmur ran round the court as it was handed back to her.

She had never seen so many eyes, so many faces, all waiting, she felt, for her to give way, to tell them about the Hawk. She felt a great desire to do so as, once at the theatre in Leeds, she had felt an urge to jump from the dress circle, right down into the pit below. Oh, why not let them wallow in the murders? They knew. No they didn't, she argued with herself, they speculated but they knew nothing, and if anyone said he was the Hawk, she could sue them for criminal libel, Temple had told her reluctantly. That was her weapon, and she clung onto it, while Henshaw cunningly drew her closer to the subject of the Hawk, like an angler dangling bait.

"You *thought* he was the Hawk," said Henshaw, with just a slight hesitation before the emphasis.

"Yes."

"Why?"

She gripped the side of the box. If she did not say enough, she would be convicted. If she said too much, they would know he was the Hawk. "He was away a lot. In the same, in some of the same places as . . . "

"As?"

"As the women who were killed. And . . . he knew prostitutes."

250

"How did you know that?"

"He took me to a pub where they were."

"Why did he do that?"

"To buy me a drink."

There was a great burst of laughter. She cried out: "Why do I always make people laugh?" and the court was immediately silent. Water was brought to her, and the judge asked if she wanted to sit. She shook her head. Henshaw went on, drawing more and more out of her, and then, after a pause, put his final questions.

"You were convinced, for all these reasons, on the day Stephen Marsh was killed, that he was the Hawk?"

"Yes."

"And what do you think now, Mrs Marsh?"

The voice was conversational, almost idle. A woman in the jury was peering at her over her grey glasses. Daybury was leaning forward to catch her reply. Faces were blending into one another. From somewhere, it was a shock, as if she had been ambushed from behind, she heard the judge's voice.

"Answer counsel's question, Mrs Marsh."

"I was ill, he was not the Hawk, he was a good man, a good father . . . "

Perhaps she was getting used to it. Or perhaps it was because Parsons adopted a sceptical, bullying attitude that first riled her and then brought out her fighting spirit, but she did better at first with him than with her own counsel.

"The children were at the pictures with a friend?" Parsons asked.

"Yes."

"You didn't want them there. Not to see their father and grandmother?"

"They said they'd rather see *Back to the Future*."

"I suggest that the real reason you didn't want them there was because you planned to kill him."

"No!"

"You packed the children's clothes?"

She shook her head. "I ironed them."

"And put them in two piles?"

"Aye. I have two children."

"You kept saying to the policeman – their clothes are upstairs."

"So they were. I didn't plan it. Anyone with two kids does a wash every day."

A woman in the jury with a bony face smiled. For the first time Annie felt encouraged. This was all a load of nonsense: grown men being paid to ask her how often she did her washing and ironing. Parsons was on about Mrs Marsh's stick now.

"You took it into the hall?"

"Yes."

"Why?"

"It were in the way."

"I suggest you took it because you didn't want her to interfere?"

"Because I wanted to talk to Stephen!"

"Ah! So you did take it deliberately?"

The questions were coming too quickly. She grew confused. "Perhaps. I don't know."

"Because you planned to kill him?"

"Because I planned to talk!"

"Talk. All right. Let's pursue that. Did you talk?"

"Yes."

"What did you say?"

"He . . . asked if it was an orange cake."

"And then?"

Her voice was a whisper. "I don't remember."

"You don't remember?"

"There was a noise in my head."

His eyebrows lifted slightly, as he glanced at the jury. "After this conversation that you don't remember, what happened?"

"I don't know."

"Where was the knife?"

"On the unit."

"On the kitchen unit next to the window?"

"Yes. Between the cake and the biscuit tin."

He smiled at her. It was as if she had given him a present. "Between the cake and the biscuit tin, thank you." He rubbed the side of his nose. "What was it doing there?"

"I put it there."

"Why?"

"Why?"

"Mrs Marsh, as my learned colleague has so well established, you are a meticulous housewife and mother, and an eminently sensible woman. High up on the wall, so as to be out of reach of small children, even when climbing on furniture, as small children will do, there is a knife rack where the police found other, similar knives, and one vacant space. That is the space it normally occupies?"

"Yes."

"Why was it not there?"

The words were coming out: she could not help herself. "I put it there to protect myself."

"Protect yourself?"

"He had attacked me before."

"Ah yes. The marks on your throat." His tone dismissed them as insignificant scratches. "Did he attack you that afternoon? In the kitchen?"

"I thought . . . "

"Go on."

Panic filled her. Since she did not know the truth, did not know what had happened in those blank moments herself, what chance did they have of finding out? All he was doing was taking her inexorably to the brink of that moment when the bird had filled her head, and she was terrified that it would happen again, that the bird would come again.

"There was a noise in my head," she repeated.

"Do you remember picking up the knife?"

"No."

"Where did you stab him first?"

"I don't know."

"Was he facing you?"

"Please don't ask me! I don't remember!"

"Was his back to you?"

"I don't know!"

"You've sworn to tell the truth?"

"Yes yes!"

"Are you telling the truth?"

"Yes yes!"

"You put that knife deliberately on the kitchen unit, didn't you?"

"Yes."

"With one intention in mind, and that intention was to kill him, is that not so?"

"Yes yes yes, he was the Hawk. Oh my God I'm sorry I'm sorry I'm sorry I'm sorry."

She swayed. A man came up, caught her by the arm, and sat her down. Dizzily she could see that half the reporters were going, while the remainder shifted about, as if they did not know whether to go or stay. She had done it now. They had finally got it out of her. Then she saw her counsel, Henshaw, on his feet. There surely wasn't more?

"I won't keep you much longer, Mrs Marsh. You said he was the Hawk?"

The court was so silent she became conscious of her own breathing. She found strength from somewhere and made one last try. "I thought he was . . ."

"You said –"

"I keep telling you! He was my husband! It was my illness that made me think . . ."

Henshaw bowed his head. "When did this noise in your head begin?"

She shut her eyes. She remembered the hot smell of the afternoon. "In the park. The children didn't come back when they were supposed to. I thought Stephen had taken them. Then the birds came. One of them spoke to me. He told me to . . . it's nonsense."

The judge looked up from his notes. "Told you what?"

"To kill him."

When she expected laughter, nobody laughed.

"That is why you made these preparations?" Henshaw asked.

"Yes."

"Tell us what happened when Mrs Marsh and Stephen arrived that afternoon."

"I heard the car. The doorbell. I saw Stephen. Then his mother . . . "

"Were you expecting her?"

"No! Of course I wasn't! That's right! I remember thinking – I can't do it!"

"You couldn't do what?"

"Kill him!"

"Why not?"

"Because Mrs Marsh was there! How could I, with her there? She spoilt the plan. I knew I couldn't do it in any case. I was playing a game with myself, I knew all the time I couldn't go through with it, I couldn't kill him!"

"You're telling the jury the truth?"

"It's the truth, the absolute truth, I swear it."

"You mean – you changed your mind?"

"Yes. Yes."

"And then what happened?"

She shivered and then beads of sweat formed on her forehead, as though she was creating the closeness of that afternoon round her. "It was hot. So hot. And that old woman. She and Stephen were trying to get me into hospital. And I knew I should go. I said so."

"And you meant it?"

"Yes. I did. I just wanted to get out of that room with her. I just wanted a cup of tea, that's all. I told Stephen to put the kettle on and I picked up the knife to cut the cake."

"To cut the cake?"

It was true. If this was about intention, about what was in her mind, then it was true that she had put the knife there because the bird had told her to do so; but it was also true that she had picked it up to cut the cake.

"Yes, to cut the cake and there was the noise, it filled not only my head it filled the room and he was lying on the floor covered with blood and I had killed him, I had killed my husband . . . "

* * *

The jury was out six hours, each one as long as a day to her. At last she was called back. Some people were still settling into their seats as if they were at the cinema, waiting for the main film to start, and then they were suddenly silent when the judge began asking the six men and six women, whose faces she knew by heart, if they had reached a verdict.

"We have."

"Do you find the accused guilty or not guilty of murder?"

"Not guilty."

She was numb. Her hands gripping the hated box seemed so much part of the wood she could not move them. She did not understand what went on next until the judge said: "I have taken into account your medical reports, and the needs of your children, and this is reflected in the length of your sentence. You will go to prison for eighteen months."

Prison! How could she go to prison? She had been found not guilty! It was explained to her, the words "manslaughter" and "diminished responsibility" were brought out, and Temple and Henshaw were looking pleased. But what had they to be pleased about – she was going to prison! Now she wanted to shout out: "He was the Hawk! I had to kill him!" But it was too late, people were taking her by the arm, telling her to be quiet, now she was no longer a sensible woman but an incredibly stupid one. And what agonised her now was not the killing, she had had to do that, but her total loss of respectability; she was going to be locked up, away from her home and her children, and she struggled and tried to hit out at the policeman like Jan, that prostitute. She would be with them, she was one of them now, and she saw, in a corner of her mind, the slight, mocking smile on Stephen's face.

20

It was a shop just off Hillthorpe's main shopping centre, and evidently just on the edge of profitability, for since Annie had known it, it had been a grocer, greengrocer, and, just before she'd gone into prison, a pet shop. Now it was a florist called The Vase, although still painted on the wall outside was an advertisement for dog food.

They didn't know her there, and she was able to look around easily enough, although there wasn't much to choose from: roses, some rather tattered carnations, and a few sprays of pungently smelling freesia. Eventually she chose a bunch of gladioli; they weren't right, but what on earth would be right?

It was nearly one o'clock and she was starving. She would have lunch out! No she couldn't do that, she told herself, not here, not in Hillthorpe, not alone. She could buy a sandwich and eat it in the car, yes that's what she'd do.

The assistant, a mousey little girl just out of school, with red, chapped hands, was staring at her, and she realised she was just standing there, holding the dripping bunch of flowers. As the girl wrapped them up, she felt suddenly angry with herself. Why shouldn't she go out to lunch? Why shouldn't she? She felt a sudden shiver of excitement, of fear, as she realised she was going to do it.

"Can I call back for the flowers?" she asked.

"We're closed at one o'clock."

Of course! Early closing! Thursday, fancy her forgetting. Everything closed, even the Home-Made Café. She'd be lucky to find a sandwich. Feeling suddenly flat, she called in at the police station. She was still on parole: remission and five months on remand had meant that she had come out in eight months, in time for summer, if there was one. It was cold and showery, more like March than July.

What should she do? She didn't feel like going home. She was not due to see the children until tea-time; under the terms of the court order, they were still with Norma and John.

There was a pub called The Castle opposite with the cheerful notice: Hot and Cold Food Always Available. It had been done up recently; pansies trailed from window boxes and in the dim interior she could see people eating at the bar. She had never been in a pub on her own in her life before, and this wasn't the moment to start. However, there was no harm in looking at the menu: she scorned it: it was all tarted up in baskets, la-di-da, Norma food, and look at those prices! But the smell of scampi and chips made her stomach contract.

"Excuse me."

She was blocking the door and two men were waiting to get in. She had to move into the pub to allow them to do so. She watched them go up to the bar and order. Well, she was in! No one had looked at her. It was fairly dark. She could have a drink and a sandwich. Lowering her head, and using the flowers as a kind of cover, she approached the bar. Of course, that was a daft thing to do! A bunch of gladioli walking to the bar naturally drew attention to itself.

A man with a red face, whom she recognised as a local solicitor and councillor, was staring at her. She felt herself reddening. If only she could get rid of these stupid flowers!

There was a girl serving at the food counter, and a man at the bar. He kept on filling a pint of draught Guinness, scraping off the head, and putting more in.

"Lager, John," said another man.

Hadn't she been before him?

"A shandy please," she said loudly.

That of course made everyone round the bar look at her! She felt totally exposed – had people shuffled slightly away from her, leaving her marooned? The soggy end of the bunch of flowers had made a wet mark on her dress. The man behind the bar, who wore a black waistcoat and a green bow tie, smiled and nodded to someone as he deftly spooned ice into glasses; the man with the lager carried his full glass past her; her neck was pricking with sweat and she was convinced she was going to stay ignored when she heard the barman say to the girl behind the food counter: "Can you get that, Sal?"

"Is it a lemonade shandy?" Sal asked.

"Yes."

The girl also wore a green bow tie and a white shirt. As she moved to pull the half (they'd brought back the old hand pumps) Annie caught her expression and knew she was wondering where she'd met Annie before. Then, as she unscrewed the lemonade cap, it hit her, and Annie saw her mouth drop open slightly.

Why, when she was going to order no more than a ham sandwich, did she say: "And scampi and chips, please"?

"Three pounds seventy-five, please."

Three pounds seventy-five! She had just a five-pound note on her! Nevertheless, she paid and pocketed her change without counting it; not that it would have taken much counting. Once she was out of the spotlight she felt better, and finding an empty table sent her spirits soaring. She had done it! She was in! She had ordered. The scampi were frying and her shandy was in front of her. She stowed the flowers under the table, and immediately thought of her bicycle basket that people had kept tripping over that night when she had first met Stephen, and tried and tried to talk to that other boy, that nice boy, what was his name? Was she still the same hopelessly gawky, clumsy girl in spite of everything that had happened to her?

When the girl in the green bow tie brought it to the table she said: "Is there sauce tartare?"

Norma couldn't have said it better. They were well cooked, were the scampi, in fact they were delicious; big, fat and juicy – and so they should have been at that price. That was a bit of the old Annie wasn't it – except that the old Annie would have been so concerned at what each scampi cost, she wouldn't have tasted them for worrying.

By, she was enjoying this! She dipped each minute breadcrumb of batter in the sauce, and rolled it round her tongue. She sipped the shandy as if it was a rare wine, savouring every drop.

Now she was looking around at people, and if they stared at her, she gave them a good stare back.

It was unbelievable! Three weeks ago, when she had been released from prison, she had been unable to leave the house. It had become nothing more than another prison, a prison she would soon have to leave, too, for the mortgage hadn't been paid for six months. Not only did she no longer have that prop of her life, the Leeds Permanent Building Society book, she owed them money.

She had the children for periods, but she couldn't cope. Their energy shocked her. After being looked after herself for so long, their constant demands bewildered her. And there was their bewilderment, and so far as Jackie was concerned, hatred. Jackie would scarcely speak to her. For a time, Matthew had thought there had been an accident, but Jackie must have told him, for one day he said: "Why did you kill Dad?"

Her mouth was so dry that for a time she could form no words. All the time his solemn face stared at her.

"I was ill."

"Are you better now?"

"Yes. Nearly."

"Is he dead then?"

"Yes."

"Does that mean he's not coming back?"

He'd stopped asking questions at last, but an hour of them was as much as she could take. The rest of the time she drank tea, or the sherry that Norma brought her, and watched television, without bothering what it was, or stared out of the window, just as if she was still in hospital or prison. Often she was fairly drunk by tea-time; it dulled things, as the tablets had done in hospital.

She scraped her plate and finished her shandy. So what

had brought her out of the second prison to Hillthorpe's premier pub, to this feast, this celebration? For that was what it was, and to prove it she bought herself a second shandy, this time actually smiling at the girl and getting served straightaway.

There had been a knock on the door. She hadn't answered it, but when it had been followed by a right thump, she had pulled the door open.

"Sorry to bang so, but I thought you couldn't hear me over the television."

It was years since she'd seen her old boss, Ernest Bradshaw, now sales director of Hallet Engineering. She felt fear immediately, for she thought some new evidence had turned up against Stephen, and it was all going to start yet again.

"Can I come in?"

"What is it?"

He looked shifty, devious, she thought. She respected nobody now and, well into her daily bottle of sherry, almost closed the door in his face.

"I've brought you some money."

That opened the door a fraction. She stared at him suspiciously: a stare that was asking him what the catch was. He shuffled and took off his hat. She had never seen him so ill at ease.

"I didn't want to send it ... it's Stephen's pension contributions."

He dipped a hand towards the inside pocket of his good grey worsted suit — that didn't come off the peg — and hesitated.

"Come in."

"Thank you."

She took him into the back room. She'd been on her own so much that she didn't turn off the television until he asked her to turn it down. He sat staring out of the window, rolling up the edge of his rather loud striped tie as he had done so often when he was dictating to her. He said the company secretary should have written really, no doubt it should all have been dealt with on a formal basis, but they had worked together, and Stephen had given so much to the firm . . .

His voice trailed away, and there was a long awkward silence. Now she remembered that he had called on her in hospital, but she had refused to see him.

She was conscious of her old slippers, of the smear of egg on her dress, of the nearly empty bottle of sherry on the table.

"Well . . ."

He drew an envelope from his inside pocket.

"Would you like some sherry?"

His glance took in the smeared label of the cheap Cyprus sherry.

"I wouldn't mind a cup of tea."

He followed her into the kitchen. He must have been acutely aware of what had happened there, because he became even more edgy and awkward. By now she scarcely thought of it, and she was more concerned about the piles of dirty dishes and the used tea-bag she trod on. Tea-bags! She'd even succumbed to them!

"I'm sorry," she said.

"For what?"

"Place is in a bit of a mess," she muttered. "I wish you'd phoned."

"Would you have seen me?"

"No," she said, "I wouldn't."

They grinned at one another and the atmosphere lightened. She found an old bit of good tea and got out two of the best cups. The aroma of the tea made her swear to herself never to buy another tea-bag. He sipped his tea appreciatively.

"I've not had a cup like this since you left."

"Rubbish!"

She flushed, inordinately pleased. At Hallet's she'd spoiled him, making his own tea for him, and never getting it from the trolley. Wasn't it there, in fact, that she'd started being fussy about good tea? When one Christmas he'd given her a special pack of fine teas?

He slipped the envelope onto the yellow table and there was a silence between them.

"It's not much, considering . . . "

"It'll help."

Another silence. He placed his empty cup back on his saucer and, without asking him, she poured another half-cup, just as she used to.

"What are you going to do?"

"I don't know, Mr Bradshaw."

She had never called him anything else. At any moment she expected him to call her Miss Tate.

Another silence. He frowned at her hard, as he used to do when dictating the difficult bits.

"I'll tell you what, and you may shoot me down, but there is this job in the sales office . . . coordinator . . . not what you had . . . you could do it backwards but . . . "

Tea slopped as she put down her cup. "You wouldn't employ me!"

"Why not?"

She laughed. She couldn't help herself. It was ludicrous, and her voice became bitter, hard again. "Don't talk daft. I've been in prison. Mental hospital."

His eyes didn't leave hers. "I'm not that daft. I went to the hospital."

"Did you? Did you? And what did they say?"

"They said there was no reason why you should not cope with a job, in their view."

"I couldn't go back there! D'you think I could possibly go back there? Of all places!"

"No. No. I can see that. Only I thought it might be difficult for you to find somewhere else and . . . I thought I'd mention it, that's all."

He drained his cup, stared at the pattern of tea-leaves, and looked for his hat.

"Everyone . . . " she said at the door.

"Everyone what? Most won't worry about it if you don't. The rest . . . well, you were always good at ignoring them, weren't you?"

He put on his hat, took it off, turned to go and then did

a strange little pirouette on the doorstep. "Are the papers still after you?"

Her suspicious feelings about him returned. "No. Not lately. How do you know . . . ?"

"I hear you said that to them." He put up two fingers in a huge V sign. "Excuse my French. Good for you, Annie. Good for you, love."

He raised his hat to her, and walked quickly back to his car, where he raised his hat again before driving off. She went back into the house and walked about, confused, but somehow exhilarated. What did all that mean? What did he know, or think he knew? Of course there were rumours, and they were bound to increase, since there hadn't been any more murders (in prison, at first, her new nightmare had been waking up every morning with the fear of finding another murder in the paper . . .). But weren't the same things that protected Stephen when he was alive protecting him now? The Hawk was a monster. People believed that. She'd heard Mrs Crowther and his brother pour scorn and disbelief on the idea. Probably his workmates did the same. He had been normal, quiet, well-liked, a man who would help anyone out.

She was the odd one. Difficult to get on with. The funny one. The maniac. The murderer.

Then what exactly did Bradshaw know, or suspect; what did he mean?

There was no way of knowing, no way of telling, and she was certainly not going to ask. She went over his every gesture, every word that he said and nuance of expression, while she poached an egg and had more tea. She was hungrier than she'd been for ages, and had another egg with some bacon. Then she cleared the dishes and washed them, ferreting them out from the top of the television and even under the bed.

All the time she wondered while she vacuumed and straightened and polished, but by the time she went to bed exhausted, she was no nearer to an answer.

She didn't wake up till nine o'clock. She'd slept through for nine whole hours! Her mind was wonderfully clear, as

if a fresh wind had blown through it. She'd decided what
to think. She thought that Bradshaw suspected the truth,
although he had no means of knowing it, beyond what he
knew of her from working so closely with her for six years.

And if he didn't, wasn't it even more wonderful that he
had come round as he did?

She stopped thinking. She got on with it. She'd done too
much thinking. She blessed him from the bottom of her
heart, and tried writing a letter refusing the job, but tore
up several versions. Of course it was absurd that she
should go back to Hallet's, perhaps he hadn't even really
meant it, but that wasn't the important thing. The
important thing was that he seemed to have unlocked
something.

The very next day, at Norma and John's, there was a
ferocious argument between Matthew and Jackie, who
were getting more and more violent with one another.

He accused her of dropping apple juice on his new Mr T
poster and then, when she picked it up to demonstrate
that the stain didn't show because it was over BA's gold
chains, he snatched it from her and tore it.

"You did that, Matthew!" Jackie cried.

"I didn't! You did it you did it you did it!"

One of his flailing fists smashed against the table when
Jackie dodged, and the sudden pain, following the
destruction of his precious picture, was too much for him
and he burst into tears, running instinctively to his
mother.

As he sobbed out his tragedy in her arms, Annie felt a
sudden release, a realisation that he had not been holding
back from her, she had been keeping herself away from
him; in killing his father she *had* robbed him of both
parents, although his need for her was just as great, was
far greater than before, and she hugged him and held
him, and kissed his wet, bawling face.

"Come on Matti," she said. "It's over, it's over now, stop
crying, it's over now."

They were clearing the glasses, the plates and the baskets,

and cloths had been placed over the food counter. Annie finished her shandy as the girl in the green bowtie passed.

"I right enjoyed that," she said.

The girl emptied an ashtray and smiled. "See you again."

No doubt it was what they said to everyone, automatically, press a button, but she found herself saying: "I shouldn't wonder."

Was she a regular, then? Wonders would never cease. She blinked at the bright light outside. It had cheered up a bit.

"I say . . ."

The girl was running after her, holding the bunch of drooping gladioli. She felt dreadful. She felt awful. Forgetting them! It was unlike her to forget a box of matches, or had been. She wasn't, amazingly, in a mood of sorrow, that was why. It was a bit bloody morbid really, but shouldn't a widow take flowers to her husband's grave on the anniversary of his death – even if she had killed him and even if – she put the flowers on the car seat beside her – they looked almost as dead as he was?

By, she was a little bit, well not drunk, not on two shandies, but lightheaded, certainly.

The car was parked opposite the Leeds Permanent Building Society office, where she still hadn't deposited the cheque. She hesitated. Flowers first, she decided, before they completely conked out.

The journey to the cemetery sobered her and, to her surprise, she found herself thinking, not of the murder, but of the early days, when they had first met, when she'd plunged out of that pub and found she had a puncture.

"Can I fix it?"

Unexpectedly her eyes blurred with tears and she had to pull in to the side of the road for a minute or two.

The cemetery was vast, a city with roads and paths, and a discoloured, weatherbeaten map inside the front gate on which had been sprayed: LEEDS UTD ARE SHIT. She managed to decipher row 5, path 3, and walked slowly between gaunt, mouldering stones on which the names could barely be read, and then white slabs of marble, some with beds of bright green chips. It was windy, and the big rolling clouds were streaked with sunlight.

It was an ordinary piece of Yorkshire stone, and already the sharp lines of his name were blunted with little threads of moss. She scraped it out with a stick, put the gladioli in the flower holder, and began methodically pulling up weeds. Once she stopped, crouched on her knees, when she remembered Stephen telling her off for making Jackie's feed too hot. Since she'd been in hospital for so long after her birth, he'd known more about it than she did.

She returned to the weeds, and was so absorbed in the task, she didn't hear them approach until they were almost on her. Jackie was bearing a bunch of bright red roses, and Norma was behind her.

Annie rose, soil dropping from her dirty hands, and the three stared at one another.

"I didn't know you were coming, love," Annie said.

The child turned away from her, clasping the flowers, eyes blinded with tears.

Annie started to move to her, but stopped when Jackie went to Norma, who took the flowers. Annie removed the gladioli from the holder.

"Oh don't do that!" Norma said.

"They're done. Finished. Those are lovely."

"Sorry, I didn't realise . . . "

"I should have thought . . . "

"No, I should have said . . . "

"It's my fault . . . "

She dropped the withered flowers by the top of the stone. Norma looked at the roses, then at Jackie, but she was shaking and crying too much to take the flowers, so Norma put them in the holder. Each time Annie moved towards Jackie, she moved away.

As Norma straightened up, Jackie said, each word blurred with sobs: "I loved him."

They all stood for a moment, unable to move or speak, the wind flapping at their coats and lifting their hair, and then Annie said to Norma: "Are you parked by the main gate?"

"Yes."

"I'll see you back there."

On the way back a rage built up in her. Fancy bringing the child here! This afternoon! It was probably one of Norma's half-baked theories of child-rearing: let the child follow its own emotions. But wasn't it her fault as well; creeping here like . . . well, like a criminal?

The marble gave way to greening, black stone, and she lingered, wanting to be alone. It was not impossible that her father was buried here, although probably he was still alive. At one period, when her mother still visited her at the home, she had told her he was Irish, then for a time she had switched to him being Cornish. She preferred that, a tall man, standing on cliffs, strong and silent, gazing out to sea. What pathetic rubbish! It was years since she'd thought of that! But, even when she'd first gone out to work, hadn't she always bought Cornish butter, although it was more expensive?

At least Jackie had not only known her father, she was still able to love him. That was important, she tried to tell herself, very important, but it did not seem to help her very much.

She had dawdled to such an extent that by the time she reached the gate, Norma and Jackie had almost caught up with her. Waiting by the car were Matthew, John and the new baby – she'd had her boy, Benjamin: a right Norma name.

In spite of Jackie she couldn't help smiling when Matthew saw her and ran towards her with an instant yell, jumping up at her.

"I didn't know you were here," he cried.

"Well you don't know everything, do you?"

"Are you taking Trouble?" Norma said.

"If I have to."

All the time Annie was aware of Jackie, with her puffy, swollen face watching them. She was half-way between the two cars, kicking savagely at stones. One flew dangerously near Annie's car. She bit back a retort. Norma shouted to Jackie while Annie opened the door of her car for Matthew. Jackie didn't seem to hear. Her shoes were scuffed and her white socks grey with dust.

Annie hesitated, her hand still on the open door. "Are you coming with us?"

Jackie kicked at another stone, and this time, to her own shocked surprise, it hit the wing with a resounding clang, and ricocheted just past Annie.

"Jackie!"

The girl turned violently to her, and what she might have said Annie never knew, because Matthew diverted her attention by saying, "We don't want her in here."

Jackie leapt towards him, pulling aside the door. "I'll come in if *I* want to!"

"Aw shurrup."

"You shurrup."

"Shove up."

"I've shoved up!"

"You haven't."

"All right, all right," Annie said, "that's enough!"

She was in. They were driving off. No doubt Norma had told Jackie on the walk that her mother had come to the cemetery in love and remorse. In Jackie's agony and bewilderment, that would have confused her still more. Perhaps it had created an opening but, really, Jackie was with them now out of hatred and jealousy of Matthew, and if it took that to bring them together, it took that.

She was tired, and the shandy had given her a bit of a headache. Jackie's knee was pressed into the back of her seat. At the Leeds road, traffic lights separated her from John's car and she drove more slowly. On the seat beside her was the cheque. There might still be time to put it in the building society, but she felt a strange reluctance to do so. The children were silent now, slumped in the back. The words came out spontaneously, without thought, almost idly.

"What about a holiday?"

Immediately Matthew was sitting up. "Whitby, Whitby!"

"Somewhere else. I was thinking of – "

But he wouldn't be silenced. "Whitby, Whitby, can we go to Whitby, that cottage, that were real!"

"In what? In this?" Jackie's tired, sullen voice was punctuated with thumps on the driving seat.

"Don't kick the seat. You can stay with Norma if you want, Madam."

What was she talking about? It would take a good slice of their money, of the cheque. And she'd done nothing about getting a job. She couldn't go back to Hallet's, she couldn't. But Bradshaw had given her the belief she could get another job.

They were in Hillthorpe, passing The Castle, whose hanging baskets had been freshly watered, leaving damp patches on the pavement. The streets were quiet and the shops shuttered, but the building society, disdaining early closing, was still open.

She slowed as she approached it until she had nearly stopped, and then astonished both herself and a man coming out, by sticking up two fingers in a strident V sign, just as Bradshaw had done on her doorstep. The customer stopped, open-mouthed, and she gestured, horrified, trying to indicate that the sign was not meant for him but for the Leeds Permanent Building Society, and not even for that, but for something which it stood for but which she could not define; but she began laughing, and when she saw Matthew doing V signs too, she drove off in a series of lurching hiccups down the High Street, leaving the irate customer staring after them.

"Don't do that, Matthew," she said.

"You did it."

"Well I shouldn't have done."

"Then why did you?"

"I don't know."

"You must know."

"You don't allus know why you do things."

Whitby. The cliffs. The moors. Why not? Why shouldn't they go over the moors to Whitby again? As she changed down to drive up the hill, she could almost hear the wind singing in her ears.

MORE TITLES AVAILABLE FROM
HODDER AND STOUGHTON PAPERBACKS

All these books are available at your local bookshop or newsagent, or can be ordered direct from the publisher. Just tick the titles you want and fill in the form below.

Prices and availability subject to change without notice.

Hodder & Stoughton Paperbacks, P.O. Box 11, Falmouth, Cornwall.

Please send cheque or postal order, and allow the following for postage and packing:

U.K. – 55p for one book, plus 22p for the second book, and 14p for each additional book ordered up to a £1.75 maximum.

B.F.P.O. and EIRE – 55p for the first book, plus 22p for the second book, and 14p per copy for the next 7 books, 8p per book thereafter.

OTHER OVERSEAS CUSTOMERS – £1.00 for the first book, plus 25p per copy for each additional book.

Name ....

Address ....

....